Y0-CDH-242

Dear Reader,

They say that people are the same all over. Whether it's a small village on the sea, a mining town nestled in the mountains, or a whistle-stop along the Western plains, we all share the same hopes and dreams. We work, we play, we laugh, we cry—and, of course, we fall in love . . .

It is this universal experience that we at Jove Books have tried to capture in a heartwarming series of novels. We've asked our most gifted authors to write their own story of American romance, set in a town as distinct and vivid as the people who live there. Each writer chose a special time and place close to their hearts. They filled the towns with charming, unforgettable characters—then added that spark of romance. We think you'll find the combination absolutely delightful.

You might even recognize *your* town. Because true love lives in *every* town . . .

Welcome to *Our Town*.

Sincerely,

Leslie Gelbman
Editor-in-Chief

OUR·TOWN

TAKE HEART

LISA HIGDON

JOVE BOOKS, NEW YORK

TAKE HEART

A Jove Book / published by arrangement with
the author

PRINTING HISTORY
Jove edition / July 1996

All rights reserved.
Copyright © 1996 by Lisa Higdon.
This book may not be reproduced in whole
or in part, by mimeograph or any other means,
without permission. For information address:
The Berkley Publishing Group, 200 Madison Avenue,
New York, New York 10016.

The Putnam Berkley World Wide Web site address is
http://www.berkley.com

ISBN: 0-515-11898-2

A JOVE BOOK®
Jove Books are published by The Berkley Publishing Group,
200 Madison Avenue, New York, New York 10016.
JOVE and the "J" design are trademarks
belonging to Jove Publications, Inc.

PRINTED IN THE UNITED STATES OF AMERICA

10 9 8 7 6 5 4 3 2 1

ACKNOWLEDGMENTS

Thanks to Shawnee Brown, of Shelby County, Tennessee, and her wonderful mules: Ada, Prairie, and Cricket, who confirmed that mules are every bit as delightful as I had hoped and more.

TAKE HEART

❧ PROLOGUE ❧

PETE ST. JOHN had never done a ·damned thing that made sense, and now it seemed he couldn't even die without screwing it up.

Ben Parrish sank back in his chair, the thin wooden slats digging through the cotton of his shirt. He didn't risk a glance at Mitchell or Eldridge. The fight would start soon enough. Instead, he concentrated on the smooth finish of the mahogany table, around which they had gathered to hear the last will and testament of their friend and onetime partner.

"That miserable son of a bitch!" Eldridge slammed his fist against the table, unsettling the coffee in his cup. "By God, he knew what that land meant . . . meant to all of us. When did he decide all of this?"

Olson, the attorney, paled visibly and cleared his throat. "Mr. St. John requested these changes less than six months ago . . . when he learned of his illness."

Eldridge was on his feet now, glaring down at the attorney as he spoke. "I say it ain't legal. He had no right to make any changes without tellin' the rest of us. That land was to be

1

divided between the three of us. Him gettin' sick don't have nothing to do with it.''

Ben traced his forefinger along a minute scar on the table-top, remembering the day Old Pete had confided the doctor's diagnosis: stomach cancer, incurable. He'd sworn Ben to se-crecy, and they had never spoke of it again—even at the last, when Pete lay dying. The old man spent his last breath re-membering the days when they had first reached the plains of Wyoming, before soldiers built forts and settlers built towns.

"We agreed to all that over ten years ago," Ben cut in. "Things change in that much time. We've all changed."

Mitchell nodded in agreement. "A man naturally thinks of the folks he left behind, knowin' his time is up and all. Pete used to talk about his family all the time, especially his brother.''

A hint of a smile touched Ben's face as he recalled Pete spinning tales of his boyhood in New York. Many evenings they had sat up until the campfire died out completely, listen-ing to the old man's yarns. Pete had always been the old man, even when he wasn't much older than Ben was now.

"I still say it ain't legal." Eldridge gripped the back of his chair. "Even if it is, why in hell would Pete leave his land to a niece he ain't never seen?''

"He expressed a sense of obligation to provide for her since the death of her father." The lawyer fingered his stiffly starched collar, coughing slightly as he gathered the remaining documents from the table. "She has no other family."

"An old maid?" Ben finally leveled his gaze on the other two men. "She'll be lookin' for a buyer."

"Not so fast, Parrish." Eldridge pointed his forefinger in Ben's direction. "Don't go trying to weasel your name on the deed just yet. I want my chance to bid for that land." He paused only long enough to turn to Olson and demand, "How much?''

"I have yet to receive a reply from the young woman's attorney. For all I know, she may already be on her way to Wyoming to claim her inheritance.''

"No woman would be foolish enough to come out here by herself." Ben rose to his feet, followed by Mitchell. "We'll buy her out and divide the land . . . evenly."

"To hell with that," Eldridge replied as he replaced his Stetson on his head. "That land is open to anyone willing take it, and by God, I won't settle for a rake-off when I can have it all."

Ben knew conflict over land was inevitable with more and more settlers coming west and staking claims. When word got out that Pete's land now belonged to an unmarried woman, every granger within a hundred miles would be looking to run her off. Once a land war got going, deeds and borders meant nothing.

"You're willing to bring bloodshed down on our heads rather than settle this quietly and keep the peace here in Wilder?" he asked.

"Peace is for Sunday-school teachers"—Eldridge paused as he turned toward the door—"and old men."

Without a second glance toward Mitchell or the paling attorney, Ben strode purposefully toward Eldridge and blocked the doorway. He leveled his gaze with the other man's and said, "If there's a range war, we might not live to be old men."

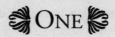

ONE

SHE HAD LOST everything. Her home, money, and now her good name. A high price to pay for trusting too completely.

Halley St. John took a deep breath, struggling to control her emotions. Anger warred with fear as she gripped the iron bars of the jail cell. Surely, they were only bluffing. Trying to scare her. But her bravado waned as the shadows lengthened against the moldy brick wall.

Hours of standing on the cement floor of the New York City Jail were beginning to take their toll; her feet ached and the muscles in her legs had started cramping an hour ago.

Glancing toward the narrow cot, Halley was sorely tempted to rest on the stained mattress, but a shudder went though her at the thought of what those stains might be. Only murderers, cutthroats, and derelicts wound up in jail. Usually.

Halley loosened her grip on the bars and began pacing the length of the cell. Thirteen steps. She'd paced the floor enough to know. Thirteen exactly.

She couldn't help but wonder how she would be charged. Trespasser? Vandal? Perhaps, even thief. All for having the courage to take matters into her own hands. Angry tears threatened at the thought of how truly desperate her situation was now.

How had things gotten so far out of control? Father had been gone less than two years, and she had let everything slip through her fingers. "No, that's not what happened," she whispered, squeezing her eyes against the stinging tears.

A pretty head shouldn't be troubled by business matters.

Her father's words rang in her ears, sounding more and more foolish by the hour. He had never taken her into confidence regarding the family's holdings. When he died, she was overwhelmed by the barrage of lawyers, accountants, and stockbrokers pressing her for decisions she wasn't prepared to make.

Halley knew she shouldn't blame her father. He had simply assumed, as she had, that he would always be there for her.

Thoughts of her father weakened Halley to the point of seeking rest on the ragged cot. She gingerly spread the threadbare blanket, finding a patch that still resembled the original color, a dismal gray, and sat down. Relief spread through her back and legs, and she cradled her aching head in her open palms.

It had been so much simpler to allow someone else to shoulder the burdens thrust upon her at the sudden death of her father. When Richard Farnsworth had so kindly offered to oversee her affairs, she thought him the answer to her worries. He saw to everything, particularly her investments. Investments, ha! That was the legal term for funneling all her money into his own pockets. There was no telling how long he would have continued fleecing her . . . if his mistress hadn't shot him. When the pungent air of that scandal had thinned, she found herself the victim of Farnsworth's manipulations. Halley grimaced, recalling the morning she learned of her misfortune through the lurid headlines.

FARNSWORTH TOOK IT WITH HIM!

CARELESS HEIRESS PENNILESS!

The heavy scrape of the entry door alerted Halley that someone was entering the cell block. She quickly rose to her feet and smoothed her dark hair back from her forehead, wincing as her fingers snagged in a tangle. Folding her arms across her chest defiantly, she refused to show any sign of exhaustion.

The guard entered the cell block, keys in hand. "I'm sorry to say, your attorney just posted bail, Miss St. John. Looks like you won't be staying overnight after all."

Relieved, she breathed a prayer of thanks, but maintained her outward demeanor of defiance. "I had no intention of staying a moment longer than necessary."

"That's too bad," he said as he turned the key, unlocking the cell. "It's not often a man like me can say he entertained one of *the* Four Hundred."

Halley recognized the subtle insult. As of now, her social standing was nonexistent, for there was no loyalty among society. With her family's fortune depleted and the stench of scandal clinging to her, life as she'd known it was over. Even now, she could hear the faint scratching of fountain pens carefully crossing her name from guest lists all over Manhattan.

Raising her chin, Halley would not be goaded by snide remarks. Instead, she gave him a cool stare as she passed through the cell, her head held high as she followed him out of the cell block.

Her father's attorney, Josiah Pittman, stood when she entered the outer waiting area. Crossing the stark room, he held his hands out to her, clearly appalled by her disheveled appearance. "Halley, my dear girl, what on earth could you have been thinking?"

"I am determined to expose Richard Farnsworth for the thief he was," she declared as he led her toward a scarred table, paired with a couple of crude wooden chairs. "I simply had to get my hands on those records."

"Hush about that, my dear." The older man turned toward the guard and said, "That will be all for now, Officer. If you would, please check on the progress of Miss St. John's release papers. She's hardly accustomed to such deplorable conditions."

"Knowing who she is, my sergeant placed her in solitary.

Otherwise, she'd have been in with the whores and the morphine addicts.''

Halley gasped, but Mr. Pittman spoke first. "Well then . . . we are most grateful for his consideration of Miss St. John's dilemma, and I will personally thank him for his kindness.''

The guard only smirked. "It wasn't kindness on his part. Those sluts would have torn her to ribbons in a matter of minutes, and he'd be the one filling out reports till doomsday.''

With one last gloating look toward Halley, the guard turned and left them alone. When he was gone, she felt panic taking hold. "I won't stay here another moment! Did you hear what he said?''

The older man merely nodded. "He's only having a little fun with you . . . making sport of your misfortune. I'm afraid you have more pressing issues to be concerned with now.''

"Do you think I've forgotten? Those *pressing issues* are what got me arrested!" Taking a deep breath, Halley lowered her voice and continued, "They're going to put me out of my home, and the bank informs me that all my accounts have been depleted. What choice did I have but to initiate my own investigation?''

"The police call it breaking and entering," Mr. Pittman corrected in a fatherly yet reproachful tone.

Tears burned her eyes, and she swallowed hard before saying, "I want everyone to know what a despicable swindler he was.''

"For God's sake, Halley, the man was shot in his underwear. I doubt he will be remembered with dignity.''

Halley took little comfort in that. She only wished Farnsworth's mistress had shot him before he had taken everything Halley had. "I simply refuse to accept that I have nothing left.''

"My dear, you must admit you've paid little or no attention to the management of your father's estate," he reminded her gently. "You've spent the last few years traveling abroad and dallying at school.''

Halley's spine stiffened. "I was not dallying. My studies simply became more extended than expected, but that gave Farnsworth no right to steal from me.''

Pittman shook his head. "You have no proof."

"I might have found proof if it weren't for the night watchman." Exasperation made her voice shaky, and she flattened her palms against the tabletop. "Mr. Pittman, are you telling me there is nothing I can do? Nothing to regain what he embezzled from me?"

"Even if Farnsworth were still alive, I doubt you would have much of a case. He was a crafty man, my dear. He knew the law and how to protect himself." The aged counselor pinned her with a piercing blue gaze that belied the tremor in his hands. "He simply took advantage of your lack of prudence."

Halley sank back into the narrow wooden chair and offered the only defense she could think of. "I trusted him."

"You trusted him because that was the easiest thing to do. Had you accepted one of the numerous offers of marriage you've had, you might not be in this predicament. A husband would have protected your fortune."

"By making it his own," Halley countered bitterly. The St. John fortune and family status had attracted many suitors, but she had found none of them sincere. "Control of my fortune meant control of my life. I didn't want to give up either."

Mr. Pittman nodded with grudging sympathy. "Farnsworth proved to be no better. Trusting him was a tragic folly."

She absorbed the weight of his words, staring down at her folded hands. "So, now, I truly have nothing?"

"I didn't say that. In fact, I've brought you good news." Pittman cleared his throat. "I have received a letter from an attorney in the Wyoming Territory, regarding your late uncle."

"Uncle Peter?" Halley managed a weak smile. "If he were still living, I know he would help me."

"He has, my dear." Josiah Pittman covered her hand with his aged one. "He's made you his sole heir, leaving you a sizable ranch in the Wyoming Territory."

"Wyoming?" Halley repeated in a whisper. Since her father's death, she had maintained the obligatory correspondence with her only uncle, never failing to write at Christmas and Easter. "But I never met him," she said out loud. "Why would he leave everything to me?"

"People like to keep property in the family," Mr. Pittman suggested. "Besides, you are the only child of his only brother. Why wouldn't he leave his ranch to you?"

Wyoming. The very thought of traveling to the untamed frontier sent a rush of excitement through her. She had read many accounts of the adventurous lives of Westerners in dime novels. People went west to start over, build new lives, and make their fortunes.

She forced her attention back to Mr. Pittman, who was patiently explaining her options for selling the land and investing the money.

"No, that's not possible," she interrupted. "This land is a godsend, and my uncle would not have willed it to me had he not meant me to make the most of it."

Halley rose to her feet, renewed determination making her green eyes sparkle. Her earlier despair vanished, and she smiled with anticipation. "Mr. Pittman, I shall go to Wyoming."

Ben Parrish turned up the collar of his coat and pulled the brim of his hat lower over his eyes. The midafternoon air held an unexpected chill for early September, and he glanced toward the horizon, half expecting to see snow clouds.

Not yet. At least another month would pass before snow blanketed the prairie. Mentally he added kerosene to his list of supplies. He had plenty of coal oil back at the ranch, but there was no sense in letting an early winter catch him unprepared.

His boots rang against the wooden slats of the sidewalk as he passed the mercantile, contemplating whether to go on to the freight office or not. Buying supplies had only been an excuse to come into town today. Like everyone else, Ben Parrish wanted to see the woman bold enough to travel all the way from New York to claim an inheritance she had no right to in the first place.

"What time's the stage gettin' in, Ben?"

Cutting a sharp glance toward his younger brother, he answered, "Ten, they said. What's it to us?"

Clayton grinned. "Eldridge says a spinster from back East

won't last two weeks. She'll probably take one look at Pete's old house and run.''

Ben flexed his fingers against the restraints of his gloves. Eldridge was most likely right. The woman would turn tail and run, leaving the land open to anyone willing to take it. And they were all willing.

"What are you going to do when she does? After all, that land borders ours.''

Ben stopped short and cast a quick look in his brother's direction. ''I told you to see to the mare when we got into town. She won't make it back to the ranch, missing a shoe.''

"I will, after the stage gets in.''

Ben shook his head. Clayton would only cause trouble. He had a talent for always saying the wrong thing. ''You can get a look at her later. Run on.''

The younger Parrish came to a halt, grudgingly looking up at his brother. ''I ain't no kid, Ben.''

"A man has responsibilities, and he sees to them.''

Clayton hesitated, but backed down as usual. Ben watched his shoulders slump as he gathered the mare's reins, muttering a curse as she nosed his shoulder. ''Come on, you,'' he growled, but ruffled her mane affectionately.

Ben looked on as Clayton made his way to the livery. At twenty, his younger sibling cast the shadow of a grown man, but Ben knew he had a lot of growing up left to do.

"Well, Parrish, didn't figure on seeing you here today.''

Ben glanced over his shoulder to see Cooper Eldridge stepping out of the saloon. There was always a challenge in everything the man said, and Ben didn't miss the one today.

He only shrugged and replied, ''Had to come in for supplies. Didn't figure to find you wasting time waiting for a stage.''

Eldridge grinned, pulling a match against the weathered boards of the saloon's outer wall. He raised the flame to the cigarette clamped between his teeth. The smoke snaked from between his lips as he said, ''Not much time. The stage ain't never late.''

"Always on time,'' Ben agreed. He couldn't help observing that this was the first time the two of them had agreed on anything in over ten years. ''Always.''

As if on cue, Tom Mitchell called to them as he rode toward the freight office. "Had a feelin' you fellas would be here. Might as well make it a welcoming party of three, I told Delia."

Ben breathed a curse as Mitchell's remark dispelled any pretense of spontaneity. Hell, he should get what he needed from the mercantile and go home.

Mitchell dismounted and clasped Eldridge's outstretched hand, and then extended his to Ben. "Who'd have thought Old Pete came from such highbrow folks? Back East society, now that's hard to picture."

Ben stuffed his gloved hands deep inside his pockets. He searched his mind for any recollection of Pete talking about his family being well-to-do. All he could remember was that his pa had been a churchgoer who made Pete wear a starched white collar every Sunday.

"What did that lawyer fella ever say about the niece?" Mitchell paused to light the cigarette he had taken from Eldridge. "She's gotta have gumption, I'll say that."

"More likely she's loco." Eldridge leaned against the doorjamb of the saloon. "I give her one night out on that ranch, and she'll run like a jackrabbit."

A sudden gust of wind rushed up the street, bringing with it a cloud of dust. Ben squinted against the onslaught, grit stinging his eyes.

"The stage should be here by now." Mitchell felt for his pocket watch. "He's never late. Never."

Gazing toward the end of town, Ben saw no sign of an approaching stage. "There's no point waiting in the cold for a stage that's behind schedule."

"We could wait inside the saloon," Mitchell suggested, replacing his timepiece. "A strong shot of rye is just what I need."

"How 'bout it, Ben?" Once again, Eldridge's voice held a tone of challenge. "Got time to share a friendly drink?"

Ben glanced down the street, toward the livery stable. Clayton would be at least half an hour with the mare. "There's always time for a friendly drink."

"A good idea," Mitchell declared as they passed through

the swinging doors. "Even if it was mine. Besides, the stage is never late. Never."

"Never! Not one time in over two hundred trips!"
Thud!
Everyone inside the saloon turned at the sound of the stage driver's angry voice. The stage was over an hour late, and there had already been talk of sending out a search party, in case there had been an accident.

"Horses gone lame! Indian attacks!" *Thud!* "This stage ain't never been late! Till now!"

Ben was the first one out of the saloon. All along Main Street, faces appeared in the windows of every business, peering out at the stage. Curiosity quickly led them away from their duties. Even the barber stepped outside his shop, followed by a half-shaven customer, just in time to see the enraged stage driver heaving another trunk from atop the stage.

"Stop that, you stupid fool! You'll ruin everything I own."

The female voice drew Ben's attention to the woman scrambling out of the stagecoach, and he breathed a curse. All this time he'd been expecting a dried-up old maid, not a shapely young woman. Her dark hair had fallen loose about her shoulders, and her face was flushed with anger. She looked wild and unrestrained. Damn, what fool in New York had let her out of his bed?

She began a desperate attempt to retrieve her scattered belongings. One trunk had spilled open onto the street and she hastily began scooping her clothing back into the battered case.

The driver glared down at her, his grip tightening on the handle of the trunk. "I even had women havin' babies on the trail, but this is the first time I've missed my schedule. You and your damned trunks, wantin' to stop and buy 'souvenirs' from every Injun with their hand out."

Halley struggled with the trunk on the street, its hinges cracked and the lid flopping like a broken arm. Soon, everything she owned would be strewn over the muddy streets of Wilder, Wyoming. Just as she turned to glare at the driver, she found him prepared to hurl another of her trunks from the stage.

"Take your hands off of that this instant!" Halley felt angry color rush to her cheeks.

She rose to her feet, her other possessions forgotten, and approached the stage. She glared up at the driver and recognized the challenge in his expression. "I'm warning you, put it down."

"Warn me? Don't no woman warn me!" He heaved the trunk closer to the edge. "I'm sick of your damned trunks anyway."

"Don't you dare!" Halley shouted. Without thinking, she seized the railing of the stage and hoisted herself onto the driver's seat. "Put my trunk down!"

"Don't scare them horses, little lady." The driver braced his muddy boot atop the trunk, rocking it precariously toward the edge. "If they was to take off, you and your fancy trunk will be in a thousand pieces."

Halley struggled to control her temper, but a mental list of the irreplaceable contents of the trunk kept going through her mind. Her mother's velvet sewing box, a clock from her father's study, and linen her grandmother had embroidered. The rest was mostly odds and ends, but it was all she'd scavenged from the bill collectors. If they were destroyed, she would have nothing tangible left of her life in New York.

Refusing to contemplate that possibility, Halley caught sight of the driver's long whip coiled like a snake across the seat. The handle was within easy reach, though she doubted her ability to wield the cutting length with any amount of accuracy. Leveling her gaze on the driver, she forced her voice to remain calm, all the while reaching for the sinister black whip.

"For the last time I demand that you unhand my property." She found the handle and gripped it tightly. "Do it now."

"What the hell is going on?" Tom Mitchell dashed out of the saloon, followed by Eldridge.

"Rone's having a little trouble with his passenger," Ben replied as the small crowd gathered to watch the spectacle grew larger.

Eldridge raised the brim of his hat. "Damn, I told you she had to be crazy."

"Pretty thing, ain't she?" Tom Mitchell elbowed Ben with a knowing look.

"I'll say," Eldridge was quick to agree when Ben made no comment. "Crazy or not, I wouldn't mind getting next to that."

Ben saw the woman's small hand grasp the handle of the whip. Damn, if she didn't intend to take a little hide off of Rone Temple's filthy carcass. As a rule, Ben believed in letting folks fight their own fights, but he knew the driver carried a bowie knife.

"Just set that trunk down easy, Rone." Ben stepped toward the stage, never taking his eyes off the driver. "Real easy. I don't want to see a speck of dust fly."

"This don't involve you, Parrish."

"It does now." He let his hand fall near his holster, an old habit, but an effective warning. He heard the woman gasp, but kept his eyes on the driver. "Set it down. Easy."

Halley felt the color drain from her face. A gunfighter! Just like in Mr. McClinton's journal, *Survival in the Savage West.* The man stepped forward, and she swore she'd never seen eyes so cold, so merciless. Despite her dislike for the stage driver, she didn't want his death on her conscience, and she let the handle of the whip fall from her grasp.

"Sir, please, he means no harm." Fear made her words sound waspish, and she fought the panic clawing through her midsection. "There's no need to resort to violence."

The gunfighter ignored her, keeping his eyes on the driver. For what seemed an eternity, the two men stared at each other, and Halley prayed her first day in Wilder would not be marred by death.

Finally, Rone Temple breathed a curse and returned the massive trunk to the luggage rack. "I'll need some help unloadin' the son of a bitch. It weighs a ton!"

"Hoist it down, Rone." A second man stepped forward. "You're just gettin' soft in your old age."

The taunt brought a string of curses from the driver, but Halley's attention remained on the gunfighter. Slowly, he turned toward her, and their eyes locked. His eyes no longer held menace, but a shudder passed through her all the same. His eyes were the palest blue she'd ever seen, so pale they appeared almost silver beneath the dark brows.

He broke the hold long enough to let his gaze travel over

her, making her painfully aware of her disheveled appearance.
She raised her chin slightly and refused the temptation to brush
the dust from her clothes. When his eyes met hers again, they
held an unmistakable glint of amusement. She felt color rise
to her face and looked away, knowing he would laugh indeed
if he saw her blush. She neatly recoiled the driver's whip and
returned it to the wagon seat, refusing to contemplate what
might have happened if the gunfighter had not stepped in when
he did.

She would have to compose herself enough to thank him
properly; rogue or not, he had come to her rescue like a gentleman.

Gathering her heavy skirts, she attempted to climb down
from the stage. There was so much to do, now that she was
actually here, but getting down from the stage was much more
difficult than climbing up. The smooth soles of her traveling
shoes slipped against the step, and her petticoat tangled around
the brake shaft.

"Oh, dear," she breathed, realizing her ankles were completely exposed. Her shaking fingers were useless as she
tugged at the white muslin.

"Hold still." The gunfighter's deep voice halted her movements. "You're going to fall."

Halley swallowed as he reached out and unsnarled the pris-
tine white of her petticoat. His large hands circled her waist
and turned her around. She placed her hands on his broad
shoulders as he lifted her down to the ground, fearing her
wobbly legs would not hold her weight. For an eternity of
seconds they faced one another, his hands cupped around her
waist, hers clinging to his shoulders.

There was not a trace of amusement left in his expression,
rather his eyes were narrowed and burning. She felt his fingers
flex around her waist, and she drew a deep breath, hoping to
bolster herself. Instead, her lungs filled with the unmistakable
masculine scent, hot and dusty. She shuddered uncontrollably
and felt his muscles grow tense beneath her palms.

Ben controlled the urge to tighten his hold around her waist,
enticed by the warmth of her flesh just beneath the material
of her dress. She smelled sweet and clean, and he felt a jolt
when her green eyes widened slightly in response. Maybe it

was the way she trembled when he touched her, or the feel of her breath against his face. Most likely, he'd just been too long without a woman, he decided as he released her and stepped back, putting a safe distance between them.

"So, you're Old Pete's niece." Cooper Eldridge stepped forward, making a quick appraisal. He grinned and slapped Ben on the back. "Ben, ain't you going to introduce me to your new neighbor?"

Halley risked a glance at the gunfighter who'd championed her cause and wondered why being neighbors seemed like such a bad idea.

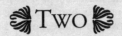

TWO

HALLEY DECIDED THAT the arrival of the Cheyenne stage was the social event of the week in Wilder, Wyoming.

The crowd had remained clustered around her while she gathered her luggage from the stage and the street. Even now, a few locals lingered before the law office, curiosity keeping them from tending to their own affairs. The attorney had finally been forced to draw the shades past peering eyes. Never had she dreamed her arrival would create such a sensation.

"A fine parcel of land you've inherited, Miss St. John. Mighty fine." Warren Olson spread a map of the territory across his desk and drew an imaginary circle around her property with his index finger. "The Platte River runs along the eastern border."

Halley paused long enough to place her wire-rimmed spectacles on the bridge of her nose before following the attorney's circling index finger on the map.

"Five thousand acres of amply watered, prime grazing land." The town's only lawyer sank back in his chair, allowing her time to study her inheritance. "And of course, there's

17

the house, but I hope that won't be too much of a disappointment.''

Her head came up at that. "What about the house? There's nothing wrong with it, is there?"

"Not a thing, not a thing," Mr. Olson assured her. "It's just that your uncle was a bachelor all of his life, and his living conditions might seem somewhat . . . stark, to a lady."

"I'm sure I shall manage just fine." She peered at the map, trying to imagine the actual size of her ranch. "After all, hardship is something one must accept with life on the frontier."

"Life on the frontier *is* hardship," he replied, lacing his fingers together across his midsection. "I can't imagine why you'd choose such an existence over a life of luxury and privilege."

"It can't be that terrible." Halley let her gaze travel the richly furnished office. "You seem to have done quite well."

Olson shook his head. "A pittance compared to what an attorney in New York or Boston would have. Your father was in pharmaceuticals, wasn't he?"

She nodded, taking one last look at the map. "He was very much involved in the distribution of medicinal supplies during the late war. The need was tremendous."

"You now have very lucrative opportunities in the cattle business." Olson cleared his throat and began sorting through the documents that would actually transfer ownership of the property to Halley. "There are a few . . . shall we say requests your uncle made toward your acceptance of the inheritance."

"Oh?" Halley peered at him over her spectacles. "Mr. Pittman mentioned no such restrictions."

"Your uncle had no way of knowing whether you would come to Wyoming or how you would manage your inheritance," Olson explained. "He simply left instructions as to how he wanted matters handled in the event you did choose to accept the land."

Choose. There hadn't been any choice for her to make. Remaining in New York would have meant a pauper's fate. At least in Wyoming she'd have a roof over her head and means to prosper. As the attorney shuffled through the papers, she resisted the nagging worry that she may have traveled to Wyoming for nothing.

"First of all, he requested that you do not change the name of the ranch or the brand he used. He also asked that the foreman, Elijah Dupree, remain in your employ." At her questioning look, he explained, "Your uncle considered Mr. Dupree a faithful friend and asked that he continue supervision of the day-to-day operation of the ranch."

"Those are both reasonable requests." Halley's voice held a note of caution. "Was there anything else?"

Olson cleared his throat and peered down at the will itself. " 'My fondest wish is that my niece will choose to make the ranch her home, but adapting to frontier life will be a great challenge for her. Before a final decision is made, I require that she reside at the ranch for thirty days.

" 'A month's time will allow her a chance to decide if she is suited to living in the West. If not, she may relinquish the property under the conditions I have set forth, with my blessing.' "

Halley sank back in the chair, perplexed. The attorney wasted no time in reassuring her. "Miss St. John, your uncle was concerned for your welfare and wanted to provide for you. However, he was uncertain as to whether or not you would have any desire to leave New York. You may indeed find ranch life unacceptable, and if so, you will have a convenient means of disposing of the property."

"I see," Halley said, more to herself than to Olson. Uncle Peter had died before the dreadful business with Farnsworth and assumed she would have the family fortune at her disposal.

"Uncle Peter sounds like a wise and prudent man." She forced a bright smile, refusing to allow her concerns to show. The last thing she wanted people in Wilder to think was that she was otherwise destitute, due to her own foolishness. Part of her reason for leaving New York was to try to leave behind that shame and start anew.

"From what you have told me, I can't imagine why I wouldn't be happy. I can hardly wait until tomorrow, when I actually get to see the place."

"Tomorrow?" The attorney looked up in surprise. "You're not planning on moving in that soon, are you?"

"Why wouldn't I?" Halley peered over her spectacles, her

delicate brows arched to meet his gaze. "There is much to do before I can fully take up residence, of course. I've already made arrangements at the boardinghouse for tonight, and now I must go to the mercantile and the livery for supplies and a sound team."

"The house has been empty for almost six months. I doubt you'll find much waiting for you out there." Mr. Olson handed her his gold-tipped fountain pen and moved the ink bottle for her convenience. "Do you know what you'll be needing?"

"Oh, yes, I've made a complete list." Halley leaned forward to gather the various documents awaiting her signature. "Mr. McClinton is most explicit regarding the importance of being well supplied."

"I couldn't agree more, and you'll find everything you need here in town. Wilder is coming to be a real boom town. Lots of folks from back East coming out this way." Olson began blotting her signatures and placing more papers before her. "Just tell Jim Tulley I sent you. He's the only decent merchant within a hundred miles, and he'll have everything you need."

Halley glanced through the curtained window of the law office toward the general store, where she noticed the man who had interceded on her behalf against the stage driver. Ben Parrish, she'd learned upon introductions, was going to be her nearest neighbor and had known her uncle for years.

He stood before the store, having removed his coat and rolled the sleeves of his shirt over his forearms. He knelt and hefted a large burlap sack that she guessed would weigh as much as she did. He tossed it easily into the back of the wagon, but she didn't miss the way the muscles of his arms bulged against his sleeves.

She looked on as he loaded boxes into his wagon, and a shiver feathered up her spine as she remembered the feel of his hands around her waist and the piercing blue of his eyes, eyes the shade of a winter sky at dawn.

She was even more intrigued to learn that he was not a gunfighter, and her curiosity still lingered. He was exactly how she had pictured the steely-eyed men who lived by the gun. Ruggedly handsome and quick on the draw, there was an aura of mystery surrounding such a man.

And there was more to a man like Ben Parrish than ranching

and driving cattle, she was sure of it. As she signed the last of the numerous documents for the attorney, Halley decided the mercantile would be her first stop.

"You sure you can't use an extra pound of nails around the place, Ben?" Jim Tulley asked as he capped the jug of coal oil. "Got in a double order last week, and that's something that always comes in handy."

Ben only shook his head as he reached into his pocket for his money. "Got plenty of nails left from the new barn."

"Suit yourself." The storekeeper began totaling Ben's order, licking the point of his pencil after each entry.

Ben glanced around the store, hoping to see Clayton. He was ready to head home and didn't feel like looking for the boy. A shiny bit of ribbon caught his eye, and he noticed a rack of sewing notions—buttons, thread, and lace. Reaching with one gloved hand, Ben traced the length of an open spool of pink ribbon.

The thought of something so soft and feminine brought a flood of memories, memories Ben thought long dead. He had put all thought of decent women from his mind, seeking only occasional comfort from nameless whores. Now he found himself imagining such a length of ribbon falling from a woman's hair. A particular woman.

Damn, if he was going to daydream, it shouldn't be about Pete's crazy niece. He'd learned his lesson early in life and wouldn't be betrayed by a pretty face again.

But her image remained clear in his mind, vibrant and real, overshadowing the faded memories of the past. It had been a long time since a woman trembled when he touched her, and he couldn't forget the feel of her fingers clinging to his shoulders.

The storekeeper gave him a curious look, and Ben crammed his hands into his pockets and looked away. Outside the store, the stage was being loaded for another journey after being hitched with a fresh team. A half grin touched Ben's lips as he pictured Halley St. John giving Rone the devil and tangling her petticoats in the brake shaft. The smile quickly faded as he remembered lifting her down, the feel of her heart beating rapidly beneath his touch, and the swell of her breast just above his thumb.

The sudden jangle of the brass bell above the store's entrance drew his attention. Again, he breathed a curse as Halley St. John herself entered the store, as if his heated thoughts had conjured her up out of thin air. She smiled when their eyes met, but he only gave her a slight nod before turning back to the storekeeper.

"Hello again, Mr. Parrish," Halley said when she stood beside him at the store's counter.

"Ma'am." His reply was crisp, almost curt. He tried to ignore the sweet scent of perfume that rose from her flesh. She began removing a delicate pair of gloves and he had to look away, not wanting to notice the bare, slender fingers.

She cleared her throat slightly, as if to reclaim his attention. "I want to thank you again, for your assistance this morning."

"No need to thank me," he said, never taking his eyes from the clerk's pencil.

Halley watched him, studying the strong set of his jaw, his broad shoulders, and solid frame. Obviously, she had been right about him. He was so accustomed to danger that an armed confrontation was of little notice to him, but to her it had been utterly chivalrous. "There is a need to thank you. What you did was most honorable."

He turned to face her then. "What you did was damned foolish. If you'd so much as flicked that whip at Rone, he would have sliced you open like a ripe peach."

Stunned, Halley could only stare up at him. She had hoped Ben Parrish would prove to be a good-natured fellow, but he seemed openly hostile, to the point of being rude. "I hope you don't think—"

"Do you really want to know what I think?"

Halley drew herself to full height, though the top of her head barely reached his shoulder, and faced him. "Yes, Mr. Parrish, I do."

His eyes narrowed and traveled boldly over her, deliberately appraising every inch, and he glanced quickly at the gloves resting on the store counter. When his eyes met hers, she barely resisted the urge to flinch from the disdain in their blue depths.

"What I think is that a woman like you has no business out here alone."

She felt her own eyes narrow and an angry warmth rise to her face. "A woman like me?"

"A pampered lady." He all but sneered. "You won't last a week, if that long."

"That is where you are wrong, sir." Halley hefted her heavy carpetbag onto the counter and gave him a knowing smile. Obviously, he had assumed she was yet another ill-advised tenderfoot. "However, I can fully understand your assumption. Mr. McClinton spoke of the Easterners who venture west, completely unprepared. Greenhorns, I believe they're called."

Ben eased the brim of his hat back from his forehead. "And you're no greenhorn. That's what you're telling me?"

"Absolutely not." Halley presented her list to the store-keeper, saying, "Good afternoon, Mr. Tulley. Your store has been highly recommended by my new attorney, and I have prepared a complete list of the supplies I wish to purchase. You do carry those items, am I correct?"

Tulley quickly scanned the list, his eyes darting up and down like a pump handle. "Yes, ma'am. I can have everything ready for you, whenever you say."

Curiosity was not one of Ben's natural traits, but he would have paid real money to get a look at that list. What necessities would a woman from the East consider vital to survival? He could well imagine her hanging lace curtains without giving a thought to the empty woodbox.

"Tomorrow morning would be ideal. Mr. Parrish?" Her voice drew his attention. "Could I impose upon you to show me to the livery stable?"

"The livery?" he echoed. "What do you want at the livery?"

"Mr. McClinton stresses the importance of having a sound beast to pull a wagon," she explained. "His instructions are most clear, and I do know a little about horses myself."

"Who's McClinton?"

Halley reached into her carpetbag, producing a large, leather-bound book. "Maxwell J. McClinton spent six entire months braving the hostile lands of central Kansas, surveying land for the railroad." She smoothed her hand across the rich grain of the cover. "He has written a vivid account of his experiences on the frontier. Before leaving New York, I had the honor of hearing Mr. McClinton speak at a luncheon given by the Literary Society."

Halley opened the cover, revealing the fly page, which read: *A Gentleman's Guide to Survival in the Savage West.* "There's an inscription, from Mr. McClinton himself. I cannot tell you what an inspiration it has been."

"And this book is what you're going by?"

She placed the volume on the counter, turning the dog-eared pages until she found her place. "Chapter Three deals exclusively with livestock, particularly horses. Did you know that one may tell the age of a horse by the length of the animal's teeth?"

"Is that so?" Ben groaned inwardly. The woman was in for more trouble than she could imagine.

"Yes, indeed. He tells of a horse trader who sells older, unhealthy horses under the guise that they are yet young and able-bodied."

Ben raised an eyebrow. "But McClinton knew to check their teeth."

Halley closed the book and replaced it in her bag. "Actually, he learned that lesson the hard way. It seems the poor nag he was cheated with had already lost most of her teeth."

Ben hefted a large bag of flour onto his shoulder and turned toward the door. "I'll show you to the livery, Miss St. John, but there's more to a horse than teeth. You've got to look at their hooves, legs, and eyes."

Halley gathered her carpetbag and hurried to keep up with his long strides. She had no intention of being cheated, and Ben Parrish seemed to be her best local resource for information. "Have you much experience with horses, Mr. Parrish?"

"I never bought one that couldn't chew his own oats." His steps halted as he turned toward her. Once again, their eyes met, but this time he didn't look away. "Like I said, you won't last a week."

Halley swallowed, hoping to find her voice, but all she

could manage was a shaky reply. "We shall see, Mr. Parrish. We shall see."

"Miss St. John!" the storekeeper called just as Ben pushed the door open, snapping Halley out of the spell of Ben Parrish's eyes. "Does this say three charges of dynamite or eight?"

She pretended not to notice the astonished look on Ben Parrish's face. "Eight, Mr. Tulley, eight."

The livery stable was located at the far end of the muddy street, adjacent to a blacksmith shop. The raucous voices of men and the stench of manure drifted through the open door. Halley gave Ben a doubtful look as he motioned for her to step through the wide entrance. Gingerly lifting the hem of her long skirt, she picked her way through the straw-littered entrance and stepped inside the teeming stable.

One could barely hear above the din of male voices, and the sweet smell of freshly cut hay perished as it mixed with the pungent odor of manure, sweaty horses, and unwashed bodies. Halley could feel her nose wrinkle in protest, but she reminded herself that one should naturally expect such in a busy livery. She turned to Ben Parrish, who seemed little affected by the condition of the stable, and waited for his suggestions regarding the purchase of a horse.

"Well, Mr. Parrish, what is your recommendation?"

The sweet lilt of a woman's voice fell like a net over the men in the livery, every one stopping midstride to turn and stare. Halley felt color rise to her cheeks as she immediately became the object of everyone's attention. She cleared her throat and hoped to appear calm and collected.

"First thing you need to do is meet the owner." Ben extended his hand to the burly man who stepped forward. "Gus Mahoney, livery owner and blacksmith, this is Halley St. John, just off the stage. Where's that brother of mine?"

"Out back, with my boy. They're just finishing up with your mare." The blacksmith cast a dubious look at Halley, his bushy eyebrows drawing together. "What ails you, Ben, bringing a lady like that into my stable?"

Taken aback by the man's gruff manners, Halley opened her mouth to protest, but Ben sent her a reproachful glance that warned her not to speak impulsively.

"Miss St. John is in the market for a horse." Ben motioned toward the series of stalls. "You got a few for sale, don't you?"

"Aye, a few good mounts in them back stalls." He surveyed Halley with a doubtful expression. "Work animals, they are, not Thoroughbreds."

Halley glanced at Ben as she followed the owner toward the back entrance of the livery. His expression gave no clue to his thoughts, and he made no move to offer his help with her selection. She forced herself to concentrate on the task at hand, determined to show herself well informed.

"Take your pick, lady." Mahoney nodded toward the six horses peering at her from their stalls. "Forty dollars a head."

Halley took note of each horse. They all seemed healthy and sturdy. Once again, she glanced back toward Ben Parrish, who offered no assistance.

"The black there, with the star on her forehead, she's gentle as a kitten." Mahoney smoothed his hand along the horse's sleek neck.

Ben looked on as Halley peered up at the mare who stood at least seventeen hands. The dismay on her face was almost comical, but he didn't smile. Instead, he merely watched patiently and waited for her to ask his opinion.

"Who is she, Ben?" Clayton whispered as he came up behind Ben without warning.

Startled, Ben gave his brother a fierce scowl "*That* is Pete's niece."

"The spinster?" Clayton let out a long, low whistle and pushed the brim of his hat back from his forehead. "She don't look like no schoolmarm to me."

Annoyed, Ben didn't respond, but he had never agreed with his brother more. Halley St. John looked nothing like a spinster, but nothing like a rancher either. She had a look of finery and comfort about her. Her life had been easy up until now, and Ben wondered what had prompted her to leave for the West.

Instead, he asked, "Where have you been anyway? I waited at Tulley's almost twenty minutes."

Clayton looked away. "I had things to see about. Besides,

you seem to have kept yourself occupied."

They both glanced back at Halley, and Ben's scowl darkened. Just when he was certain she had no idea what she was looking for, her eyes caught sight of something behind him, and her expression became one of pleased determination. Ben swiveled his head to follow her gaze, only to find a mule watching them from a stall at the very back of the stable.

"You don't want that mule, lady," Mahoney called out when he realized her intent. "I swear that ornery creature's got the devil in him."

Halley strode past Ben and stood before the wary mule, admiring his long tapered ears and soft brown eyes. There was something she liked in those eyes, something wise and compelling. She reached into her skirt pocket for a piece of hard candy and offered it to the creature. Hesitantly, the mule nosed her extended palm before accepting the candy. His long yellow teeth made quick work of the treat as Halley gently stroked his neck.

"I don't believe it." The blacksmith turned to Ben. "I can't believe it. That contrary varmint wouldn't let a soul near that stall all day, but he eats out of her hand."

"Believe it, Gus." Ben shook his head at the way Halley charmed the mule.

"Who does he belong to?" Halley inquired, wishing she had more candy. The mule seemed disappointed when she didn't offer another treat.

"Anyone who can pay for the hay and oats he eats, I reckon," Mahoney declared. "He belonged to a miner who came into town looking for excitement and got hisself shot."

Halley turned to Ben. "Mr. McClinton speaks very highly of mules. He says they are sure of foot and have fantastic stamina. What is your opinion?"

"Ben doesn't care too much for mules, ma'am." Clayton stepped forward, quickly removing his hat. "He says they're too hardheaded for any use on a ranch."

"And what do you think?" Halley cocked her head, taking an immediate liking to the younger version of Ben Parrish. "I'm going to need a strong beast, capable of carrying heavy loads."

"I think a mule might be just what you need," Clayton

replied as he stroked the mule's stubby mane.

"So do I." Halley nodded, sending Ben a lofty glance. "We haven't been introduced." She extended her hand. "I am Halley St. John."

Clayton turned pink as a cactus flower as he shook her hand, barely getting his name out, and Ben rolled his eyes. A young buck like his brother would naturally be taken by a sweet smile and gentle manners, but then so was the mule.

"Mr. Mahoney." She turned back to the livery keeper. "I shall purchase this mule. However, I want him curried, shod, and allowed to spend the afternoon in the corral. He needs fresh air and sunshine."

The blacksmith's mouth dropped open, and he cast a disbelieving glance toward Ben. "Fresh air and sunshine? For a mule?" he demanded. "Look, lady, I ain't running no Sunday school."

"I'm not asking for anything I don't intend to pay for, Mr. Mahoney," Halley blithely replied. She turned back to Clayton and asked, "What else do you know about mules?"

Ben only shrugged as Clayton continued his discussion with Halley St. John on the attributes of mules. "Why don't I settle up with you for the mare?" he suggested to the bewildered blacksmith. The sooner he was back at his ranch, the better.

"So that's who Old Pete left his land to, heh?" Mahoney asked once they were inside the office, safely out of earshot. "What's a pretty little thing like that gonna do with all that land?"

"It's none of my concern." Ben ignored the blacksmith's immediate burst of laughter. Halley St. John wouldn't be in Wyoming long enough to be of concern to anyone, least of all a man fighting to keep his land. He peered through the office window as two of the livery hands led the mule out of his stall for Halley's further inspection.

Mahoney was still chuckling as he opened the cash box. "All that land and the water rights, no concern of yours? I wonder how Eldridge and Mitchell feel about her."

"How much do I owe you?"

"Two dollars." Gus took the money from Ben, placed it in the strongbox, and slammed the lid. "I reckon she won't have as easy a time as she thinks."

"She'll have a fight on her hands, if she stays."

Gus peered through the slats of the makeshift window of his office, watching Halley with avid interest. "Maybe not. Might be different for a woman."

"How do you mean?"

The blacksmith shrugged. "If a man wants to take land from another man, it's a fight to the death. But takin' land from a woman . . . well, that's as easy as getting under her petticoats."

Again, Gus laughed as Ben scowled in disgust. He hadn't given much thought to what would happen if Halley St. John tried to hold on to the land. His concern had been the fight for control that would ensue after she fled back to the East. If she stayed, she would have to fight every land-hungry cattleman in Wyoming Territory.

Ben glanced through the office window again, suddenly aware of the way the men in the stable were eyeing her. She stood silhouetted against the bright opening of the livery, the afternoon sun outlining her generous curves and tangling in the golden highlights of her hair.

The only thing more scarce than open land was single women, and every man in the stable had abandoned their work to watch Halley with blatant interest. Too much so to suit Ben.

Jerking the office door open, he called, "Come on, Clayton. Let's get going."

Halley and Clayton both approached where he stood at the doorway, and Ben was struck by the utter delight on Halley's face.

"I'm taking Miss St. John over to the wagonwright." Clayton's voice drew his attention. "She's asked me to help her pick out a steady rig."

"We need to get home. There's work waiting on us."

"Now, Ben, that would be downright rude. She needs our help." Clayton grinned easily, enjoying his brother's stifled irritation. "After all, we're going to be neighbors."

Ben settled his gaze on Halley St. John, and wondered why being neighbors seemed like such a bad idea.

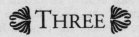

THREE

THE LATE-EVENING breeze began to stir, bringing a chill to the darkness as Ben watched Halley St. John disappear inside the boardinghouse. He breathed a curse, vowing he would have Clayton mucking out stalls for a month as payback for today. His brother's offer to assist Halley at the wagonwright had led to a call on the harnessmaker, the land office, a second trip to the mercantile, and back to the livery stable.

Clayton had then insisted on having supper at the town's only restaurant before disappearing and leaving Ben to pay the bill and escort Halley back to the boardinghouse.

From his vantage point, he could hear the bawdy laughter and tinkling of the tinny piano coming from the brothel at the end of the street. Sure as the world, his brother already had his pants down with no thought to the work that had gone undone at the ranch today.

Glancing up, Ben caught sight of a muted shadow, wavering behind an upstairs window shade. The blurred image ducked and rose, and he knew instinctively that he was watching Halley undress. He could envision her slipping the dress off her shoulders and combing slender fingers through her dark hair.

Ben couldn't take his eyes away from the silhouette, riveted in place by the thought of her bare arms and unbound hair. Too many times today, he'd found himself watching her and wondering how she would feel against him. Even now, he imagined her green eyes, eyes that sparkled so easily with delight, burning with passion.

An uncomfortable tightness began to settle in his groin, and he turned away from the boardinghouse. She was a fine-looking woman, but he wouldn't let himself get hot for her. Halley St. John was nothing but trouble. Whether she remained in Wilder one more day or a lifetime, Ben intended to stay the hell away from her. There was no room in his life for the complications a hardheaded Eastern woman would bring.

What he needed now was a stiff drink, but he had no use for the rowdy, drunken crowd at the saloon. He glanced back toward the brothel and seriously considered the offerings he would find there. Hard liquor and a willing woman went a long way to ease a man's mind. Such thoughts drew his gaze back to Halley's window, where her shadow still lingered behind the shade.

Once again, the shadow bent and disappeared for a moment. When the blur returned, her arms lifted and the shape became distorted. He realized, to his discomfort, that she was pulling a nightgown over her head. Damn, he didn't want to think about her climbing into an empty bed wearing nothing but a length of thin cotton, or silk.

Women like her wore silk, he reminded himself, soft and cool against their bare skin. Suddenly darkness filled the window, but he remained in place, bereft at the loss of her image.

He damned himself a fool, no better than a randy kid. He knew all he needed to know about such ladies, enough to know they didn't belong on cattle ranches. He remembered the way she had frowned at the conditions of the livery and wondered just what she expected to find on a ranch.

In the quiet of the darkened street, Ben again began to seriously wonder why she had really left her world of comfort and privilege for the ruthless, hand-to-mouth existence of Wyoming. She clung to that damned guidebook as if it were her only hope, as if she couldn't afford to chance a mistake.

He turned away from the boardinghouse toward the sheriff's

office, where the light was still burning. The old lawman was always good for a late-night cup of coffee, and Ben decided he could use a handy distraction from thoughts of Halley.

Still, the question lingered in the back of his mind as he entered the sheriff's office. Was she only chasing fickle dreams or was she perhaps running from nightmares?

"Evenin', Ben." The older man looked up from the newspaper he was reading, his booted feet propped on the edge of the desk. "What's got you in town so late?"

"That harebrained brother of mine," he replied, crossing the bare floor of the office to the cast-iron stove. He lifted the pewter lid of the coffeepot and grimaced. "When did you make this coffee? Christmas?"

Roy Teal chuckled as he folded his newspaper. "New Year's, maybe." He paused while Ben filled a tin cup with the potent brew. "I hear tell you're courtin' the Eastern woman."

Ben's head snapped up. "What the hell are you talking about?"

"It's all over town." Roy's grin widened. "Heard you bought her a mule. I swear, Ben, you got a way with women."

Slamming the coffeepot back on the stove, Ben scowled as the sheriff's laughter filled the tiny office. "I can thank that brother of mine for that, too. He spends all afternoon running after her and then takes off to find a two-dollar whore."

Roy's amusement subsided. "Could be you need a little of that yourself. You know what they say about all work and no play."

Ben made no comment as he sank into a wooden chair opposite the sheriff's and tossed his hat on the desk. He tasted the coffee, finding it strong and bitter, which suited his mood. The last thing he wanted to do was wallow in a whore's bed with Halley St. John on his mind.

"Speaking of all work, what's keeping you up tonight?" he asked, by way of a change of subject. "You expecting trouble?"

"No more than usual." Roy laced his fingers behind his head and leaned back in his chair. "This time of the year there's too many drovers in town with time to kill. Eldridge's boys are just itching for a fight with those nesters."

Ben stared into the darkness of his coffee, swirling the liquid. Cooper Eldridge's ranch foreman had gotten himself shot by a nester in a dispute over a fifth ace. "Cattle and farmers don't mix."

"Hell, that's for sure," the sheriff agreed with a nod. "Throw in a few miners and a cardsharp or two and you've got the makings for a real knock-down-drag-out."

Closing his eyes, Ben pinched the bridge of nose between his thumb and forefinger. "The last thing we need in this town is more trouble."

Roy nodded. "I really didn't think she'd come out here, did you?"

Ben made no reply. Hell, no one had believed for a minute that an unmarried Eastern woman would have any interest at all in the cattle business. The land was all he'd cared about, and now that was out of reach.

"She won't stay," Ben finally declared before draining the coffee from his cup. "She'll be gone before the first frost."

"And then what?"

"You're the third person today who's asked me that," Ben growled, wishing he had an answer. "How the hell do I know?"

"The squatters will be on that place like ants at a picnic," Roy informed him, "and Mitchell and Coop will be pushing their cattle right behind them."

"You act like it's my fault."

"Simmer down, Ben." Roy leaned forward and smoothed his hand across the folded newspaper. "I know it's not your fault, but that place borders yours and you'll be right in the middle when the shooting starts."

"I left Texas because I was sick of killing." Ben let his forearms rest on his knees, the empty coffee cup dangling from his thumb. "It only leads to more."

"Don't let it come to that."

"How?"

"Like you said you would. Buy her out and send her packing."

Bone-weary exhaustion far outweighed the excitement Halley felt at the prospect of traveling to her ranch the next day.

As she sank gratefully into her narrow bed at the boarding-house, the list of tasks awaiting her filtered through her foggy brain, but she was much too tired to focus carefully on any of them.

Closing her eyes, Halley's thoughts drifted to Ben Parrish ... the gunfighter. *Rancher,* she corrected herself. The rancher who'd reprimanded the stage driver and lifted her down from the stage as if she were light as a feather.

She opened her eyes and blinked against the darkness. She had literally hung in his arms, dazed by the heat of his touch. It was silly, really. She'd been assisted down from countless carriages before, but she'd never been ... *claimed.*

That was the only word she could think of to describe the way he had stepped forward, grasped her firmly, and held her closer than was necessary.

She imagined a rendering of him on the cover of a dime novel, defending her against the ill-tempered stage driver. He was every bit as rugged and handsome as the heroes of the frontier adventures. Even Mr. McClinton had declared that such fictitious accounts paled in the face of the reality of the West.

Perhaps, she mused, she should write to one of the publishers in San Francisco. With a little elaboration, the story would be as good as any she had read.

Halley smiled to herself as she imagined the book's cover: *Heroic Gunfighter Rescues Defenseless Traveler.* Pleased by her own creativity, she stretched beneath the comforter and turned toward the window.

That's when she saw him. Or at least the shadow. A man's shadow passing by her second-story window. She froze in place, her eyes widening as the shadow blocked the dim light of the quarter moon filtering through the curtains.

One must take every precaution in the interest of personal safety, and in all situations remain calm and alert.

Halley swallowed hard, recalling the passage from Mr. McClinton's journal silently. She never dreamed she would be putting his counsel to use so soon. The window creaked, and the panes rattled as the shadow became all too real. Taking no time for second-guessing his motives, Halley immediately reached for the pistol she had wedged under the mattress.

Her hands were shaking as she gripped the Colt's smooth handle, never taking her eyes from the shadow wavering before the window. The cold clammy hand of panic gripped her heart, and she could not contain her frightened cry as the sash gave way and the window flew open.

"Evenin', little lady. I can't believe a pretty gal like you ain't got nothing warm to curl up with on a cold night like this."

The voice whipped into the room along with the cold night air, the combination chilling Halley to the bone. The intruder placed one booted foot on the floor. "Now, don't you go and do nothing foolish. I mean it, darlin'. You scream and you'll be sorry in a heartbeat."

A heartbeat was all that passed. Halley raised the pistol, closed her eyes, and fired.

The lone gunshot, immediately followed by a woman's piercing scream and the shattering of glass, jolted Ben to his feet. His first thought: Halley St. John.

He and Roy raced out onto the street. The sheriff quickly looked in every direction, but Ben turned without hesitation toward the boardinghouse. Drawing his gun as he crossed the street, Ben breathed a curse and a prayer at the same time. He had known Halley's presence would cause trouble, but he never dreamed anyone would shoot her in cold blood the first night.

He topped the porch steps and tried the door. Locked. Beyond the door, he could hear frantic voices and frenzied pounding. Without hesitation, he stepped back and slammed the heel of his boot against the brass knob, splintering the door from its hinges.

"Lady, are you crazy?"

Halley knelt on the bed, holding the gun steady despite her shattered nerves. The stench of gunpowder hung heavy in the air, burning her nostrils when she dared breathe.

Her mind raced through the myriad of passages she'd read in the dime novels depicting this very scene—a ne'er-do-well held at bay by a courageous peace officer defending a cowering female. Only she was the one with the gun and she couldn't afford to cower.

Cocking the hammer of her pistol, she tried to sound as threatening as possible. "Crazy enough to pull this trigger again if you so much as breathe wrong."

The sudden pounding at the door startled her, drawing her attention from the cringing intruder.

"Just a moment," she called, her voice cracked. She fumbled to light the lamp on the bedside table and turned to take a good look at her would-be attacker. He flinched as the light flooded the room. "Get those hands up."

"What on earth is happening in there? Are you hurt?" The landlady's voice grew louder. "Open the door!"

Scrambling from the bed, Halley unlocked the door and yanked it open with the frazzled innkeeper still knocking. "There was an intruder," she gasped. "He forced the window open and came into my room."

Mrs. Porter stared openmouthed toward the broken window, the shredded curtains, and the man huddled in the corner. Her other boarders were peering out of their rooms in terror, but before she could collect her wits enough to speak, the pounding of boots on the stairs and men's voices broke the silence.

"What the hell's going on up there?" Two men topped the stairs—Ben Parrish followed by an older man Halley had never seen. The stranger made his way in front of Ben and demanded, "What happened?"

"He forced his way into my room," Halley stated, her voice high-pitched from panic. She cleared her throat and tried to sound collected. "I was forced to defend myself."

Ben shouldered his way in, his gaze sweeping the room before settling on Halley. His gun was drawn, and the icy blue of his stare chilled her. "Are you hurt?"

"No," she managed, her throat burning with frightened tears, and looked away before dabbing her eyes with the back of her hand.

Ben turned her face toward his, his fingers gentle beneath her chin. "Did he touch you?"

The temptation to lean into his touch was too strong, and Halley forced a show of bravado along with a weak smile.

Taking a step backward, she answered, "He didn't have a chance."

The sheriff turned toward the peering faces of the other boarders. "Go on back to your beds. No one was hurt, and the show is over. Mrs. Porter, we'll handle things."

The landlady would not be dismissed. "Sheriff, I won't stand for such carrying on! Glass is everywhere, and my best curtains are completely ruined."

"He could have killed me! Do you think I was worried about your curtains?" Halley's courage began to dissolve, and she looked desperately toward Ben Parrish. Swallowing hard against the tears, she repeated, "He could have killed me."

"I'm the one who almost got killed!" The intruder finally spoke as he scrambled to his feet, arms still raised above his head. "This crazy woman dang near blew my head off."

"You're just lucky I missed," Halley retorted, still wielding the pistol in her trembling hands.

"I think you're safe now," Ben admonished, taking the Colt. He holstered his own weapon and approached the intruder, glass crunching beneath his boots. "Looks like you picked the wrong window tonight, boy."

"I was just funnin', mister," he explained with a nervous laugh, his eyes darting toward the open window. "Just give a her a little scare."

Ben's eyes narrowed. "Why?"

The sheriff made his way into the room, surveying the damage to the window before settling his gaze on the intruder. "Didn't I just lock you up a few weeks back?" he demanded. "As I recall, you had a little run-in with some of Tom Mitchell's drovers. Cheating at cards, weren't you?"

"I weren't cheating." With exaggerated caution, he lowered his hands and felt his face and scalp. Shards of glass clattered to the floor, and he cursed at the sight of blood on his fingertips. "Damn, I'm cut to pieces."

"You'll live." The sheriff handed him a faded blue bandanna. "Wrap that hand good, I don't want you bleeding all over the jail."

"You ain't got no call to run me in," he said, turning to glare at Halley. "I didn't lay a hand on her."

"Lucky for you. What were you doing climbing through

her window in the middle of the night?'' Ben turned the man around and retrieved a long knife from the waistband of his dirty Levi's, the thin blade gleaming in the lamplight. "A man usually leaves his weapons behind when he goes courting."

A strangled cry escaped Halley's lips at the sight of the knife. With legs weak as water, she groped for the bedpost to keep from falling. Dear God, he really could have killed her.

Thank heavens for Mr. McClinton! Had she not read his journal, she would have known nothing about pistols or the need to have one accessible at all times.

Ben continued his unceremonious search of the man's pockets, withdrawing a pair of gleaming gold coins. "Well, look at this, Roy. Now, how do you suppose these got here?"

"That's my money," the intruder insisted. "You ain't got no right to search me."

"I'm not the law," Ben replied, tossing the coins to the sheriff. "I don't need a right."

"You can't just take money that belongs to me."

"Since when does being a cattle bum pay so well?" Ben gripped the man's arm and easily steered him toward the waiting sheriff. "Get him locked up and hold that money as evidence."

"Evidence?" the sheriff echoed.

"I'd like to see who else in town has been spending gold pieces." Ben looked on as the intruder was led toward the doorway. "The saloon would be the best place to ask."

The sheriff nodded and then glanced back at Halley. "I'll need to ask this young lady some questions. A report's got to be made, if she's going to press charges."

"She's pressing charges." Ben's reply was steady, and he turned to look at Halley. "I'll see that she's downstairs in fifteen minutes,"

The sheriff led the intruder away, followed by the angry landlady, demanding to know who would pay for the damage done to her window. When they had disappeared down the stairs, Halley turned away from Ben's critical stare. He had warned her she would not be safe, and now he would remind her of his prediction. A sob gave way in her throat, and she could hold the tears back no longer.

Even the knowledge that he was standing there watching

her make a fool of herself didn't silence her. Weary and frightened, her body shook with sobs, and she was mortified. Halley had never cried in front of anyone. She stiffened at the feel of his hands on her shoulders.

"Lady, don't cry," he whispered, turning her toward him. "You did what you had to do."

He wiped the tears from her cheek with a callused thumb, and his touch undid her frayed resolve. Halley sank against him and sobbed even harder as his arms closed around her.

Ben inhaled the sweet scent of her hair and held her gently while she cried. He tried not to think about how perfectly she fit against him, or how good she felt in his arms. Her nightgown did nothing to shield her, and he could feel her breasts, warm and pliant, pressing against the wall of his chest.

He let his hands slide over the ivory material; it was silk, just like he figured. He had no doubt her skin would be even softer and infinitely warmer beneath his fingers.

Her sobs began to subside, and she shuddered, spent from the breakdown. When she didn't pull out of his embrace, Ben indulged the temptation to slide his fingers through her waist-length hair. Slowly, Halley raised her tear-streaked face to his, her palms damp against the fabric of his shirt.

The expression etched on Ben's face made Halley forget her tears and embarrassment. His eyes narrowed when she didn't look away, and she could feel the quickening of his breath against her cheek.

She swallowed, tasting her own tears, and she knew he could feel her heart pounding as their bodies were pressed so closely together.

His long fingers tangled in her hair, cradling the back of her head in his palm while his other hand settled between her shoulder blades. He urged her closer, and her throat went dry as he lowered his head. His mouth hovered above hers, and her lips parted slightly.

"Ben! What in the Sam Hill are you doing up there?"

The sheriff's voice scattered the spell swirling around them. Ben immediately released his hold, and Halley skittered to the other side of the room, her cheeks burning. My God, she had thrown herself into his arms, like a wanton. She cleared her throat, hoping to disguise the husky tone her voice had taken.

"Tell the sheriff I'd rather wait until morning to talk with him."

"If you want that man to go to jail, you'd better sign a complaint tonight." Ben took a step toward her, and hesitated, as if weighing the consequences of coming too close. "You're a stranger in town, don't forget that. You can't leave any room for doubt that you didn't want that man in your room."

She whirled to stare at him in horror, angry color burning her cheeks. "No one would dare suggest such a thing," she bit out. "I won't stand for such tawdry accusations."

"Then get dressed, Miss St. John." Ben's face remained taut. "The sheriff is waiting on you."

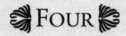

FOUR

HALLEY KNEW FROM experience that the first rule of contending with law-enforcement officials was to remain composed and polite. Even Mr. McClinton had mentioned various encounters with frontier peace officers.

She paused to take a deep breath, hoping to settle her shattered nerves. "Sheriff, that man forced his way into my room with intent to . . . assault me, and this morning you're telling me that he has been released."

Roy Teal shifted nervously in the chair behind his desk. He cleared his throat and tried to explain. "You see, Miss St. John, Tex claims he was drunk and thought he was climbing in a window at the Honey Pot."

She would not be dissuaded. "My presence should have alerted him that he was mistaken. He made no apology, Sheriff; if anything, he was all the more determined to enter the room."

"He just figured you were one of the working girls, waiting on him," Ben explained. "The Honey Pot is the local sporting house."

He crossed the small office and handed her a blue tin cup

he'd filled with coffee. A flicker of amusement passed through his pale blue eyes. "You know what that is, don't you?"

"I do indeed," she snapped, feeling the color flood her face. Anger made her voice tight, and her hands shook as she accepted the cup. Ben deliberately allowed his fingers to brush against hers, sending tiny shock waves up her arm. "He knew very well where he was."

Ben drew his hand away from hers with an almost bemused expression on his face. "He says you made no protest."

"I shot at him, didn't I?" Halley's temper was already rankled, and she refused to allow anyone to make light of her predicament. "I'd say that is a sound protest."

Retreating toward the opposite side of the room, Ben propped one hip on the sheriff's desk and grew serious. "I don't believe his story for a minute, but for now that's all we can go on. At least, until we can prove differently."

"What about the money he had?" She redirected her argument toward the sheriff. "What man with money in his pocket would feel compelled to sneak in the window of . . . such an establishment? What more proof do you need?"

"Miss St. John, my opinion of Tex is as low as yours, but he claims he was drunk and made a mistake." The sheriff sighed. "Be thankful you weren't hurt, and keep that Colt handy."

Futile anger at the situation had drained her energy and, combined with the lack of sleep, had her head pounding mercilessly. She couldn't believe the lies of a saddle tramp carried as much weight as her word. Ruefully, she imagined what would have happened had someone dared force their way into her Manhattan brownstone.

Schooling her emotions, Halley reminded herself that she would have even less clout in New York. With no money or status and an arrest to her credit, the police would have had little sympathy for her in the city. Risking a glance toward Ben Parrish, she also realized that in New York she wouldn't have had such a man charging into her room intent on saving her from danger.

She had never been so frightened in her life, but the feel of his brawny arms closing around had banished her fears. She had been aware of nothing but the heat of his body burning

through her sheer nightgown. She shuddered, the thought causing her lower body to quicken, and she felt her face flame
when he chose that very moment to meet her gaze.

The day's growth of whiskers that darkened his jaw only
added to his rugged good looks, and the narrowed expression
in those blue eyes no longer held even the slightest trace of
humor.

"In other words, it's his word against mine?" Clearing her
throat, Halley turned back toward the sheriff, but her voice
remained husky when she said, "And I'm supposed to be
grateful? He's lying, and you let him walk scot-free."

"I made sure he had enough fines against him to lose those
gold pieces," the lawman assured her. "And he'll have to pay
to fix that window—glass don't come cheap. Leastways, that
will keep him in town until I figure this thing out."

"You seem perfectly content to take his word for what happened." Halley could not keep the scathing tone from her
voice. "What is there to figure, sheriff?"

Jumping at the challenge, the old lawman leaned forward
and replied, "What I'm trying to figure out, little lady, is how
a scoundrel like Tex Whitten, who never had two nickels to
rub together, had two ten-dollar gold pieces in his britches all
of a sudden."

Glancing back at Ben, Halley felt herself becoming more
and more frustrated. "Why would his financial situation be
any concern of mine?"

"If someone was willing to pay him to scare you off," Ben
replied in the cool, steady voice Halley had learned to recognize and resent, "they might be willing to pay even more
to someone who'll finish the job."

Halley swallowed hard, her throat gone dry. "You're saying
someone *paid* that man to . . . harm me?"

"They probably figure you'll hop the first stage and head
home to New York." Ben shrugged. "After you sell the land
to them, dirt cheap, of course."

Halley opened her mouth to explain that returning to New
York was impossible, but thought better of it. She could do
nothing for thirty days. Leaving would mean forfeit, and forfeit would mean destitution.

Squaring her shoulders, she turned back to the sheriff. "I

don't scare easily, and I didn't travel all this way to turn and run at the first whiff of gunpowder. If you need me, Sheriff, I'll be at my ranch.''

"I don't think that's such a good idea, ma'am.'' Roy Teal rose from his desk. "If someone is trying to scare you off, you'd be safer here in town.''

"Ha! I daresay that is the scoundrel's intent, to keep me away from the ranch.'' She gathered her reticule and replaced her black gloves. "If anyone plans to climb in my window tonight, he'll have to ride a good distance to do so.''

"And what will you do if that happens?''

She turned at the sound of Ben Parrish's deep voice and met his challenging gaze. "I'll shoot again, and this time I won't miss.''

The narrow alley behind the saloon was littered with broken whiskey bottles and empty beer kegs, and Ben sidestepped a slimy puddle where the spittoons had been emptied. The rear entrance was open and the bartender was dutifully sweeping the back steps.

"Morning, Charlie,'' he called out. "Busy night?''

"Always.'' The bartender sneered. "Drunks and drovers, and a cardsharp for excitement. I should have listened to my mother.''

Ben hid a smile. "What did she say?''

"She wanted me to be an undertaker,'' he answered, leaning thoughtfully on the broom handle. "Steady work, good money, and no complaints.''

"I suppose none of us turned out to be what our mamas wanted.'' Ben reached into his pocket and withdrew one of Tex Whitten's gold pieces. "Anybody in here last night spending coins like this?''

Charlie took the gleaming coin and turned it over in his palm before shaking his head. "I'd remember one of these. Why?''

"Just curious where it might have come from. Was Tex Whitten in here last night?''

Again, Charlie shook his head. "He owes me money and knows better than to come around unless he can pay me off. He does his drinking over at the Honey Pot. One of the girls is sweet on him, if you can believe that.''

Ben only shrugged, satisfied at least that Whitten's story was a complete lie. Whoever had paid him to frighten Halley probably met up with him at the brothel, and he knew asking questions there would be pointless.

"Thanks anyway," he said, reaching for the gold piece.

"Not so fast." Charlie's hand snapped around the coin. "You owe me five of this."

Ben's eyes narrowed. "What for?"

"Your brother drank hisself senseless and then couldn't pay the tab. Said you'd take care of everything."

"Where is he?"

Charlie jerked his thumb toward the saloon. "Sleeping it off, and if he pukes on my floor, he'll clean it up."

"Count on it."

Ben scaled the back steps and ducked inside the dimly lit saloon. He scanned the room and found Clayton sprawled facedown across a green-felt-covered table. Grabbing a handful of his brother's dark hair, Ben lifted his face into the light.

"Just look at that grin." Charlie's comment only goaded Ben's anger. "At least, he's a happy drunk."

Catching sight of a bucket in the corner, Ben asked, "What's in there?"

"Just water from the rain barrel," the bartender replied. "I was getting ready to mop the place out."

Without hesitation, Ben hefted the half-filled bucket and dumped a good portion of the cold water onto his brother's face. Clayton bounded from the table, instantly awake and gasping for air.

"What'd you do that for?" Mopping his face with his sleeve, he stared disbelieving at his brother. "A shock like that could kill a man."

"Don't tempt me." Ben replaced the bucket on the floor and glared at Clayton. "I ought to thrash the daylights out of you."

"Aw, Ben, I just had a few drinks. What's the harm?"

"A few?" Ben lifted the near-empty bottle from the table and read the label. "You don't believe in the cheap stuff, do you?"

Clayton stiffened. "I'm old enough."

"But not old enough to pay?" He glanced at the bartender. "How much does he owe?"

"Five will cover. I don't expect to get no tip."

The rude awakening and sudden movement began to take their toll on Clayton, and he groaned aloud, clutching his stomach.

"Get him out of here!" Charlie ordered, hopping out of the way.

Ben seized the collar of Clayton's jacket and led him none too gently toward the alley. They had barely cleared the back steps before the boy was overtaken by spasms of nausea. Ben grudgingly sympathized with his brother as he retched convulsively. Clayton was in for one hell of a hangover.

"I'm sorry, Ben," he groaned, resting his forehead on the arm he had braced against the building. "I kept waiting for you to show up, and before I knew it, I was drunk."

"Buying drinks for the hostesses?" Ben filled the dipper hanging beside the rain barrel and handed it to Clayton. "They seem to drink as much as you do but never get drunk?"

Clayton drained the dipper, rinsed his mouth, and spat on the ground. "Yeah. How did you know?"

"I was twenty once myself." Ben refilled the dipper with a grin. He felt his pocket for a clean bandanna and said, "Here, take this and clean up. We need to get home."

"By the way, where were you last night?"

Ben scowled and turned toward the alley's entrance. "At the sheriff's office."

As they crossed the street toward the livery Ben recounted the events of the night before. Before Clayton could ask any questions, a woman's voice brought them both to a halt.

"Mr. Parrish!" Ben recognized Halley's voice right away. "Ben Parrish, I need to speak you."

A chaperon! Halley had laughed, at first, but the sheriff had been completely serious. Either she have Ben Parrish escort her to the ranch or remain in town, behind bars if need be.

The prospect of a jail cell sent her in search of her new neighbor. She had looked everywhere for him and was afraid he'd left town already. No one had seen him or Clayton at the restaurant, and Mr. Tulley had yet to have his first customer.

Halley dashed down the steps of the boardinghouse and called out again, "Mr. Parrish! Please, wait."

Finally, he turned at the sound of her voice, only to scowl and resume his steps. Of all the nerve, how could he deliberately dismiss her so rudely? His brother's hand on his arm was the only thing that stopped him, and she hurried across the street, carefully dodging wagon ruts brimming with murky water. To no avail—her skirt was splattered with mud by the time she reached the sidewalk where Ben Parrish and his brother were waiting.

"Thank goodness I found you." She couldn't help but notice how pale and weary Clayton appeared. In all the excitement of the past evening, she had forgotten to ask where he had been. "Have you been ill?"

The younger man made no reply and Ben finally answered, "He woke up feeling sick to his stomach."

"Oh, dear. I hope it wasn't something you ate. Tainted food can be very dangerous."

"Yes, ma'am." Clayton nodded in complaisance. "Ben was just telling about what happened to you last night. You weren't hurt, were you?"

"Not at all," she assured him, glancing at Ben, "It was a most harrowing experience, but such is life here in the West. I intend to put the whole thing behind me and go about my business."

"I thought you'd be halfway to Old Pete's ranch by now," Ben said. "Or halfway back to New York."

Halley stiffened. "I have only to claim my mule and wagon from the livery and then I shall set out for the ranch."

"You shouldn't go out there alone," Clayton insisted. "It's too dangerous. What if you get lost?"

"Mr. Tulley drew a map for me," she assured him. "He said the ranch was directly north of town and very easy to find. Were you going to the livery?"

"Yes, ma'am." Clayton glanced up at his brother. "Our horses were there overnight."

"What a fortunate coincidence," she said as they began their way down the sidewalk. "I was beginning to think you had already gone home."

Halley stepped inside the livery and caught sight of the

blacksmith at the far end of the stable. "Mr. Mahoney," she called. "Good morning."

"Mornin', ma'am." Mahoney glanced at the men following her. "Ben, what were you doing in town all night?"

"Minding my own business."

The blacksmith grinned slightly and turned back to Halley. "I hope you've come for that ornery mule. Jess delivered your wagon first thing this morning and I've got a man out back fitting a harness for your mule."

Behind the livery, Halley found her mule being hitched to the wagon. His head swiveled at the sound of her voice and she stroked his neck, noting that his coat had been curried but would need further attention. Retrieving the peppermint candy from her pocket, Halley let him nuzzle her palm for the treat.

The livery worker hitching the wagon gave one last tug on the harness and informed her, "He's all yours, lady."

"Thank you," she replied, and smoothed her hand over his wide forehead, scratching the tuft of mane between his ears. She laughed when he lowered his head to allow her better access. "You like that, don't you, baby?"

Burrowing her gloved fingers deeper, Halley began to scratch the mule behind his ears and was rewarded with an affectionate butting of his head against her arm. She was tempted to treat him with another peppermint, but Mr. Mahoney had warned her that too much candy could gripe his stomach.

Instead, she held his face toward hers and asked, "Do you know we're going home today?"

"Do you know what you're getting yourself into?"

Halley looked up to see Ben emerging from the livery. He leaned against the doorjamb and casually folded his arms across his broad chest.

She forced her attention back to the mule. "I have no delusions that things will be easy. Mr. Olson assured me that the ranch is in working order with a minimal staff. I don't intend to punch cattle, if that's what you mean."

He gave a half smile and shook his head. "I know better. Your kind doesn't do anything you can pay someone else to do for you."

"My kind?" she repeated in disbelief.

"This is all some great adventure for you, isn't it? Playing cowboy, living among the common folk. I just wonder how long before you scamper back to the gaslights and streetcars."

Silence hung between them, and Halley was convinced she'd never met a more arrogant man than Ben Parrish. Somehow, she would get to her ranch by her own means and worry about the sheriff's ultimatum later.

"Why were you looking for me?" he asked.

"I really don't know what you mean."

"You said, 'Thank goodness I found you,'" he reminded her. "What did you want?"

Before she could answer, Clayton and Sheriff Teal emerged from the livery.

"Well, Miss Halley." The sheriff spoke pleasantly. "I see you found Ben, and Clayton here says they'll be pleased to show you out to the ranch. I just can't let you go out there without an escort."

Autumn was taking hold in Wyoming. The morning air held the unmistakable bite of fall, and the trees were already a burst of gold and russet against the brilliant blue of the horizon. Halley stared across the vast high country in awe as her new wagon, heavily laden with supplies, carried her closer to the home she had never seen. Surely, this was the most beautiful place on earth.

"Want to take the lead for a while?" Clayton Parrish held the reins out to her, a halfhearted smile tugging at his full mouth. "That old mule seems to know where he's going."

Hesitantly, she accepted the reins, careful to hold them exactly as Clayton instructed. The mule plodded on without a flinch, and Halley couldn't hold back her pleased smile. The smile faded quickly when she glanced up, catching sight of Ben Parrish. He had ridden ahead of them since leaving Wilder, without so much as a backward glance.

"Don't fret over Ben, Miss Halley, he's mostly outdone with me this morning." The young man removed his rusty brown hat and combed long fingers through his dark hair. "He gets ornery when things don't go the way he wants."

"Obviously, I've imposed on you and your brother more than I should." She toyed with the reins, allowing them to dangle between her palms as Clayton had done. "I should have hired a guide to see me out this morning."

"I doubt the sheriff would have gone along with that." Clayton grinned. "After all, you're under protective custody."

The wind picked up, tugging her hair loose from the tortoiseshell combs. She should have braided it for the trip, but Ben had insisted on leaving as soon as possible, and there had been no time. Halley smoothed the loose strands back from her face and frowned at his rigid back.

"I never dreamed Mr. Parrish would have so many objections to my being released into his custody." Halley clenched the reins tightly between her fingers. "I just didn't want to stay in town, and the sheriff would not listen to reason."

"Well, Miss Halley." Clayton paused, as if searching for the right words. "You have a way of making reason sound, well . . ."

"Absurd?" she offered. "My father used to tell me the same thing. I never have learned to be patient with those who don't see things the way I do."

Clayton took the reins and urged the mule on a little faster. "I'm sure by now the old sheriff is realizing how wise he was not to press the argument. Another hour and you would have had *him* driving you out here."

Halley tried to appear indignant as she reclaimed the reins, but she couldn't resist Clayton's good humor. She found herself laughing easily as they made their way closer and closer to her waiting ranch.

Ben felt the muscles in his neck tighten every time Halley's laughter rippled across the afternoon breeze. He had known bothersome women in his time, but none rivaled her in the ability to stir up more trouble in less time. She had been in Wilder less than twenty-four hours and had already cost him a day's work on the ranch, a night's sleep, and the price of a new door for the boardinghouse.

The river was in sight now, and he was doubting his own good sense for not leaving her cooling her heels in the sheriff's office. Roy Teal wasn't about to turn her loose with folks looking to do her in, but Ben sure as hell hadn't meant to end up as her personal escort.

Glancing back toward the wagon, Ben reined his mount to a halt and motioned for Clayton to hurry up. The sooner he had Halley St. John off his hands the better. Once across the river, they would arrive at her ranch within the hour, and she would be on her own.

"How's it look, Ben?" his brother called as the wagon approached. "Think we can get the wagon across all right?"

"Shouldn't be much trouble." The river was low this morning, thanks to a dry summer. Taking a deep breath, Ben turned toward Halley. "You'd better ride across with me."

Noting the swift current, Halley scanned the riverbank. "There's no bridge?"

"Bridge washed out in the spring," Clayton explained. "There's no other way across. You just get wet coming and going."

Hesitantly, Halley climbed down from the wagon and approached Ben's horse, a fine-looking bay. She glanced back toward the river and then up at him. "Are you positive this is the only way across?"

Reaching down from his saddle, Ben gripped her arm and easily lifted her onto the horse before him. "There aren't many shortcuts out here. I could always take you back to town, if you're afraid of a little water."

"That won't be necessary," she replied in a casual tone, but Ben felt her body stiffen as the horse made its way down the slippery bank.

As they ventured into the water he tightened his hold around her narrow waist and immediately regretted the action. The feel of her firm bottom pressing even more snugly against him made forcing his attention on crossing the river damn near impossible. Clearing his throat, he motioned for Clayton to wait until they were across.

"I'll come back to give you a hand," Ben called out as he guided his mare into the current.

A sudden breeze swept loose strands of her hair across his face, teasing his senses with the delicate scent of lavender mingled with rosewater. Schooling his thoughts, Ben forced his attention on the swift current; one false move and he could drown them both.

Adjusting himself in the saddle, Ben tried to put as much

distance between them as possible, but the jostling of the horse and the rushing of the water conspired against him. Their bodies were thrown together, her back flush against his chest, and he was painfully reminded of holding her in his arms with nothing but her thin nightgown between them.

The horse stumbled, dragging Ben's attention back to where it belonged. He'd crossed this river a hundred times without a second thought. Now, with Halley pressed against him, he was addled as a schoolboy.

The bay quickly reached deeper water, and Halley gasped as the swift current rushed up to meet them. She grasped his forearms as the water pulled at her skirts, and Ben drew her securely against him.

"Don't let me fall!" Halley cried as the horse faltered in the swift current. "I can't swim."

"Don't worry, lady," he replied against her ear, unable to resist the silken texture of her cheek. "I've got you."

Pulling hard on the reins, Ben urged the mare in the direction of the bank, and the horse scrambled up the steep slope.

Without warning, Ben hefted her down from the saddle and gave her a searing look. Halley took a staggering step backward, quickly turning her back on the heated stare. Her body ached from the sudden lack of contact with his, and she smoothed her traveling suit, hoping to brush his touch away with the wrinkles. Pressing the back of her hand against her lips, Halley doubted any woman could easily forget a man like Ben Parrish.

She heard him shouting orders to Clayton, and turned to see her wagon being led into the river. The mule held his head high above the water, his ears lying flat in a show of protest, but Clayton urged him on with shouted orders of his own. Halley held her breath as the water crested the wheels of the wagon that contained all of her earthly possessions.

One sudden whim of the river would leave her without a bite of food or a stitch of clothes, save what she had on her back. With a shudder, she turned away, forcing herself to trust in Ben's ability. She glanced across the high country, absorbing the beauty of the landscape.

A sudden movement in the brush farther downstream caught

her attention. Narrowing her eyes, Halley squinted against the brilliant daylight, hoping to see what was hiding. She glanced back to see Ben and Clayton approaching the bank of the river.

Ben was in a foul mood and cursed the mule's stubbornness. Halley knew he would be even angrier if she wandered off, but curiosity got the best of her.

She had taken only a few hesitant steps when the ring of rifle fire broke the silence. Dear God, someone *was* trying to kill her. She turned toward the river, desperately hoping to find Ben already on the bank. Another shot rang out and she screamed his name.

He was shouting something at her, reaching for his Winchester as he urged his horse up the riverbank. She couldn't move, frozen in place near the brush. His words finally registered, ordering her to get down, but her limbs were like lead, and she couldn't move.

Ben slid from the saddle and caught her around the waist, knocking her to the ground. "Dammit, woman, do want to get your head blown off?"

Halley was temporarily stunned, unable to breathe with Ben's weight landing on top of her. He clamped one hand over her mouth and said with a fierce whisper, "Don't make another sound."

She nodded, wincing as his elbow dug painfully between her breasts. Her face was inches from his, and she could feel his breath on her face. Fear quaked inside her, and she wanted to bury her face against his shoulder and hide until the danger had passed. But she dared not move.

A third shot rang out, this time from behind them. Halley prayed it was only a hunter seeking game for his table, realizing she had left her pistol in the wagon. The pounding of approaching hoofbeats matched the beating of her heart.

"Ben? Ben Parrish?" a man's voice called out. "Goddamn, is that you?"

Ben hesitated. "Hell, yes it's me, you old coyote. What the hell are you doing out here shooting at folks like crows?"

"I thought you was a sheepherder I been chasin' for the last hour."

Halley breathed a sigh of relief. Life in the frontier was

proving to be *far* more adventuresome than she had anticipated, but at least this was a simple case of mistaken identity.
Still, that would have been of little comfort had someone been
killed. She struggled under Ben's weight to rise to her feet,
but when he held her down she knew the danger had not
passed completely.

"Not much sport in that, Jonas." His eyes narrowed, and
his grip on the rifle did not relax. "What the hell you got
against sheepherders?"

The old man chuckled. Risking a glance in his direction,
Halley found his gaze moving to where she lay still as death
beneath Ben's weight. A leering smile touched his weathered
face, and she quickly looked away.

"I don't give a damn about sheepherders," Jonas replied in
a sneering tone, "but there's ranchers that'll pay top dollar to
be rid of them."

Ben must have seen the conclusions forming in the old
man's eyes and immediately rose to his feet, reaching to drag
Halley up beside him. "You can get up now. Jonas is a
friend."

"I shudder to think how he might have received us otherwise," she replied as she struggled to stand, shrugging away
from his hold. Her long skirts weren't at all suited for grappling in the wet grass, but she made it to her feet without his
help. Now, if only her wobbly legs would support her weight.

Halley glanced toward the horse and rider, immediately recognizing the buckskin-clad stranger as one of the grizzled
mountain men described in Mr. McClinton's journal. Her curiosity was roused, but her pride was more than a little bruised.
"You could have killed us, for heaven's sake," she bit out.

The old man gave her a grin that was far more chilling than
any scowl. "If I was aimin' to kill you, dead you'd be." He
paused long enough to pull a small pouch from his pocket and
withdraw a generous wad of tobacco, his gaze drifting all the
while from Ben to the wagon and then back to Halley.

"Ben, you done gone and took yourself another wife?" he
finally asked as he crammed tobacco into his mouth.

Another wife? Halley turned quickly toward Ben, who stood
scowling at the old man. Surprise quelled the impulse to deny
the false assumption that she and Mr. Parrish were wed, and

prompted the temptation to demand whether he spoke of a current wife or past.

Before she could utter a word, Ben spoke. "Hell, no. This is Pete's niece, from back East."

Jonas chuckled again. "Old Pete never did do a damned thing that made sense, did he?"

Halley ignored the impudent remark and began patiently brushing blades of grass from her clothes. She was surprised that Ben didn't readily agree with the man, at least not out loud. She ducked her eyes when she realized he was watching her.

He turned back to the old trapper, nodding toward the heavily laden pack horse he was leading. "Looks like you plan on being around for a while. Don't tell me you're not setting traps this winter."

"I done got too old to freeze my ass off every winter up in them mountains," Jonas replied before spitting a steam of tobacco juice in the general direction of the ground. "A man could trap all winter and not have a dozen decent pelts. Besides, there's more money in sheep hides."

"You've hired out for wages?" The look on Ben's face was incredulous. "I remember when you wouldn't even eat at the same table with hired hands, saying a man ought to make his own way, not work for someone else."

"This country's changing, Ben. There no place for men like me anymore . . . you neither, for long."

Before Ben could reply, two more riders made their way down from the hill, their horses lathered and panting. As they drew closer the smell of kerosene and scorched wool permeated the air.

"We lost the son of a bitch," the first rider informed Jonas, his tone almost accusing. "I told Emmett we shoulda shot when we had the chance."

"Clint, I don't hold with cold-blooded killing or back shooting."

The young man spat on the ground in disgust. "I don't hold with traipsin' all over the country for nothing."

"Then you and your brother get started making camp," Jonas countered.

Halley looked on as the two men silently fought a battle of

wills. It was clear the younger man resented being ordered to do anything but lacked the confidence to risk a confrontation with a more experienced adversary.

A sudden cry broke the silence, a pitiful bleating that sounded almost like a baby crying. A frightened, hungry baby. Halley turned toward the bushes, remembering the earlier noise she had attempted to investigate. Kneeling down, she found the source of the cries and gasped in delight.

A tiny lamb gazed up at her with fearful eyes, his wool tangled in the briars. Obviously, he had meant to hide in the brush and had become caught. He bleated again as she reached to unsnarl his spindly limbs.

"You poor little thing," she whispered. Once free, the lamb bolted, but Clayton was standing nearby and managed to catch him. "Oh, the poor little thing," she repeated as Clayton placed the lamb in her outstretched arms. "Look how frightened he is."

"What's he doing out here by himself?" Clayton asked.

"He most likely run off from them other woollies." Jonas suggested.

"What other . . . woollies?" Halley stroked the frightened lamb. "I thought this was cattle country."

"It is," Ben replied, not missing the tenderness in Halley's eyes as she soothed the lamb. The last thing he needed was Halley getting crazy notions about sheep. "There's no place for sheep in this part of the country."

"Then how did he get here?" Halley began making her way toward the wagon, lamb in tow. "Someone must have brought the sheep here."

"Someone tried," Jonas corrected her. "Cattlemen pay me ten dollars a day to keep the sheepherders out, and I earn every dollar of it."

"Well, I'm not going to leave this little woolly out here alone," Halley stated, glancing back at Ben. "I'm sure there will be room for such a wee mite."

"That wee mite is mine, lady." Clint swung down from his horse and made his way toward Halley, blocking her path to the wagon. "I saw it first."

Halley took a wary step backward.

"I'm going to roast that little bastard over hot coals with a turnip stuck in his mouth." His lips curled back in a grin, revealing blackened teeth. "I'd be glad to share some supper with you. I need something sweet for dessert."

Halley's eyes widened, but her hold on the lamb tightened. Ben instinctively let his hand fall to his holster, breathing a curse.

Halley didn't flinch. "Let me by."

"I ain't telling you again. Hand him over."

A look of steely determination came over Halley's features, and the second rider chuckled at his brother's difficulty, irritating him even more. Taking two steps forward, he warned, "A mite like that ain't worth gettin' hurt over."

"That's good advice, friend," Ben stated as he cocked the hammer of the pistol he had drawn before anyone realized his intent. "Get back on your horse, and don't even think about touching her."

Halley gasped and looked to see Ben's pistol aimed directly at the man's head. His eyes were cold steel, never wavering from his target. The man froze in his tracks and held his arms up in a show of compliance. "Easy, mister, I ain't no woman killer."

"I said get on your damn horse." Ben closed the distance and held the pistol mere inches from the battered felt object resembling a hat atop Clint's head. "I didn't ask for any character references."

Moisture beaded across Clint's upper lip, and a tremble in his voice betrayed his fear. "I'm going, I'm going. Give a man room, for Christ's sake."

Ben's glance never wavered as Clint backed away and mounted his horse. With one last dark look at Halley, he turned his mount and rode off, followed by his partner.

"You boys best set up camp afore dark," Jonas called after them.

"Jonas, you're riding with trouble," Ben stated as he holstered his gun. He glanced toward Halley, who stood wide-eyed and shaking, clutching the lamb to her bosom.

"So are you." Jonas nodded toward Halley. "Worst kind there is."

❧ FIVE ❧

HALLEY COULD ONLY look on as Ben and Clayton struggled with the broken wheel. She felt utterly useless, sitting there on a rock while they toiled wordlessly to repair her crippled wagon. She couldn't imagine why Mr. McClinton had failed to mention the importance of having the necessary tools in the event of such misfortune.

"It's no use." Ben rose to his feet and wiped his forehead with the back of his sleeve. "The axle is busted all to hell, and we can't fix it with our bare hands."

When the shooting had started, Clayton hurried to bring the wagon up the bank alone. In his haste to reach Ben and Halley, the front wheel had struck a rock just below the water's surface and splintered from the impact. The wagon maker had installed an additional wheel, carried on the underside of the vehicle, but without the necessary tools to fix the axle it was useless.

"What are we going to do?" Halley ventured to ask. The shadows were beginning to lengthen, and soon the dusk would be upon them. "I had hoped to reach the ranch before night-fall."

58

"You won't see your ranch today, not by a long shot." Ben glared down at the broken axle and shook his head in disgust. He turned to Clayton and demanded, "You helped her buy this rig, why didn't you see that it had at least a wrench?"

Clayton removed his hat and brushed the dust from the brim. "Blame me all you want to, Ben, but that doesn't solve the problem. It's getting late, and we need to decide what we're going to do."

Without a word, Ben made his way to where his horse stood waiting near the edge of the clearing. Halley's mule was greedily chomping at a patch of sweet grass, still green despite the approaching autumn, and ignored Ben as he gathered his reins and led the bay back toward the wagon.

"There's only one thing we can do," he finally said, after removing his saddlebag and bedroll from the mount. "You take my horse and ride ahead to the ranch. Eli should have everything we need to get the wheel in place. Bring him back with the tools."

"But the ranch is at least another hour's ride," Clayton argued. "There's no way I'll be back before evening, and we can't fix that axle in the dark, even with a lantern."

"We'll have to wait until morning." Ben paused only long enough to hand the reins over to his brother. "Go on and get some rest. I want you back here by daylight."

"What are we going to do?" Halley spoke up.

"We're going to stay right here and wait."

"Here? We're in the middle of nowhere." Halley rose to her feet and joined the men near the water's edge. "You can't be serious."

"Do you have a better idea?" Ben demanded, turning his scowl on her. "We can't leave the wagon here—squatters would make off with everything but the busted axle."

Halley made no reply, but the thought of the endless grassland cloaked in darkness sent shivers down her spine. She'd heard terrifying accounts of prairie camps being raided, travelers butchered in their sleep by savage Indians. Perhaps even the sheep killers were nearby and would return under cover of night.

She considered making the suggestion that she accompany Clayton back to the ranch, but how cowardly that would sound. Ben Parrish had saved her life today, and no doubt regretted ever coming to her defense the day before. To ask him to wait with her wagon like a lackey while she went ahead to safety was unthinkable. No, it was her wagon and her poor planning that had left them stranded. She would stay and be brave.

"You're right, of course," she had to admit. Glancing at Clayton, she added, "Mr. McClinton made no mention in the book of wagon repair tools."

"The only thing your book is good for is propping up that axle." Ben gazed ahead, squinting his eyes against the late-afternoon sun. "Best get a move on, Clayton. You won't make it by dark, as it is."

With a halfhearted smile, Clayton gathered the horse's reins. "Don't worry, Miss Halley. I'll be back at sunup and we'll have the wagon ready to roll in no time. You'll be at your ranch before dinnertime."

Halley watched as Clayton swung himself into the saddle and turned the horse in the direction of her ranch. The horse was fast, and in mere seconds he was out of sight. She clasped her hands before her and turned to face Ben Parrish. He stood watching her, with his rifle slung under his right arm.

"You ever slept out at night before?"

"No."

He gave no reaction to her answer; none was necessary. She felt foolish enough without him pointing out her obvious lack of experience. Already, she was beginning to regret the decision that had kept her here for the night.

"Does that book of yours say anything about making camp?"

"Oh, yes." Halley brightened at the change of subject and the chance to prove herself knowledgeable. "There are detailed instructions on selecting a proper location, cooking over a fire. Everything one needs to know."

"Good," he replied. "Since the location was selected for us, you can get started setting up camp while I scout around a bit. I'll be back in about an hour."

An hour! You can't leave me here alone for an hour!

The words seemed wedged in her throat, despite her desperation to get them out. She wanted to shout, but barely managed a hoarse whisper as he turned to make his way down the ravine. She watched his agile movements until he disappeared into the thickening growth of trees downriver.

Glancing around the small clearing, Halley could almost feel the shadows creeping closer to swallow her up in darkness. She took a deep breath and turned toward the wagon, retrieving Mr. McClinton's journal and her pistol from beneath the seat.

Ben made his way along the riverbank, watching for any sign of recent traffic. The grassy bank was free of debris, but he felt no sense of relief. The absence of broken whiskey bottles and wagon tracks only meant that no one careless had passed this way. A white man always leaves a wide trail. He smiled to himself as he remembered Old Pete's adage. Pete had a saying for everything, and Ben could only wonder what the old cuss would say about his headstrong niece.

Kneeling beside the water, he breathed a curse and reflected on his own thoughts of Halley St. John. Somehow he'd convinced himself that she would never come to Wilder. He pictured the stage pulling in with no Eastern passenger, save the occasional salesman or evangelist. Every day since the lawyer read Pete's will, he'd made plans to buy the land the day it went up for sale.

That day never arrived, but Halley did. She stepped off the stage and crushed any hope of preventing a land war at his back door beneath the soles of her fancy leather shoes. It was only a matter of time before the shooting started.

The river rushed by, dragging pieces of the setting sun downstream, and Ben wished more now than ever he'd stayed out of town. Getting tangled up with Halley was the last thing he'd intended to do, but she had a way of catching him off guard, a way of worming her way into his thoughts. He wasn't looking forward to spending a night alone with her with nothing but the darkness between them.

He hadn't forgotten the way she felt in his arms, warm and pliant, clinging to him as sobs shook her body. Ben didn't consider himself a gentleman by any stretch of the imagination, and he had barely resisted the urge to kiss her until she had no doubt that comfort was not what she should seek in his arms.

The dusk was slowly giving way to evening, and the faint outline of the moon could be seen in the expanse of sky. Ben rose to his feet and turned in the direction of the crippled wagon. He knew he shouldn't have left Halley alone so long, but he'd needed a little time to sort out the events of the last day. Damn, but that woman was going to be more of a problem than he'd bargained for.

Resigned to spending another night away from his ranch, Ben turned to make his way back to the wagon. The mingled aromas of coffee and wood smoke met him as he approached the vehicle. He scanned the clearing for Halley, but she was nowhere in sight. An uneasy tightness gripped his insides. He had only meant to be gone long enough to cool his temper. Surely, she would have screamed if anything had happened. *A man wouldn't give her the chance to scream.*

A sudden hissing sound drew his attention to a small camp-fire glowing in the shadows. A coffeepot sat perched above the coals beside a covered black kettle, sputtering fragrant steam. The camp was set, neat as you please, but still there was no sign of Halley. Instinct told him to look for signs of a struggle, but there was nothing amiss.

He had barely taken five steps toward the clearing when Halley appeared from the wagon. Stepping down from the back, she was wearing buckskin trousers and an oversized shirt. She paused to reach back into the wagon for a dark hat and placed it securely on her head.

Ben watched in amazement as she turned toward the mule, who was picketed just inside the circle of light from the fire. She stroked his forehead and offered what he was certain was a piece of hard candy. He took a few more steps and the mule jerked his head around, ears flat, and brayed a series of short barks, sounding more like dog.

Halley whirled to face him, her eyes wide beneath the brim of her hat. "Mr. Parrish, you shouldn't sneak up on a person like that."

The mule tossed his head and brayed again. Halley soothed him with a gentle pat on the neck. "You gave us quite a start."

"What are you dressed up for?"

Halley glanced down at her britches and smiled. "Mr. McClinton advises that ladies sometimes don men's clothing for safety. The trousers will give the impression that two men are camped here, rather than one man and a woman."

Ben couldn't help but notice the way the buckskin outlined her feminine curves, leaving very little to the imagination. He suspected that even if Halley grew a beard, no one would mistake her for a man.

"There's coffee on the fire," she remarked in a casual tone. "And the stew should be ready by now, if you're hungry."

Ben crossed the clearing and studied the tiny campfire. He could find no fault with the depth of the pit, the precise placement of the wood, or the amount of smoke rising into the night air. He glanced up to find Halley waiting for his reaction. "The fire is fine, it should burn all night."

She smiled proudly and joined him by the fire, bringing the lamb along. She had fashioned a lead out of a length of stout twine. The animal bleated in protest, but quickly settled down on the soft bed of pine boughs.

"There, there," she whispered in a reassuring tone as she gently scratched his forehead. "I'm so afraid he'll wander off. Mr. McClinton says that wolves are a very present danger to the livestock in these parts."

"Wolves are a damnable nuisance. They kill for sport."

Lifting the coffeepot from the fire, Ben filled the two waiting cups and handed one to Halley. Their fingers brushed slightly as she accepted the coffee, and Ben studied her face in the firelight. Her features appeared even more delicate beneath the brim of her oversized hat, and the shadows emphasized the fullness of her lips.

Needing a distraction, Ben turned toward the darkness, tasted the coffee, and winced. "Where did you learn how to make coffee?"

"I watched the sheriff," she answered. "How did it turn out?"

"It tastes like Roy's, all right." Ben returned to the fire where Halley knelt, stirring the bubbling stew. "He didn't teach you to cook, did he?"

"This recipe is from Mr. McClinton's journal. A simple mixture of dried beef, potatoes, and tinned tomatoes. He shared the dish with an outfit of drovers near Abilene.'' She spooned a generous portion onto a tin plate and offered the first serving to Ben. "It certainly smells good.''

Taking the plate, he nodded in agreement. "It does.''

Ben took his place by the fire and tasted the meal. Much to his surprise, the stew was delicious. Thick and spicy, the meat was tender and the vegetables done to a turn. He looked up to find Halley watching him.

"It turned out fine . . . very good.''

She smiled again and began eating her own dinner. Damn, women required too many compliments. He couldn't remember the last time he commented on a good meal, and he sure as hell never admired the way someone built a fire. They ate in silence, and Ben's curiosity began to nag him again.

He couldn't help but notice the dainty way she held the tin plate, and damned if she hadn't spread a napkin across her lap. He could easily picture Halley dining in one of the glittering restaurants of New York, drinking wine from a crystal goblet, and smiling across the table at a man who'd never done a day's work in his life. Why would any woman willingly leave such a soft life to come to Wyoming?

Forcing his attention back to his food, Ben reminded himself that he didn't care why she had come to Wyoming. She wouldn't last, and he'd be left to face the hell that would break loose over Old Pete's land.

Halley was more than a little pleased with the results of her first attempt at frontier cooking. Of course, she was so hungry by the time the meal was ready, anything would have tasted good. Except the coffee. She couldn't imagine how anyone drank the stuff. What she wouldn't give for a good cup of tea, laced with a generous shot of brandy.

She hid a smile, remembering the disapproval on her butler's face when he detected the telltale scent of liquor in the teacups. Genteel young ladies do not sample spirits, he had informed her more than once.

There weren't many genteel young ladies who were shot at and stranded in the wilderness, all in one day. If ever she was entitled, it was tonight.

Settling back, Halley let her eyes drift toward Ben while

she ate. He hardly seemed aware of her presence, even when he refilled his plate from the kettle. His anger, at least, seemed to have subsided, but she knew he resented the inconvenience she had caused him. Not wanting to risk irritating him further, Halley decided against retrieving the brandy bottle from the wagon.

She finished eating and dropped her plate into the bucket of water she had waiting. When Ben was through, she would wash the plates and put them away in the wagon. Making camp was a great deal of work, but she was thankful she'd known what to do. She could only imagine how upset he would have been had she not managed an edible dinner and a decent fire.

Picking up the leather-bound volume, Halley began flipping through the pages of Mr. McClinton's journal. Squinting in the firelight, she marveled at the amount of information the book contained. How Mr. McClinton had so many amazing adventures and still found time to write about them was beyond her.

"Listen to this: 'How to Survive an Encounter with a Bear,' " Halley read aloud, glancing up at Ben. "Can you imagine?"

"What does your friend say about bears?" Ben asked as he slid his plate into the bucket of water, his expression doubtful.

" 'First of all, never run. Running may elicit a chase response from an otherwise nonaggressive bear. Second, in the case the bear is unaware of you, detour quickly and quietly. If the bear *is* aware of you but has not acted aggressively, back away slowly, talking in a calm, firm voice while slowly waving your arms.' Why on earth would you wave your arms?"

Ben made no comment as he crossed the clearing to the spot by the wagon where he had stowed his gear. He retrieved his bedroll and returned to the fire. "If a bear is standing on his hind legs, he's trying to identify you. Waving your arms is a sign that you're not a threat to him."

"That makes sense. One should never threaten a bear." Halley returned to the passage and continued, " 'If the bear is approaching—again, do not run and do not drop your pack. A pack can help protect your body in case of an attack. Climbing trees will not protect you from black bears, but may provide protection from grizzlies.' Which type of bears are most common in this area?''

"Both," he answered. "You're more likely to see the black bears, but the grizzly is the more dangerous."

Halley nodded and glanced around the clearing, listening for any sound in the darkness. She tried not to think about what might be lurking in the shadows and began reading from where she left off. " 'If a grizzly bear does actually make contact with you . . .' "

Her voice trailed off, and read the passage silently. According to Mr. McClinton, the possibility of encountering a bear was slim this time of the year, but she knew wild animals were unpredictable, at best.

"What does it say?" Ben prompted.

" 'If attacked, one should curl up in a ball, protecting the neck and stomach. If attacked by a black bear, do not play dead, fight back.' " Her voice was quiet and thick with doubt. "I would never have the courage to fight a bear."

Ben dropped his bedroll near the fire and began banking the fire for the night. "You held your own against Clint today, and he meant you more harm than any bear ever would."

"Who knows how well I would have done if you had not interceded?"

The question needled Ben, but he didn't answer. He had been quick to challenge the bastard, but it was more than just coming to the defense of a woman in danger. It was the thought of Clint touching Halley that had made him furious. She was starting to get to him, and the last thing he needed was to spend the night alone with her in the middle of nowhere.

"Maybe you'll think about that before you shoot your mouth off the next time," he bit out, wanting to end the conversation before it got more personal. "Now let's get some sleep. I want to get an early start."

Irritated by his rebuff, Halley snapped the book closed. She rose from her spot and turned toward the wagon, a thousand scathing retorts running through her mind. As she stored the book away in her carpetbag beneath the seat, she decided against saying anything. Once safely on her ranch, she would be beholden to Ben Parrish for nothing and could tell him to go to the devil.

Returning to the fire, she spread out her blankets and settled down for the night. She closed her eyes and tried to fall asleep quickly, but the ground was hard and cold beneath her. Mr. McClinton had suggested pine boughs as a suitable bedding, but Halley longed for the comfort of a feather mattress and four walls. Finally, her eyes drifted open and she stared up into the black night sky.

The quarter moon was rising from behind the distant mountains and seemed to have hooked itself on a particularly jagged summit. Halley marveled at the sight, scanning the expanse of the heavens, and wondered if a lifetime would be time enough to count the stars scattered across the blackness.

"I can hardly believe this is the same sky."

Ben stared at her. "What do you mean?"

"The sky in New York . . . it was never this big, or so full of stars." Her voice held a trace of awe. "One could make all the wishes in the world on so many stars."

Ben studied her for a moment, lying there beneath her blankets. "Lady, what does a woman like you wish for?"

Rising up on one elbow, Halley returned his studious look. For the first time they openly observed one another. "I could ask the same of a man like you."

When he made no reply, Halley continued, "I'll strike a bargain with you, Ben Parrish. We're both more than a little curious about one another, so here's my proposition. You answer one question for me, and you can ask me anything you like."

Ben hesitated, but curiosity wouldn't allow him to pass up such a bargain, "That sounds fair. What's your question?"

"When the old trapper asked you if you had taken *another* wife, what did he mean?" she asked without stumbling. "Were you once married or are you married now?"

The question obviously startled him, which made her want to know the answer even more. When he hesitated again, she was quick to remind him, "A deal is a deal."

"Married once. A long time ago."

"What happened?"

"You said one question," he reminded her.

"But you only gave half the answer."

"No, you asked if I was married or if I used to be married. You got your answer."

Miffed, Halley sank to her bedroll. She found herself oddly relieved that he had no chubby little wife waiting for him with a brood of youngsters hanging on her skirts. It was her own vanity that assumed his wife wasn't attractive, but she didn't believe for a minute Ben Parrish couldn't have his pick of the loveliest of women. It was just easier to picture him with a woman who didn't hold his heart.

"Now it's my turn."

His voice startled her, and she opened her eyes to find him kneeling beside her pallet, his eyes shadowed beneath the brim of his hat. Suddenly, her bargain didn't seem so clever. "Very well, what would like to know?"

"Why did you come out here?"

"To claim my inheritance. When I learned that my uncle—"

"No." His callused fingertips brushed her lips, silencing her practiced reply. He cupped the line of her cheek, denying her the opportunity to look away. "I want the real reason."

Halley swallowed hard against his palm. The flickering light of the small campfire batted at the shadows concealing their faces, and she knew he could see the lies forming in her eyes.

Silence hung between them and he traced the shell of her ear. When she shuddered, he asked, "Why would you leave the comforts of city life and travel all the way across the country to claim a run-down cattle ranch in the middle of nowhere. Why?"

Halley thought for a moment. She didn't want to lie, but too much depended on making the ranch a success. If anyone knew she had no money, no connections, and nothing to return home to in New York, they would wipe her out before she saw her first cow.

Finally, she decided on the best possible answer. "I decided to come to Wyoming because I didn't want to live the rest of my life wondering what it would have been like. I know people who live their entire lives safe and secure, always talking about what they could have done if they'd only tried. Wyoming is my adventure."

To her surprise, he let his hand fall from her face and chuckled softly. He crossed to his side of the fire and began arranging his bedroll.

She feared her carefully worded answer hadn't fooled him, but she wasn't about to admit to anything else. Finally, she couldn't resist saying, "I fail to see what is so amusing."

"You. Coming to Wyoming for adventure." He laughed again and placed his hat over his eyes as he sank to the bedroll. "You won't be disappointed."

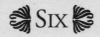

SIX

THE FIRST HINT of daylight splayed across the horizon, sending the violet shadows scurrying to their hiding places. Ben took comfort in the morning, allowing his stance to relax. Twice during the night he had been awakened by pebbles striking the ground around their camp. Something or someone was prowling around on the bluff above them, and he wanted to be awake if they decided to come any closer.

Glancing toward the river and the open range beyond, he drew a deep breath and savored the tang of sage and pine rising from the morning dew.

He turned toward the camp to see that Halley was still asleep. He watched as the sunlight reached her sleeping form, tangling first in her hair before unveiling her face. She slept peacefully, the thick fringe of eyelashes against her cheeks barely flickered as the dawn grew brighter, and he decided against waking her just yet.

Her features appeared even more delicate, and he wished she had not braided her hair. He could imagine her lying in a man's bed, clothed in nothing but the soft curtain of her unbound hair.

The sun was almost full up and Clayton should be returning any moment now with Eli. Ben was anxious to get the wagon rolling so that he could see Halley on her way and return to his own ranch. He had purposely insisted that Clayton return with Eli so that he wouldn't have to continue on with her to the homestead.

Rationalizing that work was going undone on his own ranch, he refused to feel guilty. Hadn't he already gone out of his way for Halley? Damn woman had no business coming west to begin with, and if it hadn't been for him . . .

Ben wouldn't let himself finish the thought. He was too involved with her already. The last thing he needed to do was tally up the favors he'd done her. Disgusted, he turned to make his way down the riverbank. The icy water was just what he needed to clear his head and get his body back under control.

"Ben! Ben, where are you?"

Halley woke immediately at the sound of Clayton Parrish's voice. Slowly, she sat up and tugged the blanket around her shoulders as a makeshift shawl. The morning air was cool and she shivered, despite the warmth of the fire.

She turned in the direction of the familiar voice, wondering where Ben had gone herself. Clayton rode into the clearing, followed by an older man on a roan mare. She smiled weakly, embarrassed at meeting a stranger without a chance to make herself presentable.

"Hellfire! Mornin' half-gone and not a drop of coffee or a heel of bread for breakfast." Shaking his head at the atrocity, the older man slid from his saddle with ease. "Ben Parrish ought to have his head kicked in."

Bewildered, Halley glanced up at Clayton, who sat astride Ben's horse. He grinned and explained, "This is Elijah Dupree, Miss Halley, your foreman."

She rose to her feet, smoothing her sleep-mussed hair from her face. "How do you do?"

"Howdy, little lady," Eli replied as he looped his reins over a low-hanging limb of a pine tree. "I see you survived your first night in the wild."

Halley studied the foreman as he crossed the clearing with a noticeable limp. She couldn't begin to guess his age. He seemed unaffected by his broken gate, which she suspected was the result of an old injury.

Clayton dismounted and repeated Eli's routine of looping the reins on a nearby branch. He glanced around the clearing before asking, "Where did Ben go?"

"I just woke up," she managed. Eli gave her a questioning look and she remembered his comment about the morning being half-gone. "We had quite a bit of trouble yesterday."

"Trouble is easy to come by in these parts," Eli quickly stated. "Clay told me what happened, and I'm not surprised. Jonas Flint is just the kind of scoundrel to hire out for such a dirty job."

"I'm just grateful that he recognized Ben—Mr. Parrish— before anyone was hurt." Halley hugged the blanket more closely around her shoulders,

"I wish somebody would tell me how you mistake two men and a woman driving a mule and wagon for a herd of sheep," Eli retorted. "Jonas has got eyes like a hawk. You mark my words, that old skunk was up to something."

"And I suppose you know what that is." Ben entered the clearing, buttoning the cuffs of a clean shirt. Halley noticed the hair at his collar was damp, and his face was cleanly shaven. He returned her appraisal, and she ducked her eyes, even more self-conscious about her rumpled appearance.

"You know damn well Jonas Flint ain't a man to be trusted." Eli recounted the many character flaws of their attacker. He paused only long enough to retrieve a burlap sack hanging from his saddle. "And them two fellas riding with him, they had to be no good. Wanted for something, I'll bet."

Halley watched with interest as Eli knelt before the fire and stirred the shimmering coals. He looked up at her with open curiosity, but his eyes crinkled with a smile. "You ever had fresh trout for breakfast?"

"No," she answered, returning the smile. "But that sounds wonderful."

"We don't have time for you to go fishing, old man," Ben said. "I want that wagon ready to roll as soon as possible."

"Then you and your brother get to work." Eli opened the sack and retrieved a string of fish, still glistening wet in the first light of dawn. "Let me worry about breakfast."

"I'll make the coffee," Halley offered.

"No," Ben replied without hesitation. "You get packed to leave. As soon as the wagon is fixed, we need to be on our way."

Eli ignored Ben's impatience and returned his attention to the fire. Once he was satisfied with the bed of coals, he turned toward Halley and asked, "I need a little flour and lard. You got a mess box packed on that wagon?"

"Of course, help yourself to anything you need," Halley answered, grateful she would not have to see to the cooking this morning. Needing an excuse to seek her privacy, she added, "I'll bring some water for the coffee."

Without a word, she made her way past Ben and slipped down the bank to a secluded spot. When she was certain she was out of sight, Halley wasted no time attending to her aching bladder. She then unwrapped the neat bundle of clothes she'd changed out of last night, and somehow managed to get back into her traveling suit without the benefit of a mirror.

The morning air held a chill, and her fingers were stiff as she brushed the tangles out of her hair. Securing the waist-length mass away from her face with a pair of tortoiseshell combs, Halley felt better. She hurried to gather enough water to wash her face before returning to the camp.

As she dunked the bucket into the river she was startled to find bits of ice floating on the surface. If the river was icing in September, what would she find by Christmas? Halley knew she couldn't allow herself to fear life in the frontier. There was no going back.

She scooped water from the bucket and splashed her face, gasping at the shock of frigid water against her skin. Once more she dipped her hands into the bucket, washing the sleep from her eyes. She then rinsed her mouth before emptying out the bucket and refilling it with fresh water for the coffee.

When she turned to make her way back to camp, she met Ben Parrish walking toward her. They both halted, as if surprised to see one another. She could feel the color rising in her cheeks, and she ducked her eyes as he took notice of her appearance.

Ben finally broke the silence. "I came to see if you were

all right. Eli's got the food ready, and he sent me to see what was taking you so long."

"I've never seen such cold water," she replied, wishing she didn't sound so edgy. "Will you be able to repair the wagon?"

"It's done," he answered. "Clayton's finishing up. Once we had the tools, it wasn't any trouble."

Halley nodded. "I shall purchase the necessary tools on my next trip to town."

"That's something I want to talk to you about," he said, catching her by the arm when she began walking toward the camp. "I think your next trip to town should be this morning."

"What on earth for?"

"Lady, you're in for a fight if you try holding on to that ranch." He didn't wait for her reply. "There's going to be killing over that land, and the last place you need to be is in the middle of a range war."

"It is *my* land," she stated, shrugging her arm free of his hold. "I told you before, I won't be intimidated by common threats. Besides, staying in town won't save the land."

He looked annoyed. "No, but selling it will."

Halley stared up at him, her eyes cautious. "Sell? To you?"

"I'll make you as good of an offer as anyone," he answered. "I'll even drive your cattle in the spring with mine, and let you keep the profit."

"Well, that certainly is generous of you." Halley crossed her arms over her chest and began pacing the small clearing. "When? When will I ever learn?"

"What are talking about?"

"You," she snapped. "You're no different than those cut-throats in the financial district. Dammit all, I was just beginning to think I could trust you."

"Slow down, lady. You don't understand—"

"Oh, don't I?" Halley faced him then, her anger coloring her face. "You're trying to scare me into selling the land cheap. Well, it won't work. I know exactly what to expect, hardships and all. I won't sell out before I've even had a chance to try. Who knows? I just might succeed."

Ben reclaimed her arm, struggling to keep the anger out of his voice. "And you just might get killed."

She stared up at him in wide-eyed silence. She didn't know if he meant to frighten her, but he certainly had her attention. He flexed his fingers and slightly eased his grip. "There are plenty of men who want that land worse than I do, and they won't waste time bargaining. Now, if you've got any sense at all, you'll cut your losses and head back east while you still can."

"I am staying, Mr. Parrish," she replied in an oddly even tone of voice. "And if there is to be a fight, I'll know you're not on my side."

Ben watched as the turned away from him with a flounce of petticoats and marched back to the wagon. Damn her foolish hide! Let her play cowboy, he decided. It wouldn't be long before she'd be begging him to buy her land.

Halley had read all she could get her hands on regarding life on the frontier ranch, but nothing had prepared her for the first sight of the inheritance she had journeyed so far to claim.

Abandoned was the first word that came to mind, followed by *desolate* and *deserted*. The corral stood empty, as did the pasture as far as she could see. A large black pot smoldering over a bed of coals near a rickety building was the only sign of life.

She turned to Clayton, who sat beside her on the wagon seat with his elbows propped on his knees, the reins dangling between his fingers. He gave only a shrug and a halfhearted smile, not the encouragement she was hoping for.

"The attorney said the ranch was still in operation."

Dismay made her voice thick, and she barely had the courage to take a hesitant look toward the main house. Though in slightly better condition, months of vacancy and neglect had left their mark. Broken crates, rusted wire, and various other debris littered the porch, and the window shutters hung by a nail and a prayer.

"The ranch *is* in operation," Eli informed her as he reined his mare alongside the wagon. "After Pete died, most of the hands moved on. What cattle there is, is grazing the upper pasture."

"*Most* of the hands moved on?" Halley repeated. "There's not a soul in sight."

"Cowpunchers usually take off to warmer parts afore winter sets in," Eli explained as he climbed down from the wagon. "We lost a few more a couple of weeks ago."

He didn't have to say they had left when they learned a woman would own the ranch, and Halley pretended it didn't bother her. Taking a deep breath, she climbed down from the wagon, not waiting for Clayton to help her.

"Now, don't you worry about ranch hands," Eli assured her as he dismounted. "That's my department. I've done the hiring and firing on the SJ for twenty years."

"The SJ?"

"That's your brand, Miss Halley," Clayton explained.

She turned toward the corral where he pointed. The entrance bore the letters *S* and *J*, connected with a bar at the top, painted white with a steady hand. "St. John," she whispered.

"You get yourself settled in," Eli ordered. "Me and Clayton will see after the wagon. I'll say one thing for Ben, he picked you out a fine mule."

"Mr. Parrish didn't select the mule." Halley turned her attention to Eli. "I purchased him from the livery yesterday."

Eli grinned and nodded toward Clayton. "Old Pete was always a rare judge of horseflesh. I reckon it runs in the family."

Halley smiled and glanced back toward the corral. A ripple of excitement ran through her as she stared up at the bold emblem of ownership. She hurried to gather her carpetbag, anxious to have Eli show her every inch of the property, and made her way toward the house.

A little dusting. That was all the house really needed. At least, that's what Halley kept telling herself as she looked around the shambles of what had once been a serviceable ranch house. Obviously no one had attended to her poor uncle's home since his death.

Cobwebs hung like chandeliers from the ceiling, and there were tiny telltale tracks across the grimy wooden floor. Mice! Halley shuddered at the thought, recalling the stories her Irish maid had told her about rats in Shantytown dragging babies from their cribs.

Hesitantly, she placed the squirming lamb on the floor, admonishing herself to keep a close eye on him. He gave a short bleat, unsure of his new surroundings, and followed close to Halley as she made her way to the window. She hoped a little fresh air would do away with the musty smell of a house closed up since spring.

The window held fast as she struggled with the sash, refusing to budge in the least. Halley breathed one of the many curses she'd heard Ben Parrish mutter and felt tempted to smash out the windowpanes. She had traveled all the way across the country to claim an inheritance that turned out to be an abandoned ranch, a filthy home, and a damned window that wouldn't even open.

Pressing her forehead against the resilient window, Halley closed her eyes and admitted for the first time that she might have made a mistake coming west. The exhilaration of seeing her family name proclaimed on the corral was fading. What did she know about cattle ranching? Or cattle, for that matter?

She traced a small circle in the grimy windowpane and peered out into the yard. Eli had emerged from the building farthest from the house, followed by a younger man who was as wrinkled as an unmade bed. She looked on as they began unhitching her mule. The mule's ears flattened, and he bared long teeth as they removed the bridle.

Eli laughed as the mule barely missed biting the young man on the shoulder. She enlarged her circle of vision and watched as they led the mule away from the wagon and into the barn. She suspected she would find the barn in better condition than the house.

She gazed out across the expanse of grassland and wondered what kind of future she would make out of such emptiness. Her life in New York was filled with people and festivity, but those days were gone with her fortune.

Gazing north toward the distant mountains, Halley caught sight of a wagon filled with people lumbering toward the house. She groaned inwardly. Who would be paying a call so soon? Glancing back at the squalid house, she made her way toward the door, hoping her guests would understand that she was simply unable to entertain at this time.

The wagon came to a stop just as Halley stepped out onto the front porch. Forcing a bright smile, she waved in welcome.

"Lord have mercy on us, girls." A strapping woman surveyed the house, shaking her head with pity. "Everyone out, we've got our work cut out for us."

Halley counted as one, two, three . . . four little girls hopped out of the wagon, each one eyeing her with varying degrees of curiosity. Finally the woman stepped down, leaving an older girl alone on the wagon seat.

"Bless your heart, you must be Halley," she called out as she lifted a large basket from the back of the wagon. "I'm Delia Mitchell. I told my man Tom you'd be in for more trouble than you dreamed, coming off out here on your own."

"Well, I've actually just arrived," Halley explained. "And the house is not at all ready for company."

"Company?" Delia handed the heavy basket to one of the taller girls. "We ain't company. We're here to get you settled in. Just show us where to start."

"I'm afraid I have no idea where to begin," Halley admitted in a whisper. "Everything's a mess."

"Let's just see how bad it is." Delia took her by the arm and started toward the house. She paused and turned back toward the girl on the wagon seat. "Susan, honey, tie up the horse, but leave the rest of the things in the wagon for now."

As they ducked inside the shadowed house Delia failed to suppress her gasp of horror. "Good lands! This place is a wreck. I reckon no one's been in the house since the poor man died. Pete wasn't much for housekeeping, but he did keep things clean."

Halley followed Delia's gaze from the grimy windowpanes to the dust-caked furniture, finally resting on the filthy floor. She had seen the servants back home diligently scrubbing floors and windows, but there had never been a mess like this. "Can anything be done?"

"Of course, hon," Delia exclaimed, forcing a bright smile. "All this place needs is a lot of elbow grease and determination. The furniture will have to be moved outside so we can scrub down the walls and floor. I'll get the girls started on the porch, and you had better change into some work clothes."

Halley glanced down at her dark traveling suit and agreed. She had purchased several cotton dresses, but everything was still packed away in her trunks. She would have to ask Clayton to unload her luggage first.

Before she could reply, a tiny voice piped, "Mama! Mama, come look what we found!"

Halley followed Delia out onto the porch to see three little girls huddled around the orphan lamb. He bleated loudly and they giggled in unison. "Oh, Mama, ain't he cute?" the youngest child cried before turning to Halley. "Is he yours?"

"Yes, he is," Halley answered. "I found him in a briar thicket yesterday."

"What do you plan to do with him?" Delia asked, in a tone that was almost accusing.

"Oh, I don't know, keep him as a pet, I suppose." Halley sank to the front step beside the lamb, stroking his knobby wool. "He sounds hungry. Who wants to help me feed him?"

"Me!"

"Me!"

"No, me!"

Halley laughed at their enthusiasm, the first she'd found in Wyoming for any of her suggestions. She rose to her feet, promising to return quickly with a can of milk. As she made her way to the wagon Delia followed.

"You're not serious about keeping that thing, are you?" she demanded in a hushed whisper.

"Why not?" Halley asked, looking up from the crate of supplies she was rooting through for the milk. "What difference could one little lamb make on ranch this size?"

"You might soon find out." Delia glanced back at her daughters. "Folks out here are already antsy about squatters and sheepherders. The last thing you want is everyone thinking you're going to turn this place into a sheep ranch."

Before Delia could argue further, Clayton emerged from the barn. "The mule's been put in a clean stall and fed. What do we need to do next?"

"Mrs. Mitchell has volunteered to help get the house in order." Halley finally found the tin can labeled evaporated milk. She glanced toward Delia, "I suppose we should follow her instructions."

Delia gaped at Clayton, speechless. Realizing they were waiting for her, she stammered, "The furniture needs to be moved outside so we can scrub the floor."

Clayton nodded. "I'll get started."

Delia watched him scale the porch steps and disappear inside the house. "That's Ben Parrish's brother. What's he doing here?"

"Clayton has offered to help me get the ranch back in running order. He and Mr. Parrish escorted me from town."

"Ben Parrish? I don't believe it."

"Why not?"

"Why, he's is the coldest man I've ever known. I can't believe he'd offer to lift a finger to someone taking land he wanted for himself."

Halley stiffened. "What do you mean?

"What do you think I mean? Ben had already moved some of his cattle onto the land no sooner than Pete was in the ground. I reckon he wasn't too pleased to see *you* get off the stage."

Stunned, Halley watched Delia order her daughters to forget the lamb and get to work.

Mr. Josiah Pittman
Attorney-at-Law
New York City

Dear Mr. Pittman,

Please forgive me for taking so long to write this letter. I fully intended to notify you the moment of my arrival in Wyoming and relay the details of my journey west, but I have not had an idle moment since stepping off the stage. I was twenty-four hours on the train from Colorado and two days on the stage. This letter would be a lengthy epistle if I detailed the events of such a trip.

As you instructed, I called on the attorney here in Wilder upon my arrival to settle the affairs of Uncle Peter's estate. All was in order, the land, cattle, and the house awaiting my signature. Once again, I give you my word never to take my holdings for granted.

The ranch itself is quite possibly the loveliest place on earth. There are mountains to the north, and the vast grass-lands span farther than the eye can see. The house was the worse for wear after months of vacancy, but with help, I have managed to make it feel almost like home.

I am constantly amazed by the kindness of my neighbors. Mrs. Mitchell, a dear woman with a brood of daughters, has been invaluable. My first day, she arrived with her girls and put the house in order. She gave me a butter churn she declared too small for her large family, a sample of her canning, and an obstinate Plymouth Rock hen determined to set a nest of eggs in spite of the oncoming winter.

I know you will worry over me like a wayward child, but please rest assured I have learned never to trust easily. In Wyoming, land is power, much the same as money is in New York. The neighboring ranch is owned by a former Texan whose bravery and knowledge of the land could make him a valuable ally and a treacherous foe at the same time. My heart tells me Ben Parrish can be trusted, but how wrong I have been before. Never again will I place my confidence in those who stand to gain from my misfortune.

You remain fondly in my thoughts and prayers and I will not forget your kindness toward me. I will write faithfully of my homestead adventures, but never fear that I am unaware of the perils of life on the frontier. One must always be careful, for danger lurks where you least expect it.

Yours truly,
Halley St. John
Wyoming Territory

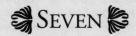

SEVEN

BEN CAREFULLY SURVEYED his handiwork with mottled pride. The new corral would be a welcome replacement, much larger and sturdier than the previous one. He had carefully selected the finest timber, dug the postholes an extra six inches deep, and done most of the work himself. If the corral failed, there would be no one but himself to blame.

Removing his work gloves, he wiped the sweat from his brow with one sleeve and glanced toward the open range.

They were out there, he knew it. Horses so wild they had no memory of the saddle or bridle. Just last fall he had caught sight of a dappled gray stallion perfectly outlined against the rising sun. The moment Ben took one step in his direction, the horse whirled and bolted toward the mountains. A horse like that could sire a generation of horseflesh like no one had ever seen in this part of the country. If only he'd had a fast mount that morning, not a herd of fevered cattle.

That was the real reason for a new corral, though he'd never admit it to anyone but himself. He'd fumed for two days over not taking out after the gray, finally rationalizing that his corral wouldn't hold a beast filled with so much hellfire. But this one would.

Tired and dusty, Ben trudged to the pump and quickly worked a steady stream of water. He filled the waiting pail and lifted the dipper, rinsing the dust from his throat. He couldn't help glancing south, toward the no-man's-land that separated his property from the St. John ranch. More and more, he found himself gazing into the distance and thinking of Halley.

Despite the ironclad fact that no woman belonged in the wild country of Wyoming, Ben couldn't help but feel the least bit proud of her for not turning tail and running. More than once, curiosity had gotten the better of him, and he'd ridden close enough to catch sight of her. From his vantage point, he watched Halley acquaint herself with frontier life.

At first, she spent most of her time setting up housekeeping. Then she began to venture out into the pastures, having Eli show her around the spread. The last time, Eli caught sight of him watching Halley inspect her sparse heard of cattle, and he hadn't been back.

Word was spreading already that the woman rancher was hiring hands for the winter, creating a flurry of speculation about her intentions regarding the land. But he knew damned well what Halley was going to do. She would run the ranch into the ground and then all hell would break loose when ranchers and squatters alike clashed to see who would seize control after she lost everything.

A sudden gust of wind from the north whipped across the emptiness, drying the sweat that had run down his neck and back, and he shuddered, again reminded that winter was not far off. He tossed the dipper back into the pail of water and returned to the waiting corral.

He tested the last post and found it sturdy. He needed only to fashion a gate and hang it with the proper hinges. His satisfaction with the finished product would be tempered by the knowledge that breeding horses would only be an indulgence. He had neither the time nor the land to spare pursuing plans he'd made when a third of Pete's land had been in his hip pocket.

Clouds were gathering in the east, and the daylight was just beginning to wane. Ben retrieved the sledgehammer from the patch of faded grass near the corral, slinging it over his shoulder as he turned toward the barn. The winter hands would not return from the range until nightfall, and the horses were waiting for fresh hay and grain.

Before he'd taken ten steps, the clop of a horse stilled his steps.

"Ben Parrish!" The familiar voice broke the silence, relieving Ben for the moment. "It's me . . . Eldridge."

The horse and rider neared, and Ben felt an odd sense of disquiet. Eldridge wouldn't ride all the way out here if he didn't want something.

"Looks like you're ready for spring roundup. Hell, we haven't seen the first snow yet." Eldridge reined his bay gelding to a halt, observing the new corral. "Looks sturdy."

"It is," Ben assured him, taking note of the man's attire. The clean white shirt and polished boots spoke volumes. Eldridge had been busy this day, but not riding the range or mending fences. "You been to a wedding or a funeral?"

"That may be up to you, Ben." He swung down from his horse, letting the reins fall to the ground. "I want to know what you're going to do about that damn woman."

"What woman?"

"You know damn well what woman I'm talking about. That harebrained spinster from back East.

Ben's eyes narrowed. "She's not my responsibility."

"Then why is that brother of yours over there all the time to see after things?" he demanded as he followed after Ben. "That woman has got to go. And when she does, there will be killing over that land . . . unless somebody takes it from her first."

"Is that what you're all prettied up for? Courting?" Anger tightened in Ben's gut, but one look at the disgust on Eldridge's face made him want to laugh. "Have any luck?"

"She's crazy, I tell you. Crazy as they come." He reached into his vest pocket for a thin cigar. "Do you know what she's doing over there? *Interviewing* ranch hands."

Ben only shook his head. "Like I said, she's not my responsibility. I've got my own place to see after . . . and so do you."

"I don't need you reminding me of that, Ben Parrish," Eldridge snapped, groping every pocket for a match. "You ought to see the setup she's got over there. Eli making those boys jump through hoops, and her making them sign an oath of conduct. Hell, half of them can't read a lick."

"Not many decent hands looking for work this time of year." Ben had matches in his pocket but decided to let Eldridge stew a little. There was nothing worse than the taste of a good cigar and no way to smoke it. "They better take what they can get."

Frustration was getting the better of Eldridge, and he bit into the end of his cigar, spitting the discard on the ground. "That's what I thought, but I'll bet there's thirty men over there looking for work. Can you believe it? Hell, I ran three of my own drovers back home."

"Might not be so bad working for a pretty woman, Coop," Ben said, finally conceding the match. "What were you doing over there?"

"As a neighborly gesture, I rode out there to see if there was anything she needed." Eldridge held the tiny flame to the end of his smoke, inhaling deeply. "Seeing as how I don't have a brother to loan out."

When Ben made no reply, he continued: "Damned if she didn't dismiss me like I was a liver-pill peddler."

"What's your point? Ben made no attempt to disguise his agitation. "Even a greenhorn knows a snake when they see one."

"Damn you, Parrish." Eldridge clamped down on the cigar, his jaw clenched with anger. "You're the one who said give her some time and she'll leave on her own. Well, she ain't! She's putting a new roof on the house and got two cords of firewood stacked neat as you please."

"She won't stay," Ben stated confidently. "She's not used to anything but security and comfort. First time she hears a wolf howl on a cold night, she'll be gone."

"And then what?" he demanded.

In an even tone, Ben replied, "You won't be the only one ready to fight."

"All right, Ben, all right." Eldridge swung into the saddle.

"Just don't say I didn't warn you. If you don't do something about her, someone will."

"Easy, Baby. Easy now," Halley crooned as she slipped the blanket across the broad straight back of her mule. After a week of patient practice, he was becoming accustomed to being ridden rather than pulling a wagon.

Eli hoisted the saddle into place and watched with grudging approval as Halley secured the front and rear riggings and tightened the cinch. "You seem to know your way around a stable."

"Oh, I learned to ride years ago . . . in England." Halley reached for the currycomb on the fence and began coaxing a bit more shine from the mule's coat once more for good measure. She had groomed the poor beast diligently, and he gleamed like a new penny. "The British set great store in their horses."

"Is that where you got that getup you're wearing?" Eli eyed her doubtfully. "You look fixed up for dancing, not riding a mule."

Halley only smiled. "It's called a riding habit."

She turned to show the clever design of the black woolen skirt, sewn with an inseam to allow a woman to ride with comfort and modesty.

"I bet you won't find too many of them English ladies riding around on pack mules."

Grudgingly, Halley had to agree with that. Nonetheless, she was proud of how much the mule's appearance had improved. She had even trimmed his bristly mane in a striking sawtooth design Mr. McClinton had described. The beast turned his head, his large eyes watching her every move. Halley smiled and reached into her pocket for a peppermint.

As he gobbled the candy the mule nudged his head affectionately against Halley's shoulder. She hugged his strong neck, saying, more to the mule than to Eli, "He's not a pack mule anymore, or ever."

Gathering the reins, she swung herself into the saddle with as much grace as possible. Riding astride was absolutely unheard of for a lady back East, but when Eli presented her with Uncle Peter's saddle, declaring it safer than a sidesaddle, she wouldn't have refused for the world.

"You be careful out there," the old foreman called as she turned the mule toward the open range. "Don't make me come looking for you."

Once clear of the grove of small trees, Halley let the mule run free. She was amazed by his speed and agility; no thoroughbred would best him. The ground flew beneath them, and she reveled in the freedom she felt. The wind whipped through her hair, and she filled her lungs with the crisp fall air.

Never had she found riding more exhilarating. The air was thick with the tangy scent of sage, and she delighted in the thunder of the mule's steady hooves, cutting gashes in the soft ground. She leaned forward and urged him on, sensing he gloried in this newfound freedom even more than she. They flew across fields of fiery wildflowers, until the fragrant meadows gave way to vast grassland.

The mule slowed of his own accord, blowing and tossing his head. Halley patted him with affection and stared out toward the expanse of open land. Her land.

She would only voice the phrase in thought to herself. The ranch had been a convenient escape from her troubles in New York, but now she was filled with a deep-rooted sense of awe and respect for the land itself. Her uncle was a man of courage to make this land his own. She had only to sign a piece of paper at the end of the month, and the law would call her the owner. She knew it would always belong to Pete St. John.

To her surprise, she caught sight of a rider coming toward her. She gripped the reins, ready to turn and run if needed.

The rider neared and she felt a faint sense of recognition. She squinted against the afternoon sun that served as a backdrop for the visitor. The mule's head came up, and his ears flattened. The rider slowly raised one arm and waived to her.

"Mr. Parrish!" she called out in relief. "I certainly didn't expect to meet you out here."

Ben reined his buckskin alongside the mule, and nodded briefly. A sudden gust of wind rushed between them, tugging at the faded bandanna loosely knotted at his throat.

"Old Pete's saddle," he observed, his gaze traveling her figure, making her acutely aware of the unladylike manner in which she was riding. "That mule must think he's died and gone to heaven."

"Why, Ben Parrish, is that a smile?" She laughed, and straightened the brim of her derby. "And all this time I thought your face would crack."

"Not everyone finds laughter as easily as you."

"I'd be happy to show you."

Halley watched as Ben's smile faded and his eyes bore down on her. She felt somewhat breathless, but managed, "Where are you bound on such a fine afternoon? Don't tell me a man like you slips away from his work occasionally to enjoy the simple pleasures of life."

"Would you be happy to show me that as well?" He reached for her gloved hand and fingered the delicate kid leather. "These gloves are too thin. You'll have blisters from riding, and they'll be of no use when winter sets in. Where did you get them?"

"New York, before leaving," she answered, staring down at their joined hands. "They're the finest material."

"You'll learn soon enough, what was true in New York won't hold up out here. It's a hard life, Halley. You should go back East where you'll be safe. Where you belong."

His hand slowly closed around hers, swallowing her smaller one in his. She couldn't help tightening her hold on his palm. Their eyes met, and she wanted to tell him that she could never go back, that Wyoming was all she had. But she dared not trust anyone with that secret. Not even Ben.

Halley stiffened and withdrew her hand. "I've already told you, I have no intention of selling the land."

Ben didn't miss the sudden tilt of her chin, and he knew there was no point in pursuing the subject any further today. "Let's ride down to the creek and water the horses."

The sun sparkled against the rushing water, and the bank was covered with fallen autumn leaves, a carpet of russet, gold, and crimson. Ben slid easily from his saddle and approached Halley where she sat mesmerized by the scene.

He reached to help her down from the saddle, his large hands circling her waist. With arms stiffened, Halley placed her hands on his shoulders, but still slid against his body as she dismounted. Their eyes met and clung, and neither moved to end the semi-embrace.

He let his palm move over her rib cage, bringing her even closer to him. He traced the curve of her waist, edging close to the gentle flare of her hip when he felt the unmistakable handle of a pistol.

Taking a step back, Ben eased the brim of his hat from his forehead. "I'll be damned. An armed woman."

Halley lifted the hem of her riding jacket to reveal the holster containing her Colt .45. "I've been practicing, and I can hit a tin can sitting on a fence post at twenty paces." A proud smile made her eyes sparkle as she added, "I shall be skilled enough to join the Texas Rangers before long."

"Is that a fact?" Ben gazed into the depths of her eyes and saw the questions Halley wanted to ask. He believed a man's past was best left behind, especially one as littered with bones as his, but he had questions of his own for her. "What do you know about the Rangers?"

"Mr. McClinton says that a Ranger can ride like a Mexican, shoot like a Tennessean, and fight like the devil." Her curiosity spilled over and she asked, "How long were you with the Rangers?"

"So, Eli's been gossiping about me?" He moved closer and let his hands fall back to her waist, easing her against him.

"He may have mentioned a few things." Gingerly, she let her gloved fingers settle against the bulk of his upper arms. "Just in passing."

"He's worse than an old woman." Ben deliberately lowered his face toward hers, allowing his words to feather across her brow. "You haven't forgotten our bargain, have you? Don't cheat by listening to Eli's rattling; you have to ask me yourself."

She swallowed, and he saw the hesitation steal the curiosity from her eyes. She was hiding something, he knew, and he wished he didn't give a damn. Her secrets kept him awake at night, wanting to know what had sent her running to the wilderness. Wanting her.

He traced the outline of her face, her skin like silk beneath his callused fingertips. "If I answer you, I can ask you anything I like."

Halley turned toward the creek and replied, "You cheated me once on that bargain."

"You didn't ask what you really wanted to know," Ben countered. Her shoulders stiffened at that and he decided against pressing her further. Better to let her keep her secrets a little longer than to scare her away for good. "So your Mr. McClinton is good with a gun?"

She turned back to him and smiled hesitantly. "Mr. McClinton says that staring down the barrel of a well-aimed pistol will unnerve even the coolest of heads," she replied, "Any rogue foolhardy enough to cross me will be sorry."

"If you can get him to sit on a fence post." Ben couldn't hold back a chuckle, though he could see how badly his amusement rankled her.

"Laugh if you will, but I am quite capable of defending myself." Halley unsnapped the cinch of her holster, drawing the weapon with more skill than he would have expected. She spun the Colt carefully on her gloved finger, pointed at an imaginary target, and pretended to fire, her arm drawing backward in a feigned reflex. "Got him . . . right between the eyes."

"If he was five feet tall and standing stock-still, you did." Ben took the pistol from her hand and opened the cylinder, revealing six gleaming bullets. She'd bested one brush with danger and now reveled in the false sense of invincibility a loaded gun gives a person. "You had better learn to hit a moving target."

"Yes, you're right." Concern furrowed her brow and she raised hopeful eyes to him. "Suppose you show me the best way to do just that."

Ben snapped the cylinder in place and returned the pistol to her outstretched hand. Turning her around, he placed his hand over hers, their fingers entwined over the Colt's smooth handle. He raised his arm, aiming the pistol toward the horizon.

"You have to know the enemy is out there before he lets you see him." Ben eased her elbow into a relaxed position, urging her to keep the pistol steady, her back pressed flush against his chest. "Listen for any sound out of place—a twig snapping beneath a man's foot, the creak of a saddle, the call of a bird at sunset."

She turned a bewildered glance toward him, her forehead just meeting his chin. "A bird?"

"Shh . . . you can't let them hear you," he continued, resting his free hand in the curve of her waist. The delicate scent of lilac made every inch of his body ache with desire, and he allowed himself the feel of her hair against his face. "You have to be still as death. Let them come to you."

Halley swallowed hard, trying not to flinch as he eased the pistol's hammer back. She could feel the warmth of his breath caress the shell of her ear and the heat of his hand burned through her clothes.

"Listen, listen," he whispered, but all she could hear was the pounding of her own heart in her ears. "You might get just one shot . . . you can't miss."

Without warning, Ben squeezed his fingers around hers and fired the pistol. Halley started and pulled herself from his grip, leaving the still-smoking Colt in his hand.

"You nearly scared me to death," she gasped, reading the disapproval in his eyes. "I wasn't ready."

Ben grasped her arm and returned the pistol to her holster. His eyes held hers, and his hold tightened when she tried to pull away. "What if I'm not around the next time you shoot without thinking?"

Without warning, he pulled her roughly into his embrace despite her feeble protest when she realized his intent. Hard and hungry, his mouth covered hers, and she winced as his fingers dug into her shoulders. An unexpected wave of heat washed through her, and Ben caught her weight against him when her knees threatened to fail.

Halley sank against his chest, her arms finding their way around his neck, as he deepened the kiss. Her derby tumbled down her back, but she barely noticed, her senses filled by the man holding her in his arms. His taste and scent, a heady mix of coffee, tobacco, and leather, were now imprinted on her senses forever.

His hand stroked up the curve of her spine until his palm circled the nape of her neck, and she shivered from the contact of flesh upon flesh. Long fingers combed through her hair, holding her head still for the first heated touch of his tongue crossing the barrier of her teeth.

A groan escaped his throat when she returned the touch, and Halley felt his arms tighten around her. She was crushed against his solid frame, every inch of her body pressed into his strength.

Dimly, she realized that she was the one prolonging the kiss, her fingers tangled in the dark hair that covered the collar of his shirt. Embarrassed, she loosened her hold and tried to pull away, but Ben didn't release her immediately. He studied her face for what seemed an eternity, as if gauging her response and reaction before setting her away from him.

Halley quickly turned to retrieve her fallen derby and began brushing the dust from the brim with exaggerated concern. Her face still tingled from the rough drag of his whiskers and she could feel her lips growing puffy already. She had been kissed before, but only under the most chaste of circumstances. This, she knew, was why proper young ladies in society were never without chaperons.

Only when her breathing had regained a normal pattern did she glance back to see Ben leaning against a tree, his arms folded casually against his chest. She cleared her throat, but her voice sounded husky when she said, "I can imagine what you must be thinking."

"I doubt that."

Placing her hat upon her head with as much dignity as possible, Halley dismissed his brash remark. "I only meant that I hope you won't misjudge me by one such slip in good sense. That is not the sort of behavior in which I normally indulge."

"That's a shame." Ben casually crossed the distance between them. "You're good at it," he said, pausing before her only long enough straighten her derby and smooth an errant lock of hair behind her ear.

Halley's face grew hot from the combined effect of embarrassment and passion. Before she could regain her composure, Ben glanced back, catching the blush warming her face. He gathered the reins, leading the horse and mule back to where she stood.

"Three years," he stated, handing her the mule's lead.

"I beg your pardon?"

"You asked how long I was with the Texas Rangers." He

swung into the saddle and peered down at her. "I always keep my bargains."

Contrite, Halley folded her arms across her chest and met his gaze. "And what would you like know about me?"

"You've already answered that question."

You've already answered that question.

The words stung, but Halley couldn't keep from repeating them to herself over and over again. She could well imagine what Ben had deduced from her shameless response to his kiss. His touch stirred passions within her she'd not known existed, and she had been powerless to resist.

For a week now she had brooded over her lack of propriety, though she'd never been a stickler for convention. Still, she was plagued to think that Ben considered her a wanton old maid who swooned if a man so much as touched her.

"Miss St. John?"

Startled, Halley turned toward the timid voice. Delia Mitchell's oldest daughter stood on the porch peering through the open door. Wiping her hands on a clean towel, Halley left the dish of potatoes she was peeling and crossed the room to meet the girl.

"Susan, hello." She smiled, grateful for the distraction. "Won't you come in?"

"Thank you," the girl whispered, and entered the house. "Ma sent me over here with some things you might need. We've been butchering this week, and fresh meat is always nice for dinner."

"Your mother is so thoughtful." Halley reached for the basket on the girl's arm and staggered at the weight. "My goodness, what all is in here?"

"She sent a haunch of pork roast, three quarts of cherry preserves, and a dozen biscuits." Susan tucked a limp strand of hair behind her ear and followed Halley to the basin. "I made the biscuits."

Halley lifted the cloth that covered the basket and found the plate of golden biscuits, their mouthwatering aroma filling the kitchen. "They do look wonderful. Let's have one with some of those preserves."

"Oh, no, ma'am. I need to get home."

"But you've just arrived," Halley countered. "Please stay. I'll make a pot of tea, and we can visit."

Susan glanced around the half of the house Halley had made into the kitchen and nodded. She sat at the square table as Halley directed and smoothed her hands across the blue gingham tablecloth.

"I'll get some water going while I finish these potatoes." Halley couldn't help thinking Susan was the unhappiest person she'd ever seen. She couldn't be more than eighteen, but her eyes held no youthful gaiety.

Halley placed two mugs on the table along with a pair of the tin plates she'd purchased from Mr. Tulley. Beside the plain dishes, she placed her mother's silver.

Susan lifted the gleaming spoon and stared at the intricately carved handle. "My lands, I've never seen anything so fine."

"Mother always prided herself on setting an elegant table." Halley filled the two cups and placed the biscuits between them. She sat down and continued: "Her china was exquisite, hand-painted from England. It would never have survived the trip."

"You left it behind?"

Halley only nodded, wishing she hadn't brought up the subject. Selling the china had brought enough to purchase her train ticket to Denver. Lifting a knife to cut a biscuit in half, Halley reminded herself to be thankful she still had the silver.

She passed the sugar bowl to her guest and said, "You must teach me how to make such light biscuits. I attempted a batch day before yesterday with dreadful results."

Before Susan could answer, Clayton's voice startled them both. "Miss Halley, you got a letter from New York."

He stepped in through the open doorway and removed his hat. "I'm sorry. I didn't know anyone was here."

"You remember Mrs. Mitchell's daughter Susan?" Halley motioned for him to join them at the table. "We were just having some tea, and Susan has made the most wonderful biscuits. You will join us, won't you?"

"Thank you, ma'am." Clayton drew a chair from the table and sat down. "I'm partial to biscuits with preserves."

"Well, you open this while I see who sent this letter."

Halley slid the jar of preserves across the table and reached for the envelope.

She had asked Clayton to mail a letter to Mr. Pittman when he left for town this morning, never expecting to have something waiting for her. She opened the envelope and immediately recognized the costly stationery and the sprawling handwriting. *Abigail Vanderburg.* Quickly, she folded the paper and placed the letter in her apron pocket. She would wait until she was alone to read letters from old friends.

When she looked up, Clayton and Susan were staring at her, waiting for her response.

"It's just a letter from a girl I knew in New York," she explained. "I'll read it later. Susan, won't you have some of your mother's preserves?"

Halley forced her attention to her teacup, stirring it well before realizing she had yet to add sugar.

"New York must be the most exciting place in the world," Clayton commented, taking a biscuit for himself. "I intend to live there someday."

"In New York?" Susan's eyes widened at the thought. "I could never live in the middle of so many people."

"That's what I want." Clayton spooned preserves onto his plate. "I read about a man who walked from one end of the city to another and didn't meet one soul he knew, and he'd lived there all of his life."

"That must be a lonely feeling," Susan observed, not looking at Clayton when she spoke. "I wouldn't like that at all."

"You get used to it," Halley remarked, her thoughts remaining on the letter in her pocket. Abigail was the kind of person you always ran into when you didn't feel like seeing anyone you knew. "Even among friends."

Clayton would not be dissuaded. "You can eat in a different restaurant every night, and there's a whole street with nothing but theaters and music halls. I'll bet you went to the opera every week, didn't you?"

Halley couldn't deny the splendor and excitement of the city. She was already longing for the conveniences of gaslights and deliverymen bringing ice to the back door. "Union Square is quite grand, but London is the city with the best theaters."

"London?" Clayton was impressed. "I've never known

anyone who's been to Europe. What were you doing over there?''

"Studying," Halley replied, somewhat embarrassed. "I was an avid student—literature in London, music in Paris, and art in Venice."

"You went all that way just to go to school?" Susan eyes were wide in amazement. "What about the schools in New York?"

"Oh, I attended school at home, but I wanted to study in a specialized environment." Halley paused to taste the biscuit, dabbing the corners of her mouth with a napkin. "What is that you like to study?"

Susan only shrugged. "Ma taught us to read a bit, but we never lived where there was school close enough to go."

"There's no school here in Wilder?" Halley couldn't believe her ears. "With all the families in the area?"

"Wilder is nothing but a cowtown." Clayton sneered. "No school, no theater, nothing."

"Well, perhaps that is something we can change," Halley stated before tasting her tea. "My family has always championed the cause of education. My grandfather served on the board of directors for several universities, and he even helped to establish scholarships for the . . . less fortunate."

"I doubt anyone in Wilder has even thought about having a school," Susan said, her voice slightly less timid. "At least, I've never heard anything about one."

"I never have, either," Clayton agreed. "I doubt anyone would know how to start something like that."

Halley nodded slowly, a plan taking root in her mind. Father had always maintained that a benevolent public image was essential to success of any kind. "Perhaps, that is something I can look into. No one can argue the fact that Wilder needs a school."

"They won't argue long with you, Miss Halley." Clayton laughed and Susan reluctantly joined in the merriment.

Halley was pleased to see the girl with a smile, her features were so gaunt and somber, but there was almost a sparkle in her eyes when she smiled. Halley wished she could borrow a cupful of Clayton's devilish humor and give it to Susan.

She sipped her tea and watched them over the rim of her

mug. Susan hung on every word of his vivid account of a trip he made to St. Louis the year before.

Clayton was a handsome young man filled with ambitions and always eager to talk about them. She doubted he would take the time to notice a quiet wisp of a girl like Susan.

Halley didn't believe in matchmaking, but she knew too well that the best things in life are often overlooked despite being right in front of a person.

🕸 EIGHT 🕸

WEDDINGS WERE ALWAYS festive occasions, and Halley was anxiously looking forward to her first social outing in Wilder. The fact that she knew neither the bride nor the groom didn't matter a whit. There would be people, music, and dancing, and she was desperate for any diversion from the monotony of the ranch.

Delia's insistence that she join them for the ceremony had been a boon, and her spirits were soaring now that the day of the party was at hand.

"Damn," she muttered, dropping her hairbrush for the third time. Her hair fell about her shoulders, soft and wavy from having been washed just that morning, and she scowled at her reflection.

She had so wanted to put her hair up for the event, but found the task much more difficult than she had anticipated. It looked so easy when her upstairs maid, Kate, had dressed the long tresses into the latest fashion.

Her frown deepened when she contemplated the possibility of seeing Ben and not looking her very best. Taking Delia at her word that *everyone* in town would be there, Halley wanted to face him poised and serene, completely unaffected by their passionate kiss.

Collecting the scattered hairpins from the floor, she doubted her ability to maintain indifference. The kiss had left her more than a little shaken. Even Eli had noticed, questioning her over and over again about her jaunt in the woods.

She wasn't fool enough to deny that she found Ben attractive. In fact, she readily admitted to herself that she found him terribly handsome, so much so that she could easily let herself forget that he wanted the land she had yet to fully inherit. Yes, Ben Parrish was a temptation and a danger rolled into one.

Still, her own vanity demanded that she appear her best, and she looked with dismay at her tousled hair, hanging in disarray around her shoulders.

She could ask Delia to help her, but there wouldn't be time. Besides, she was ashamed to admit to anyone that she was unaccustomed to styling her own hair. Resolving to practice another time, Halley combed the dark locks into a simple braid, tying it off with a velvet ribbon that matched the gown she had chosen to wear.

Carefully studying her reflection in the beveled mirror, she decided the results were suitable. Wistfully, she fingered her bare throat and thought how lovely a strand of pearls would be for such an occasion.

She crossed the tiny bedroom in stocking feet and carefully inspected the dress one last time. She had managed to save only two of her Worth gowns; the rest had been sold to fund her flight to Wyoming. She didn't grieve the loss; in all honesty, she was thankful to have spirited the clothes out of her home before the contents had been confiscated by the bill collectors.

Don't think about that now. She drew a deep breath, hoping to clear her mind of the ugly memories. Her life was here now, and she was going to a party and had a pretty dress to wear. There were many women who didn't even have that much in life.

Forcing her attention to the gown, she remembered choosing it for the opening night of an opera, the last one she'd attended with her father, and it was still one of her favorites. The beautiful green velvet fared the trip well, thanks only to the extreme precautions she had taken.

Wrapped in tissue paper, the dresses were packed in a cedar-lined trunk with lavender sachets tucked among the folds—moths were her worst fear. She tested the seams and was pleased to find them sturdy as ever. The delicate scent of lavender rose from the velvet when she shook the skirts out one last time.

Humming to herself, Halley sorted out her underthings and slipped a favorite chemise over her head. Heeding Eli's prediction that the afternoon would be warm but the evening chilly, she donned two petticoats and then her shift. She would have to hurry if she was going to be dressed and ready to leave when the Mitchells arrived.

Just as she stepped into the dress she heard Eli shouting to her from the porch.

"I see Tom Mitchell's wagon headed toward the house!" he called. "You'd best be out here waiting when he pulls up!"

Halley panicked, spearing her arms into the sleeves and desperately grappling for the buttons. She heard the wagon clatter into the lot and Mr. Mitchell call to Eli. She had barely secured two buttons before Delia's voice filled the downstairs.

"Halley? Aren't you ready yet?"

"I'm up here," she called. "I'm afraid I need a little help with my dress."

"Your dress? What's wrong?"

Halley flushed. "I can't quite reach the buttons."

"I'll be right up." The ladder creaked slightly under Delia's weight. "Tom's champing at the bit to get going. There's going to be so many folks there we'll have to hitch the wagon a mile from the house."

"I'm ready to leave," Halley promised her. "Once my dress is buttoned, we can go."

"Land sakes!" Delia gasped when she reached the loft. "That's the finest dress I've ever seen."

Halley turned to find Delia gaping at her in astonishment. Embarrassed, she smoothed her hands over the heavy velvet. "Will it be all right for the wedding?"

"All right? You'll be the envy of every female there," Delia stated, plucking a length of the skirt. She smoothed her hand over the material and shook her head in disbelief.

"Turn around," she ordered, letting the fabric fall from her hand. "Let's get you trussed up before Tom takes off without either one of us."

Once buttoned, Halley put on her nicest pair of shoes but decided against the matching bonnet. Snatching her gloves and reticule from the dresser, she hurried to follow Delia down the ladder.

The descent from the loft was doubly difficult, thanks to the heavy skirt, and Halley silently cursed her uncle's lifelong bachelorhood, knowing a wife would have insisted on suitable stairs. Delia was already out the door when she reached the bottom rung, but she took a moment to be sure the fire in the stove was banked, as Eli had stressed time and time again.

She clanged the lid to the stove loud enough to be sure he heard it and collected the wedding gift she was quite proud to say that she had made herself. Delia had helped her wash and iron flour sacks, but Halley had patiently cut and hemmed the material into tea towels for the bride's new kitchen. The package was wrapped in plain brown paper, but she had tied it off with a bright yellow ribbon rather than string.

Eli was on the porch with Tom Mitchell, discussing the prospect of raising hogs in Wyoming. He turned and studied her with a slow smile. "Well, look at you. Prettier'n a speckled pup."

"Thank you, sir," Halley replied with exaggerated graciousness and waved to Susan and her sisters in the wagon. She returned her attention to Delia, who stood on the porch with her husband. "Hello, Mr. Mitchell. It's nice to see you again."

"Yes, ma'am, I almost didn't recognize you." He grinned broadly. "Last time I seen you, you was raising hell with the stage driver."

"Tom!" Delia snapped, giving him a firm nudge in the ribs with her elbow. "What a thing to say."

"That's quite all right." Halley laughed and Tom Mitchell did the same. "I'm afraid I let my temper get the better of me that day."

"Don't be saying sorry for taking up for yourself." Eli quickly spoke in her defense. "I should have met that stage myself. I would have had that durn fool eating dirt."

"Not to worry, Eli, Ben took care of things." Tom Mitchell gave his wife a sly wink. "If I weren't a married man, I wouldn't have let him get ahead of me. Quite a treat to help a pretty woman down from a stage."

"Tom Mitchell, the things you say." Delia shook her head. "Come along, Halley, and don't pay any attention to his fool talk."

Turning to Eli, Halley asked one last time, "Are you sure you won't come with us?"

He shook his head. "Naw, missy, you go on and have fun, but behave yourself."

Ben could think of a hundred things he'd rather be doing than going to a wedding. Hell, he'd been to hangings that he'd looked forward to more than this.

As they neared the homestead Clayton grinned at the sight of dozens of buggies lining the drive. "I'll bet the whole town's turned out."

He was probably right. Frank Carney had been a good friend to most everyone in the county over the past years, lending a hand whenever it was needed. Just last year he had spent Christmas day helping Ben save a prize mare who otherwise might have died with her first foal. Ben would endure a wedding for the sake of a friendship, but not for much else.

With his reins in one hand, Clayton straightened his string tie and brushed any dust from his jacket. "I'm going to dance with every lady here," he announced. "And don't tell me I can't have any whiskey."

Ben gave his brother a sidelong glance and shook his head. "If you do too much dancing and drinking, you might end up getting hitched yourself."

"We should both be so lucky." With a grin, Clayton let up on the rein and urged his mare into a fast trot, racing toward the party.

Grinning himself, Ben leaned forward and spurred the bay into a full gallop, easily overtaking Clayton's mount. When he reached the row of buggies, he reined the horse to a halt and waited for his brother to catch up.

"You know that old nag of yours can't beat General Sherman,'' Ben reminded him. ''He can outrun any horse in the county.''

Clayton stroked the mare's neck when she came to a stop. ''Don't underestimate what Betsy can do when she puts her mind to it.''

Ben turned the General toward the gathering of wedding guests. ''Well, let's get this over with.''

The afternoon was turning almost balmy for September, and Ben was grateful for the weather's reprieve. The only thing more miserable than going to a wedding was going to one in the cold. He caught sight of Frank Carney making his way through the crowd to greet him.

''Howdy, Ben.'' Frank extended his hand to Ben then to Clayton. ''Proud you two could be here. It's not every day a man marries off his daughter.''

Carney had reason to be proud. His daughter was marrying a lieutenant in the cavalry. She would live at Fort Bridger, practically assuring her father the beef contract not only for the soldiers but for the Indian reservation as well.

''You're a lucky man,'' Ben said as Carney and Clayton shook hands.

''That I am. Well, put your horses away and join the party. There's plenty of food, and the preacher should be here any minute.''

As they made their way toward the barn Clayton grinned at his brother. ''I reckon he's set for life. Who'd have thought he'd get such a catch for that homely girl?''

''Have you seen the lieutenant?'' Ben led the horses toward the back of the barn. He unsaddled the pair and put them in a large rear stall, after seeing others had done the same to accommodate all of the wedding guests. ''He looks like he was weaned on vinegar.''

Clayton laughed and led the way out of the barn. The afternoon sunlight was dazzling after even a few minutes in the shadowy barn, and Ben nearly collided with Tom Mitchell.

''Ho, Ben,'' Tom called, stepping aside. ''What's your hurry?''

''I don't want to miss the ceremony,'' Ben lied, shaking his friend's hand. ''Good to see you, Tom. I suppose you brought the family.''

"Yes, indeed," he answered. "I got more females than one man deserves. I even brought an extra one today, one you might be interested in."

Ben was skeptical. "Who?"

"That fancy-miss niece of Pete's," Tom explained. "She and my missus are thick as thieves, and Delia wasn't going to miss a chance to show her off to the whole town."

Halley. He had wondered if she would be at the wedding, but dismissed the thought. He couldn't imagine why she'd care about going to a country wedding, especially when she didn't know the family.

"I figured you'd be happy to see her again," Tom pressed. "Seeing as how you got kind of friendly with her when she first got to town."

"Who's Ben getting friendly with now?" Roy Teal laughed as he approached the two men. "I swear, Ben, you're turning out to be a real ladies' man."

Tom chuckled as he shook hands with the sheriff. "I was telling him that Miss St. John came with us today."

Roy nodded, extending his hand to Ben. "I hear you had a little trouble when you took her out to Pete's place."

"No wonder this town doesn't have a newspaper," Ben observed as accepted the sheriff's handshake. "By the time anything got to press, everyone within a hundred miles would already know all about it."

"Hell, nothing ever happened worth telling before she got to town."

"Tom's right, Ben," the sheriff said. "That gal's a ball of fire. To hear Jonas Flint tell it, she was ready to fight one of his boys . . . over a damn sheep!"

"Is Jonas still riding with those boys?" Ben asked, hoping to change the subject. "They had trouble written all over them."

"No worse than most." Roy tugged at the tie knotted at his throat. "Damn, I hate these things. I feel like I'm choking. I think Jonas parted ways with them once they got into town. Trouble over money, I heard."

Ben could easily imagine that, but an uneasiness settled in his mind. If Clint wasn't riding for Jonas now, what was he up to?

* * *

Delia took great pleasure in introducing Halley to the other ladies, referring to her as "my good friend." As they made their way through the crowd Halley grew more and more self-conscious. Conversations came to abrupt halts and people stared openly.

"Who is that?" someone whispered.

"Have you ever seen such a dress?" another remarked.

"Mother wants you to meet the mother of the bride," Susan whispered as they neared the sprawling ranch house. "Mrs. Carney always puts on like they've got more than everyone else."

Several women were gathered on the front porch, fussing over a crystal punch bowl. Delia marched up the front steps and called out, "Howdy, Beatrice, you've got a fine day for a wedding."

A woman clad all in gray looked up with a welcoming smile. "Delia Mitchell, I'm so proud you could come. I told Frank—"

Her words halted as her eyes settled on Halley, and she nearly dropped a cup of punch. The other women followed her gaze to Halley, each gaping in astonishment.

Delia's smile was triumphant. "Ladies, I want you all to meet my neighbor Halley St. John. Halley, this is Beatrice Carney, the bride's mother."

"Congratulations, Mrs. Carney." Halley stepped forward and extended her gloved hand with practiced elegance. "I know how happy you must be. Mrs. Mitchell has told me what a fine young man your Emily will wed."

"Thank you, Miss St. John," Beatrice stammered, finally finding her voice. She took Halley's hand in a welcoming gesture. "Would you like some punch?"

"Thank you, that would be lovely."

After a few minutes of polite conversation, Delia caught sight of other guests she wanted Halley to meet and led her away. Halley followed Delia through the throng of wedding guests, returning smiles and nodding at curious glances. To her relief, she caught sight of a familiar face.

"Clayton!" she called.

He turned at the sound of her voice and shouldered his way

through the crowd toward her. His eyes widened as he drew near. "Miss Halley! You look pretty as a—"

"As a speckled pup?" she offered when he stammered, embarrassed by his own boldness. She laughed and clasped his hand. "It's so good to see you."

"Thank you," he answered, laughing himself. "I didn't know you knew the Carneys."

"I don't," she confessed. "I tagged along with the Mitchells. You remember Susan, don't you?"

Halley took a tight hold on the girl's arm and pulled her forward. A pretty blush stained her plain features when Clayton flashed a handsome smile, saying, "I remember those biscuits. I keep hoping you'll bring me another batch."

"Oh, yes, Susan, you must," Halley agreed. "I tried another batch yesterday. That's when Eli started talking about hogs. He says we need pigs to eat my cooking."

Clayton and Halley laughed, and Susan joined in, forgetting her shyness.

"I'm sorry I haven't been by this week," Clayton said. "Ben has needed me to help with the branding."

"That's quite all right. You've done so much already." Nonchalantly, Halley glanced over his shoulder, but caught no sight of Ben. "I suppose you're here by yourself?"

"Ben's around here somewhere," he answered. "He thinks a lot of Frank Carney; otherwise you couldn't drag him to a wedding."

Seizing the opportunity to learn something about Ben's past, Halley asked, "The only reason your brother is here is out of obligation to a friend?"

Clayton grinned. "I said he was here, I didn't say he was happy about it."

Toying with a bit of lace on her sleeve, Halley tried to be as casual as possible. "What's not to love about weddings?"

He only shrugged. "I suppose they remind him of his own wedding day."

She looked up at that, unable to feign complete indifference.

Clayton looked abashed. "You did know Ben used to be married, didn't you?"

Suddenly she felt guilty for tricking Clayton into gossiping. She was dying to know what had happened to Ben's wife, but she didn't want to cause problems between the brothers. Stifling her curiosity, she replied, "Oh, he may have mentioned something about it once."

"Well, it's not something he talks about," Clayton assured her. "Sometimes I think he wishes it had never happened."

"My goodness, was it really all that dreadful?" she asked before she could stop herself.

"A man doesn't forget the woman who cost him his commission as a Texas Ranger."

"Preacher's here!" someone shouted.

The bride and groom were to exchange their vows on the front porch, and the wedding guests were directed to assemble before the house. Ben joined the rest of the men in the back while the ladies gathered toward the front, nearest the porch.

The groom scaled the front steps, followed by several soldiers in blue uniforms. The minister shook his hand, and the crowd fell silent. Mrs. Carney cleared her throat loudly and her husband appeared at the far end of the porch, leading his veiled daughter.

Ben swapped wry smiles with his brother before scanning the crowd. It didn't take long to spot Halley; her green velvet dress was a beacon in a sea of calico and homespun. She stood beside Tom Mitchell's wife, staring straight ahead at the wedding party.

Carney proudly marched his daughter to her groom as his wife looked on through teary eyes. The young couple joined hands, and the father stepped aside.

"Dearly beloved," the preacher's voice boomed. "We are gathered here today to join this man and this woman in holy matrimony."

The afternoon breeze toyed with a Halley's dark hair, tugging several strands loose about her face. Discreetly, she raised a gloved hand to smooth them from her eyes, turning by chance in Ben's direction. The shadow of her hand hid the expression in her eyes, but he didn't miss the way her shoulders stiffened.

He couldn't resist rankling her a bit and raised a hand to the brim of his hat in greeting. Her hand fell to her side, and he saw the pretty blush that stained her features. He grinned slightly and winked at her, almost laughing out loud as her eyes widened in response.

She whipped her gaze back to the bride and groom, her hands clasped primly before her, but Ben wasn't fooled by her feigned prudishness. The subtle flush of color rose over her face, giving her away, and a slight frown marred her lovely face.

"Lieutenant Maxwell, do you take this woman to be your wife, to have and to hold . . ."

The preacher's words drew Ben's attention, and he listened as the groom carefully repeated the oath to love, honor, and cherish, but soon his attention returned to Halley. She was the kind of woman he had once wanted, the kind who expected vows and promises of devotion. The kind who didn't think of giving a thing in return.

He'd almost let himself forget that this was no more than a big game for her. A few weeks in the frontier, and then she'd return to her fancy city life, laughing with her rich friends about the cowboy who did her bidding. Before leaving, she'd probably try to sell him her damn mule.

Just then, she glanced back over her shoulder, and he felt his eyes narrow. Damn her, if she was going to leave, she'd better do it quick, because he wasn't a man to be played a fool.

Halley heaved a sigh of relief as the ceremony came to an end. The other guests rushed to congratulate the newlyweds, but she slipped away from the crowd, needing a moment to compose herself.

Ben Parrish had the most unsettling effect on her, and she didn't doubt for a minute that he was completely aware of it. That, of course, was her own fault for allowing far too much familiarity between them. She didn't bother to remind herself of all the reasons for keeping him at a distance; she simply wouldn't let it happen again.

Resigned to the matter, Halley turned to rejoin the party, and nearly collided with Ben's solid frame.

He reached out to steady her as she stumbled backward, gripping her upper arm. Once steadied, Halley discreetly pulled her arm from his grasp and put a safe amount of distance between them.

"Good afternoon, Mr. Parrish," she said, smoothing the sleeve of her dress. "How nice to see you."

"It's a pleasure to see you, ma'am." He fingered the brim of his hat, not bothering to hide a rakish grin. "Always a pleasure."

She swallowed, but couldn't find her voice.

"I noticed you standing over here by yourself," he continued, seemingly unaware of her lack of response. "Are you all right?"

"Of course I am, Mr. Parrish," she replied with her most practiced nonchalance. "I was merely letting the others pass to congratulate the newlyweds."

He nodded, and she couldn't help but notice his attire. The black trousers and matching jacket were a sharp contrast to the clothes he wore for work on the ranch. His face was tan above the stiff white collar, and his blue eyes were even more startling.

"How are you finding ranch life?"

She didn't miss his scornful tone, "Just fine. Why do you ask?"

"I just wondered how you were getting along without a houseful of servants at your beck and call."

"I'm not completely inept, sir." She raised her chin slightly. "In fact, I am truly enjoying the ranch."

"For now. But you'd better not wait until winter to try and get back home," he advised. "Once the snows come, the stage hardly runs at all."

Stunned, Halley realized that he had never even considered that she might stay in Wilder. He wanted her to leave, even after kissing her. He had obviously been trying to seduce her into selling the land to him.

"Don't flatter yourself, Mr. Parrish." Somehow she kept her tone even, despite the lump rising in her throat. "I've been kissed before, but even your wealth of charm will not persuade me to sell my land and leave Wyoming."

"You flatter yourself, lady." He closed the distance between them, standing mere inches away from her. "If I wanted the land, I wouldn't waste time trying to sweet-talk you out of it. There are easier ways than that.''

"Then what happened the other day was a mistake on both our parts," she retorted without a hitch. "And it shan't happen again.''

"It shan't?" he mocked. "Are you so sure? You may have been kissed before, Miss St. John, but you'd never been kissed like that.''

His arrogance tempted her to deny the truth, but she wouldn't let him goad her into claiming to be a woman of experience. Damn him! She wanted to tell him to go to the devil, but she had too much pride to create a scene.

"Mr. Parrish, what happened the other day only proves that we are both capable of making mistakes.'' She smiled sweetly to mask her anger. "I can assure you that it won't happen again.''

"You can assure me nothing.'' He eased the brim of his hat back from his eyes. "If you stay in Wyoming, you can't avoid me all the time.''

"Good day, Mr. Parrish," she managed in her most reserved tone. "I do hope that no misunderstandings will remain between us.''

Not waiting for his reply, Halley turned on her heel to find the Mitchells and enjoy what was left of the festivities, if she could.

Instead, an unexpected shadow fell over her face, and she gasped. Instinctively, she threw her hands up to ward off whatever was hurling toward her and barely missed being hit squarely in the face. Her fingers knotted in delicate petals, and to her dismay, the bride's bouquet was crumpled in her clenched fists.

A cheer rose from the throng of guests, and Delia rushed to her side. The older woman laughed at Halley's embarrassment and hugged her.

"Aren't you the sly one?" Delia eased the flowers from her grasp and tried to smooth the battered petals. "The next one to wed, and I didn't even know you had your cap set for someone.''

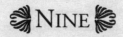

NINE

Mr. Josiah Pittman
Attorney-at-Law
New York City

Dear Mr. Pittman,

I can scarcely believe only a month has passed since my
arrival in Wyoming. Already, I feel as much a part of the
wilderness as the mountains that have stood a thousand
years. This morning I watched an eagle soar over the valley
where my home lies. 'Twas a magnificent sight. This land
is a constant revelation of wonders one would never find in
crowded Eastern cities.

The ranch is doing well, despite minor setbacks. Several
of the men we hired have gone on to warmer climates, and
the threat of rustlers is always a concern. There are those
who believe I have no right to the land, and want it for
themselves.

111

Winter is fast approaching, and I pray we will be spared the staggering losses of the past. Eli tells of entire herds freezing in their sleep. I have concluded that ranching is a constant fight to hold on to what is yours. Those who think I have no fight in me will learn otherwise. I have come to Wyoming to stay.

Halley St. John
Wyoming Territory

"Breakfast! Get it now or starve!"

Halley started at the ruckus outside her window. From the commotion, one would think every cowhand in the territory was having his morning meal on her ranch. She stretched beneath the quilts, somewhat accustomed to being so rudely awakened by now. Eli strongly disapproved of her sleeping late, and he made as much noise as possible of a morning.

She smiled to herself, imagining the old man's reaction if he had an inkling of her life in New York. By her old standards, six o'clock in the morning was the middle of the night, and when she did awaken, the upstairs maid would be waiting with a silver tray of tea, scones, and the morning newspaper. The most she ever did before ten o'clock was check the society page to be sure her name was mentioned favorably, or not at all.

Halley grimaced at the memory of the awful morning the front page instead bore her name, touting her ruin. The letter from Abigail tactfully assured her that the gossip hadn't ceased, and that there was much speculation on her reasons for fleeing to the wilderness.

It breaks my heart to tell you, dear, Abigail had written, *but I am your friend . . .*

Abigail always felt it was her duty to advise you of any unkind rumors—after she had told everyone else. She had even been kind enough to include clippings from the society page proclaiming Halley "Buffalo Bill in Petticoats." Halley decided there were some things she would never miss about New York.

Prompted by the thought, she threw back the covers and rose from the bed. The floor was cold beneath her bare feet as she scurried to the dresser for a pair of stockings. Each morning seemed colder than the last, and Halley was already dreading her first Wyoming winter.

Atop the dresser lay the wilted bridal bouquet, and she lifted the flowers, inhaling their fading scent. Later she would press the blooms in a book to save them, but for now she wanted to enjoy their beauty.

She donned a simple blue woolen skirt and plain white shirt-waist before hurriedly combing and braiding her hair. Making her way down from the loft bedroom, Halley snatched the heavy black shawl from its hook on the wall and headed out to join the ranch hands for breakfast.

"Well, look who decided to join us." Eli glanced up from the tin plate that bore the remains of his breakfast. "Ain't much left, but you might squeeze enough coffee out of them grounds to have a cup. Might wake you up by dinnertime."

"As strong as you make the coffee, I'll be awake until din-nertime tomorrow." Halley pulled the woolen shawl around her shoulders, pretending to ignore the titter of laughter behind her. The hands truly enjoyed the banter between her and the old foreman, and she did her best not to disappoint them.

As she filled a tin cup with the scalding brew, Halley noticed the plate prepared and waiting for her by the fire. Eli always claimed he scavenged her breakfast from what the men let fall from their plates, but she knew better.

"Mornin', ma'am." Each cowpuncher spoke politely and doffed a battered hat as she passed by and sat down beside Eli on the back of the wagon.

"Is that a heel print in that biscuit?" Eli's weathered face pleated around his smile. "I swore I managed to snatch that out from underfoot."

Halley returned his smile over her coffee, accustomed to the foreman's humor as she was to the bitter taste of coffee with-out cream or sugar. Reluctant to release the steaming cup that warmed her fingers, she asked, "How much longer before you decide the weather is too cold for us to eat outside?"

"Cold? Hell, it ain't close to being cold. I've seen mornings so cold, a man could take a . . . well, he could spit and it would freeze afore hitting the ground."

Eli drained the coffee from his cup and grew serious. "I've

seen many a cold day out here. One year the snow was high as the house, couldn't get out for three days.''

Halley tightened her grip on the tin cup, as if she could somehow absorb the warmth. She couldn't imagine such hardship, but here she was in the very place it had happened before. ''Was that . . . recently?''

Sensing her apprehension, he quickly replaced the concern on his face with a smile. ''Years ago, missy. All we need to worry about is branding the rest of them steers afore winter sets in.''

''How long will that take?''

''Well, I could use twice as many hands as we got,'' he grudgingly admitted. ''And there's still a lot of work ahead of us.''

Halley nibbled at a salty slice of bacon, her thoughts still focused on the prospect of being snowbound. ''Mr. McClinton writes of dreadful winters in these parts. I hope we're well prepared.''

''Old Pete always said to get ready for blizzards and pray for dandelions.'' Eli's bushy eyebrows drew together and with a knowing wink he assured her, ''We'll be ready.''

''How long did you and Uncle Peter know one another?''

Stroking his unshaven chin, Eli tried to remember an exact date but couldn't. ''A lot of years, missy. We met on a riverboat. I was working in the galley—that's the kitchen—and Pete, he was trying to earn a living dealing underhanded poker. One night two gents caught him cheating, beat him black and blue, and tossed him in the rubbish bin.''

''My goodness.'' Halley couldn't imagine anyone from her family in such a sordid profession as gambling, and she was anxious to learn more of her adventurous uncle. ''What happened then?''

''I came along to dump the trash overboard, and there he was.'' Eli made a wide sweep of his arms to emphasize the shock of finding someone in the rubbish bin. ''I hauled him out, sobered him up, and helped him get his money back.''

''How?''

Before he could reply, their attention was drawn by a horse and rider making their way into the breakfast camp. Halley smiled and waved as she recognized Clayton Parrish.

"Mornin', Miss Halley," he called, sliding down from his horse. "I could smell that coffee a mile away."

"Have a cup," Eli invited, motioning for the young man to join them. "I was just telling Missy about my riverboat days."

"Don't believe a word he says," Clayton warned Halley. "He's forgotten half of it, and what he can remember, he lies about to make it sound better."

"Boy, you're not so grown I won't box your ears," Eli warned, but he smiled as Clayton and Halley laughed. "What brings you around so early?"

"I was riding into town and thought I'd see if you needed anything." Clayton balanced his weight on an overturned bucket left behind by one of the cowhands. "You're welcome to go with me, Miss Halley."

Clayton knew Halley relished trips to town, and she suspected he was using her as an excuse for Ben to let him go.

"Thank you, Clayton," she answered. "I do have an appointment with Mr. Olson this morning and there's a letter I need to mail."

"You two are always hunting some excuse to get to town." Eli's brow furrowed with disapproval, and he glowered at Clayton. "There's work to be done, and I know Ben would have your hide if you're slacking off."

"Didn't Mr. Tulley say he had ordered some of that Tennessee tobacco?" Halley interjected innocently.

"He sure did," Clayton replied with exaggerated thoughtfulness. "Cured in whiskey, I believe. I imagine it'll be sold out before he can stock the shelves."

Eli wrestled with temptation and lost. "Get going and don't dawdle. This is still wild country."

"Good morning, Miss St. John," Warren Olson made his way into the outer office of his law practice, smiling broadly. "Always good to see you. How are you?"

"Very well, thank you," Halley answered, extending her hand, and returned his smile. She prayed her anxious nerves didn't show, but inside, her stomach was filled with butterflies. Today she would learn the remaining conditions of her uncle's will, but only after she had convinced Mr. Olson that she was perfectly content in Wyoming.

"I've seen you in town quite a lot," he commented, motioning for her to be seated. "I imagine things get pretty lonesome for you on that big spread in the middle of nowhere."

"Why, not at all," she lied, smoothing the fabric of her skirt beneath her moist palms. "I find the solitude oddly refreshing; after so many years in a bustling city, I can actually hear my own thoughts. My trips to town are usually for supplies or to post letters back home."

He raised an eyebrow, and Halley could have bitten her tongue for referring to New York as home.

"Homesick?" Mr. Olson settled himself behind the large mahogany desk and studied her thoughtfully. "That would explain all the time you spend in town. I'm afraid our humble cowtown will hardly replace the excitement you found in New York."

"Mr. Olson, I did not come to Wyoming to become a hermit." Halley struggled to hold her temper, but she deeply resented the idea of the squat little man monitoring her activities. "I see many people from the outlying ranches mingling in town on a regular basis. Does that mean they aren't cut out for life in Wyoming?"

"Please pardon me, Miss Halley, I didn't mean to offend you, but I find it hard to believe that a well-bred city woman would be content living among longhorn cattle and drovers."

Halley swallowed hard and caught her bottom lip between her teeth in an attempt to squelch the panic rising within her. If he advised her to return to New York, she would be forced to admit she had nothing to return to. Wyoming was all she had, and even that wasn't guaranteed.

"You are entitled to your opinion, sir, but I have every intention of remaining here in Wilder."

To her surprise, Olson only chuckled. "If Pete were still with us, I'd owe him twenty dollars."

"I beg your pardon?"

"He wagered twenty dollars that you'd take to frontier life like a duck to water. He said you had the pioneer spirit . . . always traveling to school and looking for adventure."

Relief spread through her chest, and at last she drew an easy breath. She smiled and sank back in the chair. "So the ranch is mine?"

Olson kept smiling and reached for the documents neatly stacked on his desk. "Yes, ma'am, come spring, the SJ will be yours—lock, stock, and barrel."

"Come spring?"

Clearing his throat, the attorney selected a document from the stack. "Now, don't be concerned. This is all a formality, and your uncle wanted what was best for you."

He gave her a reassuring smile and began reading aloud:

" 'The reading of this document signifies that my niece, Halley Elizabeth St. John, has indeed traveled from New York to reside at the SJ ranch and wishes to remain in Wyoming. I regret that I did not know her better in life, as she must be a young woman of courage and fortitude.

" 'My decision to bequeath the ranch to her was not a spontaneous one, and the fact that she has accepted this inheritance suggests that there are circumstances in her life that I could not have anticipated. Therefore, precautions will be taken to ensure that the ranch will be properly managed and her interests protected.' "

"Mr. Olson," Halley interrupted. "I am beginning to get the impression that Uncle Peter did not truly wish for me to have the ranch. I do not understand the need for so many . . . precautions."

Warren Olson smiled in sympathy. "Your uncle was a very influential man, and I imagine he relished the idea of maintaining some sense of control over his property even from the grave."

"That is hardly fair to me." Desperation began to creep into her voice and she sat back, willing herself to remain calm.

"Miss St. John, surely you have noticed the tensions mounting between the cattlemen and the ever-invading farmers. There are those who would take that land from you, and you have no experience in running a ranch. Don't you see that Pete only wanted to ensure that you would be protected?"

"I suppose." She shifted in her seat. "Please forgive my interruption and continue."

Clearing his throat, Olson did just that.

" 'I have chosen a trustworthy adviser who will oversee the management of the property, cattle, and future holdings of my estate, until such time as he feels his guidance is no longer needed. My niece shall consult him on all matters relating to the ranch, regardless how trivial. The adviser will have the authority to prevent any such actions that would place the ranch at risk. He may also seize possession of the property if my niece proves to be unfit or unable to maintain her inheritance.' ''

Halley opened her mouth to speak, but words failed her. It was as if Richard Farnsworth had risen from the dead in time to grasp her only hope for solvency. The attorney droned on about the importance of learning to manage the ranch and making prudent decisions.

Despite the chill of the day, she suddenly felt suffocated in the small office. She withdrew a handkerchief from her reticule and discreetly dabbed at the moisture beading on her forehead.

'' 'In conclusion, I will be satisfied if Halley endures one winter and sends a herd to market.' ''

"Mr. Olson," she managed at last. "Just who is this adviser?"

The attorney felt his pocket for his timepiece and observed, "I have asked him to join us, and he should be here any minute."

Rising from his desk, he peered into the outer office. "Good morning, sir," he called in a pleased tone. "You are just in time."

"I hope this is as urgent as you said." Ben's deep voice filled the room. "I've got a man waiting to buy horses, and he's anxious to spend his money."

"Come in, please." Olson followed Ben into the office and closed the door. "Miss St. John, I believe you know Ben Parrish."

Ben stared out of the attorney's window and watched Halley cross the street. Her back was to him, but he had seen the tears shimmering in her eyes as she had marched out of the office. He wished she had slapped him or cussed him; anything would have been better than the look of betrayal and the accusation in her eyes.

Warren Olson cleared his throat. "That didn't go well at all, did it?"

He turned on the portly attorney. "You should have told

me what this was all about before now. And her, too.''

"Mr. St. John left very explicit instructions—''

"Pete is dead. He can't run this county from his coffin.''

Olson opened the bottom drawer of his desk and produced a bottle of brandy along with two glasses, which he filled without asking Ben if wanted a drink. "He wanted you to protect his niece from those who would take the land.''

"Don't give me that bullshit, you knew him as well as I did.'' Ben accepted the brandy, but chose to remain standing. "The old cuss couldn't stand the thought of anyone being a bigger man in this town than he was, and he's using her to keep his boot on all our necks.''

"Pete St. John was a difficult man, but he was fair,'' the attorney retorted after taking a sip of the brandy. "He considered you a friend, and you will be well compensated.''

Ben drained half the brandy from his glass, grateful Halley had left before Olson revealed the remaining details of the will. If Ben succeeded in establishing Halley in the cattle business, he would be rewarded with a generous portion of land. Just enough to start a decent herd of horses.

"I was his friend,'' Ben said. "But that doesn't mean I think he's right. I told him so more than once.''

"Your frankness is most likely what prompted him to appoint you as Miss St. John's adviser,'' the attorney observed. "He didn't want anyone to mislead her or make allowances to spare her feelings.''

Ben glanced back toward the window, catching sight of Halley just as she ducked inside the general store. "How do you think she feels now?''

Halley slipped into the shadows of the back corner of the general store, pretending to inspect the selection of galvanized washtubs. Other shoppers mingled in the next isle, discussing the unreasonable price of sugar. She gripped the cold metal edge of a fifteen-gallon tub and swallowed hard against tears.

Crying would only further the humiliation she felt at the thought of the smugness Ben and the attorney must feel. Foolish woman, she could hear them saying, she really believed that ranch was hers. Something in her insides twisted at the thought of them gloating over her reaction.

Her first instinct had been to tell them both to go to blazes and take the ranch with them, but pride was a luxury she'd lost with her fortune. Without a word, she had stormed out of the building, barely resisting the urge to slam the door hard enough to rattle the windowpanes.

She had wanted to run from town and hide in her tiny loft bedroom until spring, but she had ridden with Clayton. They had agreed to meet at the general store, and she would have to wait for him.

"Clayton!" she gasped aloud. No wonder Ben had so generously allowed his brother to help out around her place. How convenient for him, taking her ranch with a complete inventory tallied by his own brother.

Halley stepped aside to allow an elderly man to pass through the isle, leading a small boy toward the front of the store. She looked away from their questioning glances.

Obviously, she had learned nothing from her misfortune in New York. She had readily trusted Ben Parrish, sought his advice, and given herself over to the romantic whimsy she had created to justify the attraction she felt toward him. What a fool he must have seen her for, clinging desperately to him and returning his kisses with the thirst of a drunkard.

She dabbed at the moisture threatening her eyes, hoping her face held no telltale redness. She remembered the tobacco she had promised Eli and made her way to the front counter. She shuddered and drew a deep breath, determined to appear as if she had not a care in the world.

"I declare, Miss Halley, ranch life agrees with you." Jim Tulley scurried behind the store counter, scooping cornmeal from a large wooden barrel. "Don't you miss the big city none at all?"

Halley forced herself to smile at the storekeeper. "I do feel a wee bit homesick from time to time. I've been so busy trying to learn my way around the ranch, I just haven't had time to miss New York."

"I'll bet New York misses you."

Cooper Eldridge's deep voice resonated throughout the store, and Halley turned to see him striding purposefully toward her. He was always smiling, she noticed.

"Your leaving broke many a heart, I'd say." He leaned

against the counter and tipped his hat, still smiling.

"None that wouldn't mend easily."

Halley didn't return the smile, simply because he expected her to do so. She had so often wished Ben Parrish would smile at her that way, and chided herself for such foolishness.

"You gettin' settled in all right?" he continued, oblivious to her stoic response. "Must be lonesome for you."

"I feel right at home, thank you."

"You know, Miss Halley, I've been meanin' to pay you another call." He leaned forward, deliberately lowering the tone of his voice. "I'd like us to get better acquainted."

Halley wasn't at all surprised by his boldness, but if he meant to flatter her, he had failed. She didn't dislike Cooper Eldridge, but she was certain he was not someone to be trusted. "I'm looking forward to getting to know everyone in Wilder. After all, this is home for me now."

"You ought to come to the town council meeting tomorrow night," Tulley suggested as he began boxing the order he had just filled. "You'll meet lots of folks that way and learn a little about the town."

"Town council?" Halley glanced back at Eldridge. "Where is this meeting?"

"Right here," the storekeeper explained. "I close up at six, and everyone gathers in the back. Plenty of room, and we always have coffee and cake afterward."

The thought of mingling with a large group of people was appealing. The solitude of the ranch was welcome at times, but stifling after hours of monotonous silence when Eli and the hands were out on the range.

"I'd be happy to see you home once the meeting is over," Eldridge offered. "It wouldn't be safe for a lady to travel alone after dark."

Halley studied his face and found him quite handsome in his own way. His light hair and dark eyes were nothing like Ben's somber features, and he didn't tower over her. For the first time she returned his smile.

She nodded. "Very well, gentlemen. I will see you both tomorrow at six o'clock."

*   *   *

"I swear, Ben, I wouldn't have believed it, if I hadn't seen it with my own eyes." Frank Morgan shook his wet hair as he rinsed the soap from his neck. "Forty horses at seventy-five dollars a head, that's three thousand dollars!"

"It was nothing but good, old-fashioned horse trading." was Ben's only reply as he accepted the whiskey from his foreman. He uncorked the bottle and took a long drink of genuine Kentucky bourbon, not the rotgut served in the saloon.

Warmth spread through his chest as he sank deeper into the copper bathtub, sloshing soapy water onto the floor of the bathhouse. He tried not to think about how much money he could have made if he'd had more horses to sell.

"Big Sal herself sent that bottle," Frank continued, working a coarse brush across his back. "I told her you had come into town with us."

"Thank her for me, will you?" Ben took another drink before corking the bottle and tossing it across the room into the other man's bathwater.

"I'm sure she's counting on you to do that." Frank laughed and pulled the cork, taking a long gulp.

Without comment, Ben closed his eyes and let his head rest against the rim of the tub. Big Sal would wait till doomsday before he would pay her a call. She was the raunchiest woman he'd ever seen. Nearly six feet tall, with hair the color of tarnished brass, and a pipe always clenched between her teeth.

Still he intended to have a little fun tonight. Frank had convinced him he needed a night in town, if for no other reason than to keep the ranch hands from walking out on him.

"Ben, you've been meaner than a damn bull lately," Frank had informed him. "What's the matter with you?"

Not what. Who.

Frustration welled up inside him at the thought of Halley St. John, and he wished he'd held on to the whiskey. No woman had ever made him cuss more, and now he found himself in the unlikely role of her keeper.

Damn Pete St. John anyway! The old coot had known how much Ben wanted to venture into horse trading.

And damn his own lack of good sense. Seeing after the ranch would have been no problem, if he had stayed the hell away from Halley to begin with, instead of giving her pointers on target practice. Damn, he could still taste her sweetness, and he couldn't forget the look on her face after that kiss. She had wanted more than just a kiss, and it scared the hell out of her.

"You better have another drink." Frank's voice drew his attention. "You're getting that ornery look on your face again."

He accepted the bottle and combed wet hair back from his face with his fingers. Kissing Halley was a mistake he wouldn't have to worry about making again. Ben doubted she'd come within ten feet of him now.

The bathwater was cooling off and the water streaming down his neck was cold. Frank was already getting dressed, and he knew he shouldn't linger. Fingering the cork, he decided against having another drink. For now, anyway.

"Come on, Ben," Frank said as he tossed a towel at his boss. "Why don't you just forget the council meeting? Big Sal's waitin' on you."

"Then she should have sent more liquor." Ben was beginning to regret the trip to town already. He wasn't looking forward to spending the next few hours in a smoke-filled saloon playing cards with ill-tempered drunks. "Why the hell would I pay to hump a woman I wouldn't be seen with in broad daylight?"

"When did you get so damn choosy?" Frank peered into a cracked mirror hanging on the wall and began combing his tawny hair. "I suppose you're taken with the fancy type these days. Can't say as I blame you."

"I'm not taken with anyone."

"Pretty as a picture in one of them mail-order catalogs." Frank ignored the interruption and hunkered closer to the small mirror. "All done up in lace and silk ribbons and smelling good enough to eat. I reckon a woman like that could put a man in a foul mood."

Ben's eyes narrowed, but the door burst open before he could reply.

"Damn, if you girls don't smell pretty." Eli closed the door behind him, grinning broadly. He surveyed Frank's neatly combed hair and clean shirt. "I believe you'll take first prize."

"That I will," Frank agreed, never looking away from the

mirror. "What brings you to town, old-timer?"

"Old-timer! Why, I'll have you know I can hold my own against the likes of you any day." Eli plopped down on a rickety stool in the corner, and his eyes lighted on the bottle in Ben's hand. "Pass me a little of that vanilla you been dabbing behind your ears."

Ben tossed him the bottle and rose from the tub. Without a word he began drying himself with the rough towel. His mood was definitely not improving, and he was tempted to demand to know when Frank had gotten close enough to Halley to know how good she smelled.

Satisfied with his reflection, Frank turned from the mirror and claimed his hat from a peg on the wall. "Don't piddle at your council meeting too long," he warned with a knowing grin. "Big Sal will drag you out of there."

Before Ben could reply, Frank ducked down the rickety staircase, his laughter reverberating behind the closed door. He turned to find Eli grinning with delight at his agitation. "So what did bring you to town tonight?"

"I want to talk to you, Ben Parrish." Eli's usual humor disappeared and his bushy eyebrows were drawn together over an expression of intense concern. "About that little gal."

Ben's hands stilled over the buttons of his shirt. "So talk."

"She come home crying yesterday. She didn't want me to know it, but she went in the house and didn't come out, even for supper." Eli leaned forward on the stool. "I went in to see about her, and I could hear her up in that bedroom, plumb heartbroke."

Ben had nothing to feel guilty about, but that's exactly how he felt. He turned his back on Eli and began stuffing the tails of his shirt into his pants. "Why are you telling me this?"

"I want to know what happened in that lawyer's office."

Ben turned at that. "How do you know about that?"

"Your brother saw you coming out of Olson's all horns and rattles, and I know that Missy had an appointment with that law wrangler. Clayton said she wouldn't say a word on the way home."

Ben buttoned the cuffs of his shirt. Twice the night before he had started to ride out to her place hoping to convince her that he had known nothing of Pete's will, but he knew she would believe nothing he said.

"It seems Pete wanted someone to oversee the ranch if Halley decided to live out here." He toweled his wet head and smoothed the hair back with his fingers. "An adviser, he called it, someone to keep the ranch running until she proves up."

"And that someone is you?" Eli gave a short laugh and turned up the whiskey. He was still smiling as he wiped his mouth with the back of his hand. "That ought to make things interesting. Now I'll have something to bet on besides how high the snowbanks will be."

"I don't want anyone to know about this." Ben leveled his gaze on Eli, wishing he'd kept his own mouth shut. He crossed the room with Eli right on his heels. "I'll get her through the winter, and that's all. Come spring, she's on her own."

"Does that mean you won't be smoochin' on her in the woods no more?"

"Miss St. John, I am so pleased to meet you."

"Thank you, Mayor." Halley smiled and took Edmund Riales's outstretched hand in hers.

"I'm sorry I wasn't here when you arrived, but I had taken my wife to care for her sister in Laramie," he explained, leading her to a seat nearest the general store's potbellied stove. "Well, well, well. Old Pete's niece, all the way from New York City."

"Your sister-in-law isn't ill, is she?"

"Oh, nothing serious. She just had a baby, but she's frail and my wife worries about her."

More men filed into the mercantile, and Halley became aware of the fact that she was the only female present. She recognized Gus Mahoney from the livery, and Warren Olson arrived and rushed to speak with her.

"Miss St. John, how good to see," he said, taking her hand. "I deeply regret how upset you were by the conditions—"

"Mr. Olson, please," she interrupted, raising her hand to stop his words. "I would rather not discuss this now. I, too, am sorry I became upset. I should not have left so abruptly. Perhaps we can arrange another meeting?"

"Of course, anytime you say," he replied as Cooper Eldridge made his way to the back of the store and claimed the seat beside Halley.

"Howdy, Olson," he said casually as he sank into the wooden chair. He turned to Halley and commented on her dress. "You're the prettiest thing this town has seen since the Montgomery Ward catalog."

Halley managed a bland smile at the contrived compliment and glanced toward the front of the store. A few more townsfolk were filing in, and among them Halley recognized the sheriff followed by Ben.

She turned around in her seat, already feeling the telltale warmth flooding her cheeks. She should have known he would be at the council meeting; maybe she had even hoped he would be here. Her senses sharpened, and she caught the deep timbre of his voice, despite the din of conversation.

Gus Mahoney stood not two feet from Halley, and she started when he called out, "Howdy, Ben! Where you been? It's time to get started."

Halley stared straight ahead, refusing to swivel her head around like a schoolgirl. She might feign indifference, but her senses betrayed her. The masculine scent that had haunted her now demanded her response, and she could feel those pale blue eyes all but touching her.

"Howdy, Ben." Cooper Eldridge spoke cordially.

"Coop," he replied. "Miss St. John."

Halley winced at the formality and forced herself to meet his gaze. "Good evening, Mr. Parrish."

"You haven't been out riding lately." He stared down at her, his eyes even more startling against the dark growth that shadowed his jaw. "I thought you enjoyed the outdoors."

"I've been busy," she answered quickly, forcing herself not to look away. She wondered if he was growing a beard, but didn't dare ask. "Besides, Eli doesn't think it's safe for me to ride alone."

"You should tell him about your target practice."

Halley could feel her face color and he flashed a wicked smile. She cleared her throat and forced herself not to look away. "Isn't it time for the meeting to start?"

"It sure is, and we're in for a long night." Gus broke into

the conversation, handing Ben a sheet of paper. "Lots of folks means lots of gripes."

Ben scanned the list and scowled. "Damn," he breathed. "Range patrols? Only fools are anxious to draw first blood."

"Do unto others before they do unto you," Gus suggested. "You and I both know what will happen if them squatters keep traipsing in where they're not wanted."

"That's what I've said from the beginning." Cooper Eldridge balanced his Stetson on one knee. "Those bastards need to be cleaned out. Pardon me, Miss Halley."

Gus laughed. "You ought not to sit by a lady, if you can't mind your words."

"Having a pretty lady present lends a little class, don't you think, Ben?"

Ben's gaze raked over her, and he smiled knowingly, as if admiring something the others couldn't see. "You're right about that, Coop."

Halley had to look away at that. She knew her eyes would betray her, revealing her aching memory of that kiss. He delighted in embarrassing her, but there was nothing she could say without revealing the incident.

"Well, let's get started," Mr. Mahoney directed, and made his way to the back of the store.

The six council members sat in a semicircle facing the assembly. Jim Tulley and Gus Mahoney represented the merchants, while Ben and Tom Mitchell spoke for the cattlemen. Mayor Riales and the town barber filled the two remaining positions. Ben took the center seat, facing Halley.

"All right, folks, we got a lot to get done, so quit your yammering," the blacksmith barked. The room fell silent under his terse command. "First up, a proposal for a range patrol to clean out squatters, sheepherders, and coyotes."

Halley bit back a smile at Mr. Mahoney's blunt summary of the first item on the agenda. Several members of the audience rose to speak in favor of the proposal, citing recent incidents of fence cutting and muddied watering holes.

"My cattle can't drink where them stinking sheep have been," one man complained.

"Fences don't do no good," another reiterated. "They just cut 'em down and keep going."

Mahoney raised his hand, bringing an end to the discussion. "You've all had your say, but I ain't heard how you plan to pay for this patrol."

"The town can't afford to hire that many men." Mayor Riales spoke quickly. "I say the ranchers should pay for these patrols, if they want them."

Voices rose in agreement and protest, and Eldridge leaned over and whispered to Halley, "You just let me know if you have any trouble at your place."

Halley suddenly felt smothered by his nearness and glanced up to find Ben watching her, his expression unreadable. She looked away and forced a reply, "Thank you, Mr. Eldridge, I will."

The meeting droned on with lengthy discussions regarding the need for an ordinance against spitting on the sidewalks, and the mayor announced the installation of an official town clerk, to oversee the issuance of various licenses and permits.

Finally, Gus Mahoney raised his hand and demanded, "Any more new business?"

"Yes, Mr. Mahoney." Halley spoke clearly. "I wish to know what action has been taken toward the establishment of an educational program for the children here in Wilder?"

Mahoney's expression went blank, as if he had not understood the question. The other members of the council, save for Ben, also offered the same puzzled stares. "We ain't done nothing about a school," Mahoney finally answered. "No need for one, lady. Now, on to the—"

Halley rose to her feet and smiled pleasantly. "Mr. Mahoney, I was not finished."

"Let her talk, Gus." Ben's deep voice intervened before the blacksmith could refuse.

"I feel there is a great need for a school system. Most of the families have small children, and those that don't soon will." She paused long enough for her words to be absorbed, before adding, "You have three boys of your own, Mr. Mahoney. Surely, you want them to have an education."

Several men stood to voice their agreement with Halley's proposal. "The little lady's right, Gus," a man in the corner spoke up. "My young'uns is near school age, and I say we ought to think about such things."

"How would we go about getting things started?" Jim Tulley asked sincerely.

"It really won't be difficult," Halley assured him. "Wilder is already part of an established school district. We need only to write to the elected school superintendent and petition for our portion of the county school fund."

"You mean there's money already set aside?"

Halley paused to verify her notes. "Yes, the county school tax is apportioned to the various districts based on the number of students."

"And they'll just give us this money 'cause we say we want a school?"

"Well, not exactly. The board of directors will have to approve the petition, and the superintendent will make recommendations regarding the textbooks and which branches of learning should be taught."

A thoughtful silence fell over the assembly. Finally, Gus Mahoney turned to the mayor. "Did you know anything about all of this?"

Edmund Riales sat staring dumbfounded at the young woman who'd strolled into his town council meeting knowing more about territorial government than he knew about pouring water out of a boot. Ben felt oddly proud of Halley, standing up and speaking so eloquently. He finally prodded the mayor with a question of his own. "What do you say, Ed? If she's right, we'd be foolish not to give it a try."

"Our district's board of directors will meet this month," Halley continued. "We could send a representative to present our petition and determine what appropriations Wilder would be entitled to."

"I say we send this little lady right here," a man in overalls stated. "I want my youngsters to know their letters. I'll bet she knows as much as any of them birds setting on that director's board."

Halley's eyes widened and she whirled to find the person who'd nominated her. "I didn't mean to imply that I should be the one to go, but rather someone who can speak for the town. The mayor, perhaps."

"Hell, he didn't know there was a school board." Gus Mahoney laughed at his own humor. "Get Ben here to go with you. He's on the council and can speak for the town.''

The voices rose in agreement, and before Halley could pro-test, a motion to send her and Ben to the upcoming meeting of the county school district board of directors was made and seconded.

''All those in favor say aye!'' Gus ordered.

''Aye!'' the men chorused loudly.

Mahoney glared at the mayor. ''Opposed?''

Halley felt smothered by the silence and forced herself to look at Ben. Much to her irritation, she found a look of wry amusement on his face.

''Motion carried!'' Gus announced. ''Miss St. John, good luck and we'll expect a full report when you get back.''

❧ TEN ❧

"YOU WON'T FIND a sturdier building in town, ma'am."

Halley nodded with approval, standing in the center of the vacant print shop, but took note of the many minor improvements that would be required before the abandoned building could be made into a schoolhouse.

"These loose boards will have to be repaired." She tested the damage with the toe of her button-top shoe. "We can't have the little ones tripping."

"No, ma'am, we don't want that," Ross Carson agreed. The banker had learned of her effort to establish a school and suggested the empty building to be put to good use. A father of two school-age daughters, his enthusiasm had a strong foundation. "We'll have things in good shape."

"My case will be much stronger if the directors know we have a suitable facility."

"When is your meeting?"

"This Wednesday," she answered. "We must leave at first light in order to arrive in Logan Falls by ten o'clock."

"Ben Parrish is going with you?" Carson knelt to inspect the damaged flooring for himself. "Hard to picture a man like

131

that caring about anything as tame as a grade school.''

Halley had tried not to think about making the trip with Ben; she dreaded spending an entire day with a man she wished never to speak to again. Most of her anger had passed, but the hurt and resentment were still there.

''Someone had to represent the town council,'' she finally offered by way of explanation.

She crossed the floor and raised one of the many glass-pane windows, pleased that none was broken. ''At least there will be plenty of light. What about the heating?''

Carson pointed to a dangling stovepipe and explained, ''The owner left the old stove behind, and Murphy bought it to use in the barbershop. A new one can be installed in a week's time.''

''And the wood?'' Halley pressed, anticipating the questions she would have to answer before the school board.

''Each child's family can share the responsibility of providing wood,'' he stated. ''I'm prepared to furnish half a cord to get things started.''

Halley smiled. ''How old are your little girls?''

''Nine and six,'' he answered proudly. ''My wife has been teaching them to read, but with the new baby she doesn't have the time.''

''There's no doubt a school is needed here in Wilder,'' Halley stated. ''I do appreciate your interest.''

''I'm just sorry I couldn't be at the council meeting last week, but my wife needs my help in the evenings,'' he explained. ''What about a teacher?''

''I plan to place a notice in a Denver newspaper. I'll send a telegram this afternoon,'' she said, closing the window. ''It will be most important to find a qualified person. Someone who is mature and experienced with children.''

A sudden knock at the door drew their attention, and Mr. Carson hurried to open the door. ''Mrs. Mitchell, what a pleasant surprise.''

''How are you, Mr. Carson?'' Delia Mitchell shooed her brood of girls inside and quickly closed the door behind her. ''I just saw your wife last week, and I couldn't get over how much that baby is growing.''

The banker's face beamed at the mention of his son. ''Yes,

ma'am, he's going to be a strapping boy."

The Mitchell children wasted no time in inspecting the would-be schoolhouse, their giggles and questions filling the empty building.

"Where will we sit?"

"Will there be picture books?"

"I want to be by the window!"

"Hush up, girls," Delia ordered. She glanced around the empty building and nodded with approval. "This should do fine, once you get it fixed up. My man Tom hasn't stopped talking about the way you spoke right up at the council meeting the other night. Another Daniel Webster, he called you."

"I may have bitten off more than I can chew." Halley sat down on the windowsill. "They want me to petition the school board for the needed funds."

"Well, I think that's a fine idea." Delia sat down beside Halley. "We need someone to show the menfolk in this town a thing or two."

"Ladies, if you will excuse me, I must return to the bank." Ross Carson smiled, taking one last look around the building. "Miss St. John, please feel free to call upon me for any assistance you may need."

Halley returned his smile. "Thank you, Mr. Carson." When the door had closed behind him, she turned to Delia. "So, what are you doing in town?"

"I've got a little trading to do with Widow Canfield. She just loves my cherry preserves, and I'm hoping to swap a few jars for enough wool to knit myself a red shawl." Delia's eyes sparkled with anticipation. "I saw your mule out front and thought you'd like to come along."

Halley had nothing with her to trade, but she welcomed any distraction from her worries over cattle ranches and schoolhouses. "Thank you, I would."

"I understand Cooper Eldridge saw you home after the council meeting the other night." Delia's eyes darted to her daughters, who were completely absorbed in a debate over who would sit closest to the window. "Tom said Ben Parrish looked like he'd swallowed a hornet."

Halley only shrugged. "Mr. Eldridge was only being neighborly."

The other woman laughed out loud, and Halley forced her most innocent smile. "Why, Mrs. Mitchell, whatever are you implying?"

They both laughed at that, but Delia soon sobered and covered Halley's hand with her own. "You be careful with those men, girl. Where you come from, a man minds his manners, but out here they take what they want without asking."

Halley felt the color rush to her face at Delia's blunt words. "I've dealt with overly amorous suitors before."

Delia's eyes widened. "What did he do?"

"Nothing," Halley assured her, mocking Delia's wide-eyed expression. "I simply meant that I know what to do in such a situation."

"Halley, you're a handsome woman, trying to hold on to a ranch with no man," Delia stated flatly. "You're putting down stakes in this town, and it won't be long before you'll have to start fighting to keep that place."

"Why should I have to fight to keep something that rightfully belongs to me?" Halley demanded, rising from the windowsill. "My uncle wanted me to have the ranch, and I shouldn't have to prove anything to anyone."

"You have to keep your eyes open, girl, no matter where you live." Delia pinned her with a knowing look. "You can't tell me that folks in New York were too good to cheat or steal. People are pretty much the same all over."

Again, Halley only shrugged, not liking the comparison. She'd lost everything in New York to someone she'd trusted, and now she faced the prospect of having everything snatched from her grasp whether she trusted Ben or not.

Wednesday morning dawned bright and cold. Halley was dressed by sunup and stole out to the barn to check her mule before Ben arrived.

"Morning, Baby," she cooed, presenting him with a bright orange carrot. She stroked his sleek neck while he gobbled greedily. "I'm sorry you can't go with me today."

At the sound of her voice, the lamb began a frantic bleating, and she opened his stall. He trotted out on spindly black legs, his cries unceasing. She bent to pet his woolly back, but he would not be quieted.

She wasted no time preparing his breakfast, using one of the few remaining cans of milk. She would have to purchase a new supply soon. He was growing fast and wanted to eat constantly.

Once he was happy, she scooped a generous portion of oats for Baby and poured them into his trough. Mules, she had learned, would eat only their fill, whereas horses would gorge until they made themselves sick.

The barn door burst open, admitting a chilling blast of air, and Halley turned to find Ben entering with it. He was huddled deep inside a sheepskin coat and his hat was low on his brow.

"Good morning." She managed a cool tone, refusing to give him the satisfaction of seeing how upset she was still. "You're earlier than we agreed."

"I had a few things to talk over with Eli," he remarked casually. "There's a lot of work to do, if we're to get this place ready for winter."

Stung, Halley focused on the drag of the currycomb across the mule's coat. Ben was certainly wasting no time asserting his authority over her ranch, and without consulting her.

She could hear the soft thud of his boots against the sweet-smelling sawdust Eli kept spread across the barn floor. His shadow fell across her face, and she glanced up to find him standing mere inches from her. She hated the fact that she still found him handsome, even more so with the rakish growth of whiskers.

"Eli and I have already discussed the work that needs to be done in preparation for the winter months," she finally replied, failing to keep the resentment from her voice. "I'm sure he has matters well in hand."

He closed the scant distance between them, and her arm brushed his with the next stroke of the currycomb. He covered her hand with his, showing her how to hold the brush at an angle to coax a greater shine from the mule's coat.

"There's a lot of strays out there," he murmured against her ear. "They'll have to be branded before winter or you'll lose 'em to rounders in the spring."

The heat of his breath feathering her skin made her knees weak, and it took every ounce of restraint she possessed to keep from lolling her head against his shoulder. Righting herself, she rounded to the opposite side of the mule. "We haven't had a large enough staff."

"I'm going to send some of my boys over to ride with your ... staff for a few weeks." He studied her over the mule's broad back, and a knowing grin touched his features. "Unless you were planning on asking Cooper Eldridge to help you out."

With a saucy tilt of her head, she smiled slightly. "I hadn't considered that; perhaps I should."

"Don't be foolish, Halley." The humor faded from his expression. "I had nothing to do with what Pete wrote in his will, but I'll do what I have to to keep things like he wanted."

"How terribly noble of you," she snapped. "I'm sure my dear uncle will rest easy knowing you are meddling in every aspect of my life."

"Don't play games with Eldridge just to spite me," he warned. "He's not one of your gallant society beaux, and you could find yourself in a corner sooner than you think."

"Mr. Parrish, I am only required to consult with you on matters pertaining to the ranch." She turned to replace the currycomb, but his big frame blocked her path. "With whom I choose to socialize is my business."

"Did you kiss him good night?"

"What if I did?" She had been sorely disappointed in Mr. Eldridge's groping attempt at kissing. She had no intention of kissing him again, but she was more than a little pleased by Ben's apparent jealousy.

"Coop had his heart set on this place and was none too pleased about you coming out here to take this ranch." The warning echoed Mr. Olson's, and she felt her eyes widen. "He'll do whatever he thinks will get him what he wants."

"And what about you?" she countered without hesitation. "Were you pleased to learn that I would be coming to Wilder? I'd say you are now in the most advantageous position to remedy that problem."

Tossing the currycomb aside, Halley made her way out of the barn into the autumn chill. She shivered slightly and smiled when she saw Eli waiting beside the wagon, her coat slung over one arm.

"I reckon this flimsy thing will do for today, but you'll

need something heavier when the snows come.'' Eli helped her find the sleeves of her coat and admonished her to keep it properly buttoned. ''A starving moth would turn his nose up at that.''

She heard the barn door close and glanced up to see Ben heading toward the wagon. Quickly, she looked away and accepted Eli's assistance into the wagon.

''Please see after Baby for me,'' she asked, settling her skirts around her. ''Let him spend some time in the corral, and you know where I keep his candy.''

''That mule is a work animal, bred for pulling plows or hauling freight. I reckon he can get through one day without peppermint candy.'' He scowled at her pleading expression. ''Oh, all right. Never saw such foolishness over a goldurn jackass.''

''Thank you.'' She heard the wagon creak and felt Ben's weight settle on the seat beside her. Without the slightest glance in his direction, she spoke only to Eli. ''We should be back before dark.''

''I packed you a bite to eat.'' Eli scowled as he produced a large basket and placed it in the back of the wagon. ''You won't get nothing decent in them eating houses.''

Ben slapped the reins across the wide rumps of the wagon team and the vehicle lurched forward, causing Halley to be thrown against his solid frame. She glared up at him and righted herself, putting as much distance between them as possible.

Logan Falls was at least three hours away, and Ben decided they were making good enough time to afford a stop. He knew of a watering hole at the halfway point, and he didn't want to tire the horses needlessly.

Halley had scarcely looked at him during the trip, her attention focused on the notebook in her lap. She scribbled hastily or reread her notes from a previous page, her lips moving silently. Ben was willing to bet the school board was in for a presentation like they had never heard before. Halley, he decided, could talk the devil out of his pitchfork.

The wagon rocked along the bumpy road, and Ben realized how important this was to her. Clayton had blabbed about her travels to Europe and how she had studied the fine arts, but today, she sat poring over her notes as if bringing a school to a frontier town like Wilder meant the world to her.

"We'll be stopping a few minutes," he said, finally breaking the silence.

She glanced up, as if trying to gauge the distance they had covered.

"We're almost halfway," he offered. "I want to water the horses and let them rest a minute."

She nodded and closed her notebook. Removing her wire-rimmed spectacles, Halley pinched the bridge of her nose between her fingers.

"Headache?"

She nodded, placing the glasses in their velvet case. "I hope I have all the facts right. Mayor Riales wasn't any help at all. How on earth did he get elected?"

Ben only shrugged. "He was the only one with nothing better to do."

"I don't believe that for a minute." Halley carefully placed her glasses and notebook into her carpetbag. "Wilder is a growing town. Someone better qualified has to be found."

"Are you going to wear your glasses to the meeting?"

Surprised, Halley said, "I really hadn't thought about it. Why?"

He studied her face. "The glasses make you look wise, like a teacher."

"Really?" Halley wanted to make the best possible impression on the school board. "I always thought they made me look like an old maid."

Ben studied her fine-boned features, marred only by pinkish indentations left by the glasses on her nose, and decided no one looked less like an old maid.

"Why haven't you ever gotten married?" The question was out the moment it formed in his mind, and he groaned inwardly as delight flashed in her eyes.

"Before I answer, let me decide what I want to ask you." She paused dramatically and glanced toward the sky as if seeking divine guidance. Finally, she nodded with a satisfied smile and replied, "I never married because I never had to."

"Never had to?" That was the last thing he expected her to say.

"I didn't *need* a husband for money or status," she explained. "So, I couldn't see tying myself down to man who would expect me to give up my freedom and play hostess for his benefit."

He shook his head, never failing to be amazed by her views. Halley St. John was unlike any woman he'd ever known.

"Now for my question." She leveled her gaze on him. "Why *did* you marry?"

Directing his gaze on the road ahead of them, he slapped the reins across the backs of the plodding team and they lurched forward. He didn't look at her when he answered, "I was in love."

Halley sat staring at her notes, but her eyes wouldn't focus on the words. She was stung by Ben's answer, mostly because she knew it was the absolute truth. The thought of Ben being in love rankled her pride, and she wondered about the kiss they had shared. Did he compare her with his wife? She kept her eyes on the page, afraid to look at him and find the answer.

The wagon topped the hill and Halley gasped in surprise at the sight of a flock of sheep gathered at the watering hole. "Look!" she cried. "There must be at least a hundred!"

"At least," Ben agreed, and reined the horses to a halt. "Damn!

A man wearing an oilskin duster advanced toward the wagon, a shotgun slung under his arm. Halley glanced toward Ben, his eyes narrowed and menacing.

"Ben, please," she whispered. "Just tell him we need to water the horses."

He turned a hard stare on her. "You keep quiet and let me do the talking."

Halley was well aware of the potential danger and nodded. Such confrontations were becoming increasingly common and deadly. The cattlemen were determined to keep the sheep-herders off the open range, and open grazing land was worth fighting for.

"Mornin'," the man offered as he neared the wagon.

Ben nodded, but said nothing.

"Where are you folks headed?"

"We've got business in Logan Falls," Ben informed him. "The horses need watering."

"My name is Summers," he offered, casting an appraising gaze toward Halley. "I got a pot of coffee made. You folks are welcome to a cup while the horses rest."

Ben nodded in acceptance and urged the horses on the remaining distance to the creek. He said not a word as he set the brake, wrapping the reins around the brake shaft, and climbed down from the wagon. He slowly circled the wagon to offer his assistance to Halley.

At Ben's direction, she followed Mr. Summers to the makeshift camp while he watered the horses. Halley accepted the cup of coffee Summers held out to her, managing an audible thank you. She unwrapped the basket of biscuit-and-bacon sandwiches Eli had packed and offered one to their host.

"Thank you, ma'am," he said, reaching for the basket. His hands were dirty, and he was careful to touch only the biscuit he removed. "It's good to visit with decent folks. Hadn't seen anyone but saddle tramps and coyotes since leaving Cheyenne."

"I've never seen so many sheep." Halley sipped her coffee and studied the bleating flock as they clustered at the water's edge. "How ever do you keep them all together?"

"I don't." He motioned toward the top of the hill, where a spotted dog sat surveying the sheep. "Bud, there, that's his job. Just watch him."

Sure enough, a shaggy member of the flock began trotting away from the group. The dog sprang into action, rounding the corner and barking furiously at the wayward ewe. She stood her ground, determined to reach her destination. A few short barks from Bud, however, changed her mind.

"That's amazing," Halley breathed. "Did you teach him to do that?"

"Some, but it's mostly instinct, ma'am," he told her. "A good dog is worth a year's wages."

Ben joined them by the tiny fire, bracing his boot on the log beside Halley. Summers filled a tin cup from the coffeepot and he accepted it without a word.

"Where exactly are you headed?" Ben finally asked.

"I was hoping to make it down to Utah before winter set in."
Summers took a bite of his biscuit and chewed thoughtfully.

"You've got a good bit of ground to cover." Ben propped
the hand holding his cup on his knee. "Winter's not far off."

"The nights are already miserable." Finishing his biscuit,
Summers reached for his coffee cup and drank deeply.

"I'd hate to get snowbound in the middle of nowhere."

"If I were you, I'd be getting these sheep out of these
parts."

Ben's voice was deceptively neutral, but Halley didn't miss
the hard set of his jaw. Summers placed his cup on the ground
and met Ben's narrowed gaze with his own.

"I reckon, I can have my sheep where I please."

"I wouldn't bet my life on it."

Silence fell, save for the bleating flock, and Halley's breath
lodged in her throat. She glanced up at Ben's hardened features and again at Summers.

Ben had told her to keep quiet, but she desperately wanted
to change the threatening subject. Forcing a cheerful tone to
her voice, she asked, "What is leading you to Utah?"

Summers gave her a startled look, distracted from his bud-
ding anger. "My wife's brother has a place just below the
Uinta River, plenty of grassland."

"Your wife is there?"

He nodded. "I sent her ahead by stage. She's a dainty thing,
and I didn't want her making the trip with the flock."

"I'm sure she misses you terribly," Halley sympathized.

"It's not good to leave a woman alone," Ben commented
almost to himself.

Halley glanced up at his impassive face. Her curiosity had
backfired, causing him to think of his wife and reveal nothing.
She had hoped to learn that his marriage had been a youthful
mistake that meant nothing. Instead, her prying question had
resurrected painful memories that might have remained buried.

"She wrote me a letter before I left Colorado."

Startled, they both glanced back at Summers, and Halley
wished she had not raised the subject of his wife.

He fingered his pocket and produced a battered envelope.
"I reckon she's ready to have her husband where he belongs.
I always wished I'd learned my letters."

Halley paused thoughtfully before offering, "May I?"

He hesitated, but extended his hand. "I'd be much obliged, ma'am."

She took the letter and carefully unfolded the creased paper. She began reading the neatly written words aloud." 'My darling Frank, I have arrived safely and the trip was not nearly as difficult as you feared. Peter and Ellie met me at the stage, and you know I cried when I saw how the children have grown. Utah is more beautiful than Ellie's letters told, and you will be very pleased with the section that is ours.

" 'We have already put a garden out, and the hills are lush with wild berries and chokecherries. There will be plenty, and with hard work we will never do without.

" 'I have news to tell you that shouldn't be written in a letter, but I fear it will not wait until you join us.' "

Halley looked up to see the color draining from Summers's face and she quickly read on, " 'By the time you arrive, our little one may already be with me, and I don't want him to be a stranger to you. Frank, darling, please hurry as best you can. Your loving wife, Amelia.' "

Halley could have cried herself when she saw the telltale dampness that made the herder's dark eyes shimmer in his weathered face. "Oh, Mr. Summers, you're going to be a father."

Summers hung his head, burying his face in his dirty palms. "God forgive me. I was too dang proud to ask anyone to read that letter. Now the babe is probably born already, and Meena thinks I've forsaken her."

Ben glanced over Halley's shoulder. "This letter is only four months old. How long will it take you to move these sheep?"

He shrugged. "A month, if I push 'em hard. But four months is so long. The poor woman doesn't even know I'm on the way."

"I can write a letter for you, and mail it from Logan Falls." Halley made her way to the wagon and returned with her notebook. "Do you want me to tell her you may winter here in Wyoming?"

Summers shook his head. "No, ma'am. You tell her I'll be in Utah before that babe gets here."

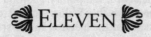 ELEVEN

HALLEY WAITED UNTIL the last member of the school board had disappeared into the hotel at the end of the street before laughing out loud.

"We did it!" she cried, and threw her arms around Ben. "We really did it!"

He returned her embrace and said, "You did it, Halley."

That was true. Halley had stood before the stern-faced board members and presented the most logical case for establishing a school in Wilder. She had countered every objection with substantiated fact. In the end the vote had been unanimous and funds were approved for the school, textbooks, and a teacher's salary.

"I still can't believe it," she said, her palms resting on his shoulders. "Just wait until I tell Mr. Mahoney."

Ben laughed and covered her hands with his. "Just wait until Gus tells the mayor. Wilder, Wyoming, will never be the same as it was before you came to town."

"And I shall never be the same, either." Immediately, she regretted the somber words and forced a bright smile. "Wyoming is proving to be everything I had hoped for."

His doubtful expression told her that he wasn't at all fooled by her cheerfulness, but he only nodded. Their smiles faded, and his fingers closed around hers. "This is no way for the newly appointed member of the school board to carry on in public."

Halley righted herself, grateful he had not pursued the subject. "That was the greatest shock of all. I suppose I made a better argument than I meant to."

Ben hadn't been at all surprised when the chairman had asked Halley to accept a temporary position on the board to represent and supervise the Wilder school district. The appointment was just until the election in the spring, and Halley had been advised to prepare to run for office.

"Just wait until I tell Eli how wrong he was." Her smile returned at the thought.

"How wrong he was?"

Rolling her eyes, she explained, "He told me the school board would shoo me home to my kitchen. I'm afraid he can be very narrow-minded at times."

"Eli can be as contrary as a stump," Ben agreed with a slight grin. "But Pete always said there wasn't a better man to have on your side when you got cornered."

Halley glanced up and down the main street, noting the varied storefronts—a bakery, three restaurants, a newspaper office—even a dress shop. Compared with Wilder, Logan Falls was a veritable metropolis, and she couldn't bear the thought of leaving without peering in a few of those windows.

Ben had displayed little interest in the town, and she knew he would be anxious to return to his precious cattle and chores. Smiling slightly, she cleared her throat.

"It seems the meeting didn't last as long as we had feared," she ventured. He made no comment, so she continued: "In fact, we still have half the day left."

"We can get an early start for home," he concluded. "I might even get a few hours of work in before dark. I know damn well Clayton has slacked off with me gone all day. Probably spent the whole day reading one of those mail-order catalogs."

"Don't you ever do anything spontaneous?" She studied the somber set of his jaw and the level gaze in his blue eyes and tried to remember just once seeing him laugh. "Something just for fun?"

With a doubtful expression, he eased the brim of his hat back and gave her the slightest smile. "You want to have fun with me? I thought you were mad at me."

"I *am* mad at you," she assured him. "But not enough to go home without seeing the town. Besides, I have to post Mr. Summers's letter."

"This isn't New York, Halley," he reminded her. "You probably won't find much to see besides a pair of old hounds sleeping in the shade."

"Fun is where you find it, Ben Parrish." She hesitated before taking his arm and smiling up at him. His steps fell into rhythm with hers, and she couldn't resist adding, "You have only to take the time to look."

Ben could see the disappointment stealing into Halley's expression, and the arm tucked into his elbow hung limp between them. Two of the businesses she had wanted to visit were closed for the afternoon, and the bakery was sold out of its daily supply of confections.

"I just don't understand where all the people in this town are," she finally said. "All of these stores . . . and no shoppers?"

They turned the corner, and Ben caught sight of a small crowd clustered around the entrance of a building painted a bright shade of yellow. Gently he nudged Halley and motioned toward the group of people. "I'll bet everyone is in there."

"The Sun Theater, Afternoon Matinee." Halley read the banner with an unmistakable tone of delight in her voice. She glanced at the delicate timepiece pinned to her dress. "It's already late. We should be getting back."

Ben chuckled at her stoic attempt at practicality and tightened his hold on her arm, leading her across the street.

"Two, please," he said to the balding man inside the ticket booth.

"Rafter benches or down in front?"

"Down in front." He passed his money through the tiny slot and accepted the tickets.

The darkened theater was crowded; Ben was certain everyone in town had come to the show. The benches were filled with rowdy drovers, and he led Halley toward two empty seats in the second row. Once seated, she studied the program in the dim light.

"The first act will be Professor Baldree, master of illusion and sleight of hand." She leaned toward the light to see better, and he couldn't resist leaning closer in pretense of reading the program along with her. "Then there will be a song-and-dance performance, followed by a dramatic recitation."

Ben could almost taste the sweet scent of her flesh, and he had only to lean a few inches closer and his mouth would easily graze the delicate nape of her neck. His body readily responded, and he shifted in the narrow seat.

Halley glanced up and found him staring at her, their faces inches apart. She swallowed and a sudden intake of breath parted her lips slightly. Her eyes widened, and she righted herself in the seat, putting a respectable amount of space between them.

He reached for the program and scanned the list of performers. "Looks like my idea of fun is a lot different than yours."

Before she could reply, the stage lights flared and the curtain went up, bringing a thunderous chorus of applause from the drovers in the rafters. With visible effort, Halley turned her attention to the stage, joining in the applause as Professor Baldree made his way to center stage.

The matinee was predictable but entertaining, better than what normally made its way to smaller towns. Ben enjoyed watching Halley more than the show; she laughed easily and graciously applauded the second-rate actors.

The performance culminated in a dramatic recitation of speeches from Shakespeare. A distinguished man clad all in black strode purposefully toward center stage. His hollow gaze swept the audience, and only when silence filled the frontier playhouse did he begin.

Halley gasped softly and cupped her hand over her lips. Ben slid her a questioning glance, but she said nothing. The actor's polished voice resonated throughout the theater, and even the raunchiest cowboy listened in appreciative silence.

When he had finished, the actor bowed to the applause with great dignity and left the stage before the tattered curtain fell.

When it rose again, the rest of the troupe stood onstage, taking bows and waving to the cheering crowd.

The audience began filing out of the theater, and Halley rose from her seat, following Ben toward the exit. Halfway down the aisle, her steps halted, and she glanced back toward the stage.

"What's wrong?"

"The actor, the one who recited Shakespeare. I'm positive I've seen him in New York. He was one of the most respected performers in the theater." A frown caused her brows to knit together, and she scanned the program for a familiar name. "A few years back he fell prey to drink and disappeared from the scene."

"Might not be the same man."

"No, his performance was wonderful. It had to be him." She glanced over her shoulder toward the now empty stage. "I wonder if I should go backstage and speak to him.

"I doubt he'd want to be reminded of his past." When she gave him a quizzical look, he added, "Not everyone comes to Wyoming for adventure, like you."

The rain had started half an hour before they neared Wilder, and Halley's dress was soaked despite the wagon's awning. Ben seemed unaffected, and she managed not to complain, huddling beneath an oilskin slicker he had found tucked under the seat.

Lightning flashed as they approached the barn and the mares reared in fright.

"Whoa, there!" Ben shouted over the storm, pulling hard on the reins. The horses fought against the restraint, desperate to escape the storm. Ben turned to Halley, his face taut. "You'll have to open the barn door. If I let up on the reins, they'll bolt."

She nodded and hurried down from the wagon, already drenched. She scrambled to the barn and struggled to open the heavy doors. When she finally succeeded in prying them a few inches apart, the wind tore them open wide and nearly knocked her to the ground.

Ben urged the mares inside the barn, and Halley quickly followed, struggling to close the heavy doors behind her. Ben drew the wagon to a halt and set the brake. He bolted down from the seat and easily pulled the barn door closed, shutting out the storm.

"Damn!" he breathed, mopping his forehead with a soggy shirtsleeve. "I'm soaked."

"To the skin," Halley added, looking down in dismay at her sodden clothing. "I've never seen such rain."

"You'd better get to the house and into some dry·clothes." Ben began unhitching the weary mares. "You'll catch your death."

"What about you?"

"I'll be fine," he replied. "I've slept in worse rain than this."

Halley removed her ruined bonnet and briefly mourned its loss. She had purchased it at her favorite shop on Fifth Avenue. She didn't grieve so much for the hat as for the knowledge that she would never shop in that little store again. She clutched the soggy brim between her fingers and, to her horror, felt tears burning in her throat.

Memories flooded her mind, and she remembered the warm spring day she had been shopping with a friend who was planning a wedding. She would never return to that world. She had accepted that, but it still tore at her heart to lose the tiny pieces that kept her connected to it.

"These horses are exhausted," Ben called as he led the mares to their stalls. "Tell Eli to let them rest tomorrow."

She could only nod, blinking back tears, but reality wouldn't be swept away. The ranch had been her haven, but the precarious terms of her inheritance had stripped away her security. If she lost this time, she would truly have nowhere to go.

Ben crossed the barn. "Halley, what is it?"

"I don't know," was all she could manage. Her voice trembled when she tried to explain. "It's just been a long day."

He hooked his finger under her chin and forced her to look at him. The genuine concern in his eyes undid her and she crumpled against him. Pride deserted her, and she accepted the comfort of his embrace, burying her face against his shoulder.

"Oh, Ben," she sobbed. "I want to go home."

Shocked, Ben took her in his arms and held her while she

cried it out. Her tears were never hysterical, but the pitiful sobs of someone whose heart has been broken.

"Halley," he whispered as the tears subsided. "What brought this on?"

"I'm sorry," she said, pressing her palms against her flushed cheeks. "I'm just . . . tired from the trip and all, and a little homesick, I suppose."

"It's more than homesickness." Ben traced the outline of her lips with his forefinger.

His fingers left her mouth and trailed the column of her throat. He cupped the back of her dampened head, holding her still for the first coaxing touch of his lips against hers. His mouth was tender, his breath warm as he pulled back to study her face.

Halley gazed up into his eyes and shivered at the desire she saw in their blue depths. Her arms closed around his neck, and she raised her lips to his, hungry for the taste of him. A muted warning ran through her mind at the danger of allowing herself the luxury of his kisses. Ben evoked passion in her, and she had barely been able to pull away once. Tonight, she needed that passion more than ever.

What began as a gentle kiss quickly turned to hunger and desire. His arms tightened around her and their wet clothes clung from the heat of their bodies. Halley gave way to the moment with reckless abandon, accepting the demanding pull of his lips and the brand of his tongue.

She combed her trembling fingers through his wet hair and reveled in the silken texture, so different from the rough drag of his new beard against her face.

His hands slid down the expanse of her back and cupped her bottom. His mouth became more demanding and he pressed her fully against his arousal. She moaned aloud, a strangled cry of fear and excitement.

Catching her around the waist, Ben slowly dropped to one knee, easing her astride his thigh. Halley shuddered at the feel of his solid muscles thrust against the thin shield of her muslin underclothes. She resisted the intrusive thoughts that warned her not to go too far, recklessly abandoning herself to the moment.

He deepened the kiss, his tongue seeking her own, urging

her to match him thrust for thrust. She was a willing student, shy at first, but soon mastering the task.

Only when she felt his fingers tugging at the buttons of her bodice did the reality of what was happening strike home. She nearly fell to the floor, dragging herself to her feet, and backed away from him. She was horrified at the picture she made, straddling him like a trollop.

He was breathing hard, and he advanced the distance between them, reaching for her.

"Ben, no," she managed, flattening her palms against his chest. "We can't do this."

She watched the battle of emotions within his eyes, lust, anger, understanding, each vying for first position. Finally, scorn won out.

Pushing her away, Ben silenced her stammering explanation with a searing glare. "Don't play games, Halley. You wanted that kiss as much as I did."

His horse was saddled and ready in a nearby stall, and Ben gathered the reins to leave. He led the bay toward the barn door, his expression taut.

"How do I know what you want?" Halley's wounded pride refused to let him leave unscathed. She raised her chin defiantly. "Perhaps you're merely after my land."

"When I want this land, I'll take it." His hand stilled on the latch, and he gave her a look that chilled her to the bone. "The same goes for you."

The rain was still falling in torrents when Ben reached the boundaries of his own property. He urged his horse on faster in the direction of the house, toward the warmth of a fire and the solace of dry clothes. A decanter of fine Tennessee whiskey was waiting in the parlor, and he intended to get dog drunk tonight.

Icy drops of rain pelted his face, sluicing in cold rivers down his already soaked clothing, but did little to cool his anger. Damn that woman. Tonight he'd seen a side of Halley he'd sooner forget. She stood like a haughty queen, her chin raised in defiance, staring daggers at him for daring to touch her.

Yet the horror in her eyes assured him she had never been

that intimate with any man, and he had every intention of showing her even more. He could still feel the firm flesh of her bottom against his palms, the thin underclothes hiding nothing from his grasp. Another minute and he would have had her flat on her back in the hay, with those slim legs wrapped around him.

The storm was gaining momentum, and thunder pounded overhead. The dark shape of mounted horses took form riding toward him, silhouetted against a backdrop of lightning. Recognizing Frank Morgan's mustang, Ben reined his mount in to meet them.

"Ben!" Frank shouted. "Where the hell have you been?"

"What's wrong?" He knew from the anxiety on his foreman's face that something had gone wrong.

"Rustlers!"

The word seemed to hang between them momentarily before being swept away on the storm.

"When?"

"Not more than an hour ago." Frank motioned toward the ravine. "At least ten of 'em . . . riding hell-for-leather. Didn't take much to spook the cattle, what with all this thunder."

Ben cursed his own foolishness. This was exactly what he deserved for leaving his land and cattle to go on a do-gooder's mission with Halley. "Which way were they headed?"

"North, when we caught up with 'em." Frank leaned away from the rain. "Once the shooting started, they scattered every which way."

Ben glanced toward the ravine, watching the rain wash all the tracks away. "And the cattle?"

"We were able to turn most of them back, but they were pretty spooked." Frank managed a rueful grin. "We'll be chasing strays for a month."

"Anybody hurt?"

"Got one of 'em down in the bunkhouse. Jess winged him with a rifle, and he took a tumble down the ravine. He's busted up, but Creek says he'll live. Kinda figured you'd want to talk to him when you got back from your tea party."

Ben ignored Frank's sarcasm and turned his horse toward the bunkhouse, all hope of dry clothes and whiskey gone.

A young cowhand was waiting to take their horses, and Ben

wasted no time in dismounting and tossing his reins to the boy. Frank was on his heels as he ducked inside the rough-hewn quarters where the hands that had hung on for the winter slept.

The bunkhouse was dimly lit by one kerosene lamp, and a makeshift clothesline was strung across the center of the room, sagging with an assortment of long johns and Levi's drying before the potbellied stove. The lingering aroma of frying bacon mingled with the cloying scent of fresh blood.

The bespectacled cook glanced up from the leather-bound volume he was reading, his disapproving gaze settling on the muddy tracks their boots made across the worn plank floor. Creek Renfrow regarded the bunkhouse as his domain, and even Ben refrained from infringing on it.

"Got a fresh pot of coffee on the stove," Creek said, carefully marking his place in the book he'd read a hundred times. "Looks like you could use something a little stronger."

Ben declined the offer with a wave of his hand and made his way toward where Frank pointed. He stood over the narrow cot and stared down at the would-be rustler. To everyone's surprise, he only chuckled. "When did you give up running out the sheepherders?"

"Clint and Jonas had a falling-out," the boy managed in a hesitant voice. "He said the old man was keeping all the money, and we was gonna be the ones killed."

"If you keep crossing my path, you *will* end up dead."

The boy's eyes widened in his paling face. "I didn't know this was your place, or I never would have gone along with them. I ain't fool enough to go up against a Texas Ranger."

Ben's ignored the murmured surprise of several of the men gathered in the bunkhouse. He didn't make conversation about his past, and he didn't ask questions of the men who worked for him as long as they put in the work he expected.

Strips of torn cloth had been fashioned into a bandage around the boy's bony rib cage, darkened by blood seeping from the wound. A crude sling on his arm hindered his movements, and he grimaced with pain, his breathing labored.

"What's your name, boy?"

"Emmett . . . Emmett Pruitt," he managed.

"In the future you'd better know who you're riding

against." Ben leveled his gaze on the frightened boy and asked, "Who hired you?"

"My brother Clint said all we had to do was make off with a few steers just this once . . . easy money."

"Thieves for hire," Creek snorted, joining Ben at the cot. "Hope they paid you enough to get hung."

Emmett struggled to raise up on one elbow. "Please, mister, you got to believe me. They said a woman owned the spread. I didn't know—"

Ben's amusement vanished. "Who hired you?"

"I don't know who the real money is. Fella come right up to us in the saloon and asked if we was interested in riding with him for a little money."

So, it was starting already. Now that winter was well on its way and the range was almost deserted. What cattle Halley didn't lose to rustlers could easily be claimed by starvation and exposure.

The boy shifted slightly and winced at the effort, and Ben noticed the angular line of his collarbone jutting against his pale skin. Pity was not an emotion he was accustomed to feeling, but he couldn't help but wonder when the boy had last had a decent meal. Instead, he asked, "How's that arm?"

"Hurts pretty bad," Emmett admitted. "Snapped like a twig when I fell off the horse."

Ben nodded. "Creek, give him a little of that whiskey and a bite to eat."

"How 'bout I read him a bedtime story to boot?"

Ben made no reply as he shrugged into an oilskin slicker. He crossed the room and stepped out into the rain, Frank once again on his heels.

"Are you crazy?" the foreman demanded. "Coddling rustlers? Ben Parrish, you know he deserves the rope."

"The man who hired him deserves the rope," Ben corrected. "How do you suppose we'll find out who that is if we hang the one person who can tell us?"

Taken aback, Frank shoved his hands into his pockets. "I can't ask the hands to bunk with a rustler."

"Put him in the barn," Ben countered. "Just keep him out of sight. That brother of his will come looking for him, and he'll know more than Emmett ever would."

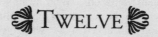

TWELVE

"Mr. Mahoney!" Halley was forced to shout over the din of hammering. "Mr. Mahoney!"

For three days now she had been overseeing the transformation of the abandoned print shop into a suitable schoolhouse, and her patience had reached its limit. The repairs had been far more extensive than she had anticipated, and everything had cost twice as much as she had budgeted.

She ducked under a ladder, confident her luck could get no worse, and maneuvered herself within hearing range of Gus Mahoney. Once again she drew a deep breath and called out, "Mr. Mahoney! We have a problem."

"What now?" the blacksmith demanded, looking up from the section of lumber he was sawing.

"The cause of the damage to the floor has been determined." Halley picked her way across the floor, the hem of her skirt gathering sawdust like a magnet. "I thought you'd like to know."

"What is it?"

"The damage to the roof." Exasperated, Halley gestured over their heads. "It leaks! And the leak has damaged the flooring . . . which we now know was not properly cured before being laid.''

Peering up, Gus could only shrug. ''It'll have to be replaced.''

''And how much will *that* cost?''

''Miss Halley!'' a voice called, drawing her attention from the roof. ''Come quick!''

She made her way out onto the porch, where Mrs. Porter's son waited, his face marred with concern. ''What is it, Brian?''

''Look down here.'' He knelt on the porch, peering through the cracks. ''It looks like a nest of some kind. Raccoons, I'll bet!''

Halley leaned against the porch railing, grateful it didn't collapse. ''I'll wager it's better built than the print shop.''

''Now, hon, don't fret over a few loose nails.'' Mrs. Porter made her way toward the building, an enormous wicker basket slung over her arm. ''Brian, you get up from there and fetch that other basket, and be careful.''

Hazel Porter had been delighted at the prospect of a school and readily assumed the duty of providing the noon meal for those working on the renovation. Though she couldn't drive nails or climb ladders, no one, she declared, could make a better pot of chicken and dumplings.

''I'm afraid it's more than loose boards.'' Halley descended the steps and followed her toward the makeshift table they had set up under the pine trees. ''I wouldn't be surprised if the whole building gave way around my ears.''

''Oh, it can't be all that bad,'' Mrs. Porter assured her as they began unpacking the first basket, placing dishes of steaming baked beans and perfectly browned potatoes on the table. ''The place has been empty for almost two years. Naturally it needs a little fixing up.''

Mrs. Porter produced two golden loaves of bread and instructed Halley to begin slicing them. She placed a platter of sliced ham in the center of the table, accompanied by a dish of shredded cabbage, properly dressed with vinegar and caraway seeds. ''Besides, folks in this town want a school.''

Halley knew that Hazel was only trying to cheer her up, but her concerns over the school would not be swept aside. ''Yes, they do, and I'm the one who promised to get it for them. It seemed like such a good idea at the time. I never dreamed it would turn into such a mess.''

"Here comes Ross Carson,'' Mrs. Porter noted. "Just in time to eat, imagine that.''

Glancing up, Halley caught sight of the banker crossing the street. He had helped her draw up the budget for the project, and now, she hoped, he might see a solution to the problem.

"Good afternoon, all,'' Carson called, tipping his hat toward Halley as he approached the table, his eyes scanning the bounty with delight. "I trust things are going well?''

Halley almost laughed out loud. "No, Mr. Carson, I'm afraid we've encountered far more setbacks than we'd anticipated.''

"A project like this is bound to meet with a few complications.'' He filched a deviled egg when Mrs. Porter turned her back to open a jar of pickles. "Nothing serious, I hope.''

"If by 'serious' you mean expensive, the answer is yes.'' Despite her irritation over the renovation, Halley hid a smile when Mrs. Porter cast a questioning gaze at her platter of deviled eggs. Coughing slightly, she purged her voice of any humor. "In fact, the entire roof may need replacing.''

Discreetly licking egg yolk from his fingers, the banker glanced toward the roof, and Halley could almost hear the figures going through his mind.

"Yes, ma'am, that could be a problem. As it stands now, we've all but exhausted the funds allotted for standard improvements.''

He produced a small notebook from his pocket and began quoting figures. "The only funds available are what we set aside for the teacher's salary. Have you promised the position to anyone yet?''

Halley shook her head. "I've only received a few responses to the advertisement, and they weren't at all suitable.''

"We could use the remaining funds to complete the renovation,'' Mr. Carson suggested hesitantly. "Of course, that would leave us without a teacher.''

"A teacher won't do us any good without a school,'' Mrs. Porter pointed out. "We can get the place fixed up and have school next year.''

"No, we can't do that.'' Halley thought of the contract she

had signed with the school board, accepting complete responsibility for the funds and their use. Spending the money without holding classes would make her liable for fraud!

She glanced back inside the building and thought of the townsfolk who had so generously given of their time, motivated by the promises she had made of an education for their children. "I guess this year I'll just have to teach the children myself."

"You?" Mrs. Porter looked skeptical. "You live too far to be riding into town every day, especially with the snows coming."

"School will be out before the weather grows truly fierce and then resume again in the spring. Perhaps, by then we'll be able to hire a teacher."

"You'd be welcome to stay with me," Mrs. Porter said. "I've always got an empty room or two during the winter."

"Yes, that would be the simplest solution." Halley knew she couldn't travel back and forth every day, and the boardinghouse was just across the street from the school. "I just hate to be away from the ranch that long."

"Who'll see after your place?" Mr. Carson's eyes lingered on the platter of ham slices, and he finally looked up when she didn't answer. "Eli's getting too old, and he can't get around well on that bad leg."

Halley knew the answer, the only answer. She would have to ask Ben to oversee the ranch while she stayed in town to teach school, and was he going love that! Especially after she had reacted so indignantly toward his suggestions to Eli, informing him that she could run her property just fine without him, thank you very much.

"There's nothing else I can do," she finally said aloud, more to herself than the others.

"Let's have a bite to eat first," Mr. Carson suggested, reaching for a plate. "It's not good to worry over money on an empty stomach."

"I swear we've rounded up every stray in Wyoming." Clayton groaned as he followed Ben inside the house. He rubbed his eyes and yawned as they entered the front room. "I don't think I could take another day out on that range."

Ben started to remind him that they would be returning before dawn tomorrow, but decided against it. Clayton had held his own without complaint, and he didn't need to be reminded that the worst was yet to come.

"You'd better get cleaned up," he advised instead, "unless you're too tired to eat supper."

Clayton's eyes widened. "Are you kidding? I could eat a whole side of beef, hooves and all."

Ben had to laugh at that. "Then you'd better get going, or you'll be lucky to get the horns."

Ben watched his brother's shoulders sag with exhaustion as he disappeared up the narrow stairs. Tonight would be the first in two days either one of them had slept in his own bed, and Clayton was definitely feeling the effects of that hardship.

He noted his own mud-splattered clothes, but the cut on his hand needed immediate attention and his clothes would have to wait. The strip of torn cloth he'd wrapped around his palm was stiff with dried blood, and the wound was beginning to throb.

What he really needed he realized, was a strong drink, and turned toward the parlor. Just as he reached for the half-empty decanter, a knock sounded at the front door. He swore under his breath and hoped he wasn't needed back out on the range.

He heard the door open as he tossed the liquor down his throat, warmth spreading through his chest. There was a soft exchange of voices in the hall, followed by silence. Relieved, he lifted the decanter and refilled his glass.

"Ben?"

The sound of Halley's voice startled him, and he turned to find her standing in the parlor doorway, her hands clasped primly before her. Despite his exhaustion, Ben felt an immediate quickening of desire, as if only minutes, not days, had passed since they had clung desperately to each other.

He'd pushed himself without mercy, hoping that weariness would make him forget the feel of her in arms, but the sight of her was all the reminder he needed. His voice was ragged when he said, "Halley, what are you doing here?"

She gave him a hesitant smile. "I'm sorry to call unexpectedly, but I need to talk with you."

"Come on in." He let his gaze sweep over her form, noting

her freshly ironed clothes and neatly combed hair. To her, his appearance was probably horrifying, but he refused to offer an apology or explanation. He did, with reluctance, put the whiskey aside.

When she stood inside the parlor, Halley peered over her shoulder toward the foyer. "Who was the lady who answered the door?"

"Mrs. Gunter? She's my housekeeper."

"Housekeeper?" She glanced around the parlor and then back at him. "You have a housekeeper?"

He didn't miss the subtle thinning of her lips or the unspoken resentment in her eyes. He knew it was on the tip of her tongue to repay him for accusing her of being lost without a houseful of servants, but something kept the words in check. Miss St. John wanted something from him, and she wanted it badly enough to mind her words.

He couldn't resist adding, "She's been with me for years."

She considered his words without reply, as if trying to determine if he was teasing her.

"I was just going out to the kitchen for some coffee. Care to join me?"

She found her voice. "Do you have a cook as well?"

He hid a smile at her sarcasm. "Sure do, but he mostly stays out in the bunkhouse."

She followed him into the kitchen without a word, but he caught the sly way she inspected the house, her eyes scanning every gleaming piece of furniture, every sparkling fixture. When they entered the kitchen, she barely contained a gasp of surprise.

"What a lovely kitchen," she murmured, staring first at the gleaming cast-iron stove and then at the elegant sideboard. "And it's so large."

"It suits me." He began unwinding the tattered bandage around his hand, cursing as the cloth stuck to the open wound. Gingerly, he tugged the bandage back from his palm, causing the cut to bleed anew.

Her eyes widened at the sight. "What happened to you?"

He shrugged. "I got careless."

"You? I find that hard to believe." She crossed the kitchen floor and peered down at the gaping gash across his palm.

"Ben, that looks serious. Shouldn't you see a doctor?"

He laughed. "I'll just get Creek to throw a little axle grease on it and tie it up with a bandanna for a few days."

"You'll do nothing of the sort," she countered, and turned toward the pump. She filled a basin with water and motioned for him to wash his hands. "Careless treatment of such injuries can easily lead to infection. My father firmly believed that filthy conditions killed more soldiers during the War Between the States than enemy bullets."

"I'll bet that made him popular with the army brass."

Halley ignored his flippant remark, turning without comment to retrieve a clean linen towel from the cabinet.

Her initial shock at the size and beauty of Ben's home had shifted to curiosity. She had noticed the staircase off the parlor and wondered how many rooms were upstairs. The downstairs alone was as large as her entire cabin, and she was shocked to realize how quickly she had adapted to the smaller space.

With a dubious expression, Ben began rolling up the sleeves of his shirt. Halley looked on as he lathered his hands with a sliver of lye soap. He worked the lather up his forearms, and she felt her pulse quicken at the sight of the taut muscles flexing. She quickly looked away and began searching the cupboard for some type of disinfectant.

Finally, she located a bottle of iodine and turned to find him watching her as he dried his hands on the towel. She reached for his hand, and she knew he felt the tremble in her fingers. Forcing herself not to meet his eyes, Halley turned his wounded palm up for her inspection.

Gently, she dried his hand and applied iodine with a soft cloth. He swore the moment the saturated rag touched his flesh and tried to withdraw his hand.

"Hold still," she ordered, holding fast. She meticulously cleaned the wound and wrapped a fresh bandage around his hand. "You really should be more careful. How did this happen?"

"I found a steer hung up in some barbed wire." Ben closed his bandaged hand around her fingers. "He fought me for all he was worth, even though I was trying to help him."

Halley swallowed. "I suppose being caught in a barbed-wire fence would make one very distrustful."

"Even if they got *themselves* caught?"

Halley met his gaze, and her breath caught in her throat; looking into his eyes was always a mistake. She longed to lose herself in their blue depths and allow him to shoulder her burdens. Now she would have to trust him if she was going to go through with teaching school.

She didn't look away, praying her faith would not be misplaced again. The ranch was all she had in the world, and she was going to ask Ben to hold it in his hip pocket, trusting him to return it.

"Does it matter how they came to be in such a predicament?" She moved to back away from him but found herself pinned against the counter. "All that matters is not having it happen again."

"That's the chance you take." Ben closed the scant distance between them and cupped her face with his uninjured palm. "The steers have to live on the range, and the range is full of barbed wire. You can only hope someone comes along to cut them loose."

She moved to set herself apart from him, but he anticipated her reaction and let his hand fall to her shoulder, refusing to permit her escape.

She willed herself to resist his hard, hungry kiss, but instead, his lips barely grazed hers, coaxing and gentle. His tenderness was far more persuasive than any demands he could have made, and she raised her lips to meet his kiss. He caught her weight against him and her palms smoothed a path over his chest, her fingers clinging to his shoulders. His mouth became more demanding, and she tasted whiskey on his tongue.

His touch made her weak and dizzy, and she needed to be strong and clearheaded. Twisting from his arms, she looked away, trying to sort her jumbled thoughts. He refused her reprieve, turning her to meet his heated expression.

"Why do you always run from me?" he demanded, his eyes searching hers for any shred of truth. "Don't you trust me?"

"You don't need my trust." She stiffened and tried to pull away once again. She might trust him with her land, but dared trust no one with the knowledge that she was stranded in Wyoming. "With or without it, everything I own is at your disposal."

Immediately, he released her and turned toward the stove. He lifted the coffeepot and filled a waiting cup without offering one to her. "I suppose there's a reason you're here."

"Yes, I . . . I need your help."

He turned to find her standing ramrod straight, her chin tilted in defiance. He crossed his arms over his chest. "I'm listening."

"It's the school," she began hesitantly. "There have been many unexpected costs in repairing the building, and now the roof may have to be replaced."

"And you want me to put a new roof on your schoolhouse," he concluded, raising the coffee cup to his lips. "I thought you inspected that building."

Piqued by his smug expression, she bit out, "Well, I didn't climb up on the roof."

"Maybe you should have before you made all those promises to the school board."

Squaring her shoulders, Halley replied, "Mr. Carson assured me that it was the sturdiest available building in town."

"Did he tell you that it is the only available building in town?"

"This town needs that school," she whispered, "and I'm going to see that one is delivered. If you won't help me, I'll manage somehow."

"I've got a ranch to run," he reminded her. "Now it looks like I'll be running yours as well."

Halley looked away, unsure how to respond. She felt foolish enough without having to admit that she had no money left to pay a teacher and would have to take the job herself. "I have no intention of neglecting the ranch."

"Well, you can't manage a cattle operation and piddle in town all day."

"Piddle!" she repeated. "Is that what you think I'm doing? You have no idea how much work has been involved in this, and I happen to think it's been very worthwhile."

"You can play do-gooder to your heart's content, but leave the cattle business to those of us who are serious." He set his coffee aside, never taking his eyes from her. "If you're not cut out for Wyoming, Halley, do yourself a favor and go home before it's too late."

"Isn't that what you've wanted all along?" Halley realized she was shouting but didn't care. "From the moment I arrived, you've done nothing but discourage me at every turn."

"I've tried to save you needless disappointment," he countered, gesturing to his muddied jeans and torn shirt. "Just look at me. And today was a good day! I was lucky not to get gored by that steer, and I've been kicked and stepped on, had bones broken—"

"I get the picture," she cut in. "I realize how hard life on a ranch can be, but I can't quit just because I'm a woman."

"Why are you fighting so hard to hang on?" Genuine bewilderment knitted his brows, emphasizing the tired lines framing his eyes. "A woman with any sense would have gotten right back on that stage and headed home as fast as she could."

"Is that what your wife did?"

His expression hardened. "That's none of your damn business."

"I think it is." Bargain or no bargain, she wanted some answers from Ben Parrish. "That's why you've been trying to send me away, isn't it? She left when things got tough, and you think I'm no better."

Deafening silence fell between them, and she waited for his answer.

"That's not what happened." He drained the coffee from his cup. "I sent a telegram telling her the house was ready, along with enough money for a train ticket to Cheyenne."

A rueful grin touched his lips. "I met every train for three days."

Halley had never regretted anything more than she regretted the spiteful reference she'd just made to Ben's wife. She was jealous of any woman he had ever cared for, and so she'd imagined a whining shrew with whom he had gladly parted.

He turned his back to her, bracing his palms against the counter. "A cattle ranch is no place for a lady. At least, that's what her letter said."

"Ben, I'm so sorry." She moved toward him, hesitantly resting her hand on his arm. "I didn't know. . . ."

He shrugged away from her touch, refusing to look at her. "Well, now you do."

His rebuff hurt, and she knew it was well deserved. The hard set of his jaw was enough to assure her that she had pushed him away when she needed him the most. She would have to put pride aside if she was ever going to regain his trust.

"But don't you see?" she pleaded. "I *want* to stay in Wyoming, but . . . I need your help."

As if he knew what that admission cost her, Ben turned toward her and he lifted her chin. "Is that such a bad thing, Halley?"

He lowered his mouth to hers, claiming her lips as she sank against him. His taste was a lusciously wicked mixture of coffee and whiskey, and she felt herself succumb to the intoxicating rush of sensations it aroused.

Lifting his head, Ben studied her face with a wary expression, as if he expected her to bolt and run. Instead, she raised her lips to his, her arms finding their way around his neck.

He let her control the kiss for a moment before claiming her mouth with a hunger that took her breath away. She could merely hang in his arms, her legs useless beneath her, and submit to his urgent demands.

"Mr. Parrish?"

The voice startled them both, and they turned to find the stern-faced Mrs. Gunter eyeing them with disapproval. "Vill dere another place for dinner?"

Mortified, Halley attempted to pull away from him, but he held her tight. With complete composure, he answered the housekeeper's question. "Yes, Mrs. Gunter, there will."

There was just something exciting about opening a packing crate, even if you knew what was inside. Halley returned Mr. Tulley's smile as he offered the crowbar, allowing her the honors. With her second attempt, the lid gave way, baring nails like crooked teeth, and the scent of new books filled the back room of the general store.

Delighted, Halley set the crowbar aside and retrieved one of the many volumes, inhaling the odor of bookbinder's glue mingled with that of the packing straw. "*Worthen's Fundamentals of Mathematics*," she read out loud, and began flipping through the crisp pages. "I'll have to spend some time with this one, I'm afraid. Arithmetic was never my favorite."

"Just start with the basics," Tulley advised. "Those youngsters won't know this is your first time teaching."

"I hope you're right." Halley had more than a few misgivings about teaching. More than anything, she had brooded over not telling Ben, but he had just been so damned smug. Even his offer to help with the renovation had held a patronizing tone.

She would have to convince him that the school was more than a fanciful whim on her part. When he saw how much the people of Wilder wanted and needed the school, he would be happy to look after the ranch while she held classes.

Mr. Tulley withdrew a second book, tendrils of wispy straw clinging to his shirtsleeve. "*Hick's First Reader.*" A sentimental mist clouded his eyes and he slowly turned the pages. "Lord, I remember this; seems like only yesterday. Mother would pack baked apples in our lunch pails, but I always ate mine before I even got to school."

Halley closed the volume in her hands and thought of her own school days at Miss Van Adams's School for Fine Young Ladies. In addition to the basics of learning, society children were instructed in the rudiments of manners, dancing, and the arts. She had adored learning to paint, but detested the tedious piano lessons.

Mr. Tulley chuckled as he flipped through the reader. "I remember old Miss Brower. Lord, she was a sour woman. We used to catch frogs and snakes and put them in her desk drawers."

"Snakes?" Halley echoed, and he laughed out loud at her horror. "The poor lady. I can't believe you were so mischievous."

"They were only grass snakes," he amended. "But she sure would start screeching."

Halley smiled at the thought. "I'm certain Miss Van Adams would have fainted dead away if she'd ever found such creatures in her desk."

The bell over the store's entrance clanged loudly, startling them both from nostalgic thoughts. Mr. Tulley brushed the straw from his shirtsleeve and excused himself to attend the customer.

Halley retrieved the reader he had set aside and began scanning the table of contents. The stories were of a boy named Joe and his dog, Blue, and their adventures on a farm, helping Joe's grandfather.

"Tulley! Where the hell are you?"

Right away, Halley recognized Cooper Eldridge's voice, and she was glad she had hitched her mule in back of the store.

"Right here, Coop." Mr. Tulley's answer was patient. "What's your hurry?"

Halley listened as the jangle of spurs filled the store along with the murmur of men's voices.

"I need cartridges, and I ain't got time to go home for 'em."

She could hear Tulley placing items on the counter and then the unmistakable sound of weapons being loaded.

"Are you trailing grizzlies?" the storekeeper asked.

"Grizzlies, hell! I got over fifty head of cattle missing, maybe more." Money clattered on the counter. "Wrap up some of those soda crackers and a few slices of that hoop cheese."

"Shouldn't you alert the sheriff?"

"Hell, Roy Teal ain't caught a cold in six months, let alone cattle rustlers." Coarse laughter filled the store. "I intend to settle this myself."

The bell sounded again and Halley started at the sound of a familiar voice.

"Got fresh horses from the livery, and Mahoney said he's to get paid for feed and boarding our own mounts."

The intruder! The book in her hand slipped, and she barely caught it before it fell noisily to the floor. Tex Whitten was working for Cooper Eldridge! She couldn't believe it. She had told Mr. Eldridge all about her harrowing experience at the boardinghouse. Why would he hire such a scoundrel?

"Good enough." Eldridge's reply was curt. "Mahoney's always been a damned tightwad. Hell, if I don't have enough problems."

Paper rustled and the cash register chimed open. Mr. Eldridge instructed his men to purchase whatever provisions they wanted for the ride, vowing not to tolerate any complaints.

"If it ain't coyotes and rustlers cuttin' the herds, it's a damned woman taking the land." His voice held an unmistakable tone of disgust. "I hope they got windows in hell so Pete St. John can see what a harebrained spinster he left that ranch to."

"She needs what every old maid needs, boss. Get her skirts up over her head and let her have it."

Halley recoiled at the intruder's crude remark, clutching the book with icy fingers.

"Well, I don't expect you'll be the one giving it to her, seeing as how she nearly shot yours off." Eldridge's reply caused an eruption of laughter and brought a string of curses from Whitten. "Get your gear, I'm ready to ride."

The stomping of boot heels rose and faded as the man passed through the doorway, letting it slam behind them. When the jangling of the bell faded into silence, Halley stepped from the storeroom into the light.

She glanced toward the door and then at Mr. Tulley.

Coughing slightly, he began wiping the counter. "I'm sorry about that, Miss Halley."

"Why didn't you tell him that I was here?"

"It's good to know what folks say about you when they think you aren't around."

❧ THIRTEEN ❧

LOLLING HER HEAD from side to side, Halley was beginning
to believe that the crick in her neck was permanent. She had
fallen asleep reading the night before and woke up stiff and
sore.

She closed her eyes and drew a deep breath, hoping the
crisp morning air would clear her head. Having moved her
studies out onto the porch, she sat facing east to attain the best
light. Glancing toward the faded grassland, she longed to
sneak away with Baby for a quick ride. The mule did so love
to run on autumn mornings.

Forcing her attention back to the lessons, Halley turned to
the place marked in the book. "Fractions," she groaned, adjusting her shawl more securely about her shoulders. "How
can I teach something that makes no sense?"

"Morning, missy." Eli's voice broke through her thoughts.
She looked up to see him crossing the lot toward the house.

He made his way up the steps, his limp more pronounced
on cold mornings. "You're up early."

She nodded and reached for her coffee cup. "I've been up
awhile."

He settled himself across from her on a cane-bottom chair. "What'cha reading?"

"I'm looking over books for the school." She tasted the coffee and made a face. "Arithmetic."

He made a face in return. "Never did take much of shine to book learnin'. I figure the good Lord put all I needed to know in my noggin."

Grateful for the interruption, she closed the book and asked, "You never went to school?"

"Oh, a time or two," he recalled. "In those days, most teachers were menfolk, and the one we had couldn't abide no mischief. 'Course, that's what little boys are best at. Well, I decided learning to read weren't worth getting whupped three or four times a day."

"Goodness, I don't blame you."

He adjusted his position in the chair and folded his arms over his belly. "So, are you going to have a female teaching the young'uns?"

"As a matter fact, the teacher will be a lady." She met his gaze. "Can you keep a secret?"

"What?"

"I'm going to be the teacher."

"You?" he exclaimed, doubling over with laughter. "Now, that I'd like to see!"

"What's so funny?" she finally demanded when the peals of laughter continued.

He tried to answer, but only laughed all the harder. At last he was able to contain himself long enough to wipe his eyes and say, "Lordy, I can just see you as the schoolmarm."

"Well, I'm more qualified than the women who answered the advertisement," she insisted, decidedly insulted by his amusement. "Most of those women were more interested in the number of eligible bachelors in town, as if teaching school were a means to catch a husband."

"Think it'll work for you?"

The old man always found his own jokes entertaining and broke into another bout of laughter.

"You missed your calling, Eli." She rose from her chair and went into the house to refill her coffee and fetch him a cup. "You should have gone on the stage with Eddie Foy."

"Oh, Missy, I'm only funnin' with you," he called after her. "Are you bringing me a cup of that coffee?"

"Yes, I am," she answered. "Have you had breakfast?"

"Well, that was a few hours ago."

She placed two biscuits on a saucer, broke them in half, and spooned cherry preserves over them. Palming a napkin, she balanced the two mugs of coffee in one hand and carried the saucer of biscuits in the other.

"You'd make a better waitress than a teacher," he couldn't resist saying as he accepted the coffee and biscuits. "Don't ranching keep you busy enough?"

"I'm not ranching," she countered, licking a smear of preserves from her thumb. "Mr. Parrish is running the place, remember?"

"You ain't still got your nose out of joint over that, have you?" He sipped the coffee, eyeing her over the rim of the cup. "Ben just gives me little reminders of what needs doing."

Halley only shrugged, retrieving the math primer. "Well, I'll have to ask him to see after things completely while I teach school."

"You're serious about that." He bit into a biscuit and studied her with preserves clinging to his stubbled chin. "How did you get your tail in this crack?"

She tossed the napkin toward him. "How do I ever get myself into these things? I opened my big mouth!"

Wiping his chin, Eli chuckled softly. "Lord, if you ain't Pete St. John made over. That man was always telling folks how they ought to be doing things."

"Well, Wilder does need a school."

"'Course it does, missy," he reassured her. "And you'll make a fine teacher."

"Let's hope so, because I'm all there is."

Mr. Josiah Pittman
New York City, NY

Dear Mr. Pittman,

Please pardon my delay in answering your letter. You

are so kind to worry after me here in the wilderness, but I can honestly assure you that I am neither lonely nor repentant of my decision to come west. If fact, my life has become such a whirlwind of obligations that this very letter will necessarily be brief.

Since my last letter, I have become involved in the founding of a school here in Wilder. As most things that sound so good and simple, it has turned out to be more of a chore, as they say out here, than I ever dreamed.

The territorial school board was more than willing to see a school established, and they were more than generous with the funds appropriated for the necessities. All seemed lost at the end when extensive repairs were required, but my neighbor saved the day, donating lumber and nails left from a barn he built just last year.

The news that will make you smile is that the schoolmarm will be none other than myself. After so many years as a student, I will be the one preparing lessons and grading papers.

My only regret is that teaching will require my being away from the ranch for over a month. In a very short time I have grown accustomed to the beauty and solitude, content to awaken to nothing but sound of my own thoughts.

As I write this the schoolhouse is near completion and classes will begin in less than a week. A grand party is planned to celebrate, a dedication of sorts, with plenty of food and dancing. My friend Mrs. Mitchell assures me it will best any in New York.

Again, I apologize for not writing sooner, and I hope my next letter will not be so hurried.

Halley St. John
Wyoming Territory

Halley stood in the center of the schoolhouse, her hands clasped behind her back. She had never been more proud of anything in her life.

Somehow they had pulled it all together. The loose flooring had been repaired, and the roof had been mended without having to be completely replaced. The desks and chairs had been stacked against the walls for tonight's party, but the teacher's desk sat on the platform facing the classroom. Behind the desk, a blackboard hung on the wall with unbroken chalk cradled in the railing.

On impulse, she scurried across the room and wrote her name in bold, practiced script. Below that, she neatly printed the words WELCOME STUDENTS AND PARENTS.

She was looking forward to tonight's celebration of the school, anxious to meet as many of the children as possible.

The men of the town had worked all day on the final renovation of the abandoned print shop and now there would be a buffet supper and dance to commemorate the occasion.

Only one thing kept her spirits in check. School would be starting Monday, and she had yet to muster the courage to tell Ben she would be teaching. She hated confrontations and always made things so much worse by waiting until the last minute.

At worst, he would be furious and refuse to help her. The best she could hope for would be for him to think her foolish and lecture her on the evils of shirking responsibility.

"Miss Halley?"

She turned toward the doorway, startled by the girl's voice. "Hello, Susan, you're here early. The party doesn't start for another hour."

Susan stepped inside and closed the door behind her. "Ma wanted to get here before Mrs. Porter did. She says there's no way that woman is going to run this party."

They laughed and Halley shook her head, constantly amazed by the ruthless competition to be hostess. She took in Susan's appearance, pleased that the girl had chosen to wear a dress she had given her. "You certainly look pretty. I knew that color would be perfect for you."

The door flew open and Delia backed in, carrying a box overflowing with what Halley suspected were meticulously prepared dishes. "Susan, help your pa with those turnovers, and don't let him snatch one when he thinks I'm not looking. And hurry! I won't have that woman acting like she's the only one in this town who can boil water."

* * *

"My hens have been laying eggs with double yolks," Delia Mitchell announced, gloating, to the other women. "That's what makes the batter so rich."

"Well, I've always been partial to your applesauce cake," the banker's wife replied. "I'm determined to get the recipe out of you one of these days."

The other ladies laughed in chorus; Halley had been warned that Delia never divulged her secrets in the kitchen. She glanced down the makeshift table, heavily laden with an unlimited variety of delicacies, and feared the planks would not stand the strain.

"When I make *my* applesauce cake, I always use nutmeg," Mrs. Porter couldn't resist saying. "You need to use plenty of nutmeg and cinnamon."

Delia's lips thinned. "Too many spices overwhelm the flavor of the cake."

"Raisins are nice, too," Hazel continued, undaunted by Delia's irritation. "And you might add a few chopped walnuts next time."

"Cider's here!" Gus Mahoney burst through the doorway, a large wooden keg balanced on his shoulder.

Delia met him halfway across the room, her hands braced on her broad hips. "That better not be hard cider. You pulled that stunt last year at Peg Murphy's wedding. Half the town was drunk as skunks."

"And you the worst of all." Gus placed the cider near the table, quickly tapping the keg. "I never seen a married woman fight so hard to catch the bouquet."

Everyone laughed and Delia colored to her the tops of her ears.

Families bearing food, lanterns, and chairs were still arriving as children swarmed through the building, wide-eyed in anticipation of the new school, and claims were made and challenged on seating assignments.

"I can't believe how much food is here." Halley looked on as yet another platter of chicken was placed on the table, along with an enormous crock of sweet butter. "There's enough to feed an army."

"But there won't be a bite left," Mrs. Porter assured her. "One thing folks around here can do is eat!"

"Everyone is excited about the school." Susan placed a stack of folded napkins on the table. "They're all so proud of you, Miss Halley."

"I want them to be proud of the school," Halley replied, "not me."

Delia patted her shoulder affectionately. "Of course, folks are proud to be getting a school, and having an excuse for a dance just makes it that much better."

The fiddler was tuning up in the corner, and men were already filing down the buffet, filling their plates with roast beef, boiled ham, dumplings, cabbage and turnips, and the unending variety of desserts. Halley had taken on the chore of slicing the cakes into serving-size sections, and her fingers were sticky from the many gooey frostings.

"Didn't I tell you we'd get this place in tip-top shape?" Ross Carson lead the procession, his plate piled high. He smiled at Halley. "And you were so worried."

"It was a miracle," she maintained as she offered him a choice serving of vanilla cake layered with butter-cream frosting. "I'm glad you were right."

He accepted the cake, only to point toward the far end of the table and ask, "Is that raisin pie?"

"Would you rather have that?" She sliced into the flaky crust, exposing the dark, fragrant filling of raisins and dried apples.

"I think I can manage both."

His wife appeared at his side, scanning the food on his plate. "Ross Carson, you're not having two desserts, are you?"

"Well, Hannah, who's counting?"

Everyone laughed, and Hannah Carson steered her husband away from the table, but only after grudgingly accepting the slice of pie from Halley.

"Evenin', Miss Halley," Clayton said with a smile as he reached for a thick square of yellow corn bread. "Is there any of your spice cake left?"

"We saved a slice just for you." Halley winked at Susan, who hurried to retrieve the last fragrant serving of Clayton's favorite cake, rich with molasses and chopped walnuts. "How are the back steps coming?"

"Almost finished." Clayton spooned a generous portion of

roasted potatoes onto his plate. "Ben wanted the edges sanded once more, to make sure they're even."

Halley paused, looking up from the sponge cake she was about to slice. "Ben is here?"

"Yes, ma'am, he got here just a little while ago."

"I thought he was reluctant to leave the ranch."

"Oh, Ben worries more than most," Clayton explained. He leaned forward and gave her a conspiratorial grin. "But I told him how important this night was to you and that he had better show up."

Halley smiled weakly. Ready or not, she would have to reveal her plans to teach school and her need for Ben to oversee her ranch. She glanced toward the blackboard where she had written her name, welcoming all students and parents. She had better tell him now, before he walked in and found out for himself.

Susan returned with the cake and held the saucer out to Clayton, blushing crimson when he smiled and thanked her.

"Clayton, help Susan find a seat," Halley insisted, steering the girl from behind the table. "She's been helping me all evening and hasn't had a bite to eat."

"But I can't leave you to do everything," Susan protested as Halley thrust a hastily prepared plate of food in her hands.

"Nonsense, there's hardly anything to do until everyone leaves." Halley wouldn't hear any argument. "Then you can help us clean up."

Once the young couple were seated across the room and absorbed in their own conversation, Halley quickly glanced at the dishes remaining on the table. The feast had been scavenged in a matter of minutes, and she knew Ben wouldn't find much if he waited.

She prepared a plate with the best of the remains, filled a speckled blue cup with coffee, and rushed toward the back door. Once outside, she found Ben kneeling before the back steps, meticulously working sandpaper over the wooden boards.

"Good evening," she began hesitantly. "You're just in time for supper."

His head came up and he gave a quick smile before returning to his work. "I told Clayton I'd finish these steps so he wouldn't have to come back tomorrow."

"I'm sure he'll appreciate that."

Clayton had deliberately dragged out every job for which he'd volunteered, always deciding he'd better return the following day.

"He'll think of something," he assured her.

"I really appreciate your helping the way you have." Halley placed his plate and coffee on a nearby bench and clasped her hands behind her back. "Can't you stop long enough to eat?"

"I'm finished," he informed her as he tested the top step beneath his weight. "Try it for yourself."

Halley scaled the six steps and stood beside him on the top step, nodding her approval. "You've done a fine job."

She bounced her weight lightly on the wooden boards. "The steps must be sturdy with all the children bounding out to recess."

He looked down at her with a skeptical grin. "What do you know about children?"

"I've been around children." She rolled her eyes and shook her head in exasperation. "Honestly, do you think New York City is really so very different from anywhere else in the world?"

"Are the folks there much like you?"

She ignored the remark. "One of my best friends had a baby of her own last year. A precious little girl, but she cried constantly."

The evening breeze picked up, teasing her hair loose from its combs. Ben reached out and smoothed the strands back in place, his fingers lingering against her face. "Don't you want babies, someday?"

Halley felt the color rise in her cheeks, and she was thankful for the darkness and crisp night air. Pretending to inspect his handiwork, she descended the steps, testing each one with her weight.

"You'd better eat before your supper gets cold," she advised, nervously arranging the napkin and fork she had placed beside his plate. "I didn't know if you preferred ham or chicken, so I brought both."

"Wouldn't you rather go inside?"

"Oh, no," she blurted out, and then added, "It's such a nice night, and there are so many people inside . . . all that noise and smoke."

Ben joined her and gathered the plate as he straddled the bench. He motioned for her to take a seat at the opposite end, and she did so with as much composure as she could muster.

He jabbed the sliced ham with his fork and ate heartily. She hoped the food would put him in a receptive mood.

"Mrs. Gunter sends her regards," he remarked casually, tasting the coffee.

"Ha! I'm sure she does." The breeze picked up, and Halley belatedly thought of the shawl she'd left inside. "Every time she looked at me, I could feel daggers."

"She's just old-fashioned," he said in dismissal. "She thinks things should still be the way they were when she was a girl."

Halley rolled her eyes. "That's certainly one thing I don't miss about New York—nosy servants!"

"Tell me why you left New York." He reached out and placed his thumb beneath her chin, turning her toward him. "And why you think you can't go back."

"You're still jumping to conclusions over a few tears." She wouldn't meet his eyes. "I was merely homesick, and exhausted from the trip to Logan Falls."

He wouldn't let it go. "Halley, there's a difference between homesick and no home to go back to."

She still couldn't look at him. "How would you know?"

"Takes one to know one."

She glanced up at that, startled, and her curiosity immediately had the better of her. She remembered what Clayton had said about Ben's wife causing him to leave the Rangers. She assumed this was why he'd come to Wyoming, but it hadn't occurred to her that he couldn't return. She thought before speaking, choosing her words carefully. "Did you—"

"Bargain still holds." He smiled at her over the coffee cup. "And I asked first."

"Well, I'm not telling you anything. You'll just have to get used to the idea of me being in Wyoming."

"I'm beginning to like the idea. I may even decide I want to court you."

She laughed. ''Eli will be glad to hear that. He says I'm in danger of being an old maid.''

''So, the old coot's looking to marry you off?''

''Not exactly.'' Halley rose to her feet and glanced up at the night sky. ''He suspects I'm too contrary to make a suitable bride.''

''Is that what those fancy New York gentlemen want?'' he asked. ''A meek little mouse, afraid of her own shadow?''

''I doubt they give much thought to the bride herself. Perhaps as an afterthought, once the major criteria have been met.'' She recited the edicts, chapter and verse. ''First, a girl must have her debut. And depending on how successful that is, then a prospective suitor determines how well connected her family is. It must be a delicate balance of power, position, and profit.''

She laughed out loud at the look of astonishment on his face. ''Is that so hard to believe?''

''Those folks must have more money and time than good sense.''

From inside the refurbished schoolhouse, the fiddle cried a mournful song, and the drum of stomping feet quieted.

Halley glanced back at Ben. ''I don't know how they found room for dancing. The place is packed.''

He rose to his feet and crossed the distance between them, his hands extended. ''We can dance right here.''

She hesitated only a moment before placing her hand in his. He drew her into his arms and she realized her mistake too late. The music drifted through the night, the fiddle pleasantly out of tune, and Ben led her through the motions of a waltz.

Their bodies barely touched, but her flesh tingled from the nearness. His palm splayed across her waist and she miscounted her steps, nearly tripping over her own skirts. She forced a smile. ''I'm a little rusty.''

''Not rusty, you've just never danced with a man who took your mind off the music.''

Her smile disappeared. It was true. She'd danced a hundred waltzes, but couldn't remember more than a few names of her partners. Her attention had always remained on the music and the surrounding couples.

But here, on a grassy lot in Wilder, Wyoming, beneath a

starry sky, nothing existed but the man holding her in his arms. Realization took hold, making her even weaker. She was falling in love with Ben Parrish.

His embrace grew deliberate, their bodies swaying in time to the gentle breeze stirring between them.

"Kiss me, Halley," he whispered against her lips. "Don't think, just kiss me."

She wanted to. She wanted to ignore every argument running through her mind and allow herself to be absorbed by his strength.

"Ben Parrish!" a voice called out from the darkness, startling them both. They turned to see Frank Morgan turning the corner of the building. "You'd best get home, Ben. We've had trouble."

"What kind of trouble?"

"That boy's brother showed up, just like you said and he wasn't alone." The reply was ominous. "Ten of them riding hell-for-leather and they were heading straight for Cooper Eldridge's place."

❧ FOURTEEN ❧

"MISSY, I TELL you it ain't nothing to fret over."

Halley glanced back at Eli. "I don't see how you can say that. Mr. Parrish is in pursuit of men no better than outlaws. He could be killed."

"*Mister* Parrish can take care of himself," Eli snorted, and turned his attention back to his coffee. "If I was a woman, I wouldn't be staying up all night wringing my hands over a man I wasn't even on a first-name basis with."

"I am not wringing my hands." Halley turned back toward the window and stared out into the blackness. It was raining again, and the fire in the hearth popped and hissed. "It's just that I would feel responsible if anything happened to him."

"How's that?"

"Clayton said that those men had originally been after my cattle, probably trying to run me off."

"The boy talks too dang much." The old man tasted his coffee and reached for the sugar bowl. "Besides, Ben was chasing outlaws before he ever knew about cattle or cattle rustlers, and he rode for your uncle many a year before getting his own place."

180

"Really?" Halley sank to the table, her curiosity roused. "How did Mister . . . Ben come to work for Uncle Peter."

Eli chuckled and leaned back in his chair. "Lord have mercy, I can still see him. He rode into our camp one rainy night, just like tonight, on a nag someone was probably glad to see stole. He was soaked to the bone, half-starved, and looked like he'd been wrestling sticker bushes. Walked right up to Pete, cocky as a rooster, and said he was looking for work.

"He barely knew one end of a cow from the other, but he wouldn't be put off. He could ride better than any man in the outfit, and he just kept trying till he caught on. By the time we reached these parts, Pete asked him to stay on as foreman."

Halley knew she shouldn't ask the next question, but Eli was in a talking mood. "Did Ben ever say anything about his wife?"

The old man laughed. "I wondered how long you'd hold out afore asking about that. What has Ben told you? Not much, I'll bet."

"One look at that house, and you know that it was built for a family." Halley fingered the handle of her empty cup and decided against refilling it. "He did say that she had refused to come to Wyoming."

"Sure did." Eli leaned forward and lowered his voice, "Pete read the letter, and told me it had to have been written by a mighty heartless woman."

Halley nodded thoughtfully. "What I don't understand is what made him leave Texas, if she didn't want to come with him."

"Saying you'll do something is sometimes easier that going through with it." Eli pinned her with a piercing look. "This country's hard on folks—womenfolk especially."

She stiffened at the statement. Glancing up, she asked, "You're not going to start telling me that I don't belong here, are you?"

"That ain't what I'm saying at all," he snapped, pointing a gnarled finger at her. "But you ought not to get so uppity when folks want to know you can make it out here before they start counting on you."

Taken back, she could only nod. After a moment she asked,

"How did Clayton come to live here?"

"Now, that's where things get complicated." Eli drained his coffee cup. " 'Bout five years later Ben got a letter from Texas saying his ma had died. By that time he had filed for his own land and had a sizable herd. He had no choice but to bring the boy out here."

Eli drew his pipe from his pocket and began refilling the bowl with fresh tobacco. A match flared and soon the room was filled with the sharp tang of smoke.

"For a Texan, I ain't never seen no one more ignorant about horses than that boy." He chuckled at the memory. "First day, an old nag bit a plug out of him, and it was six months before Ben could get him to go near the corral."

Silence fell between them, and Halley thought of Ben, heartbroken and alone for so many years, and her heart ached for what he must have gone through. Perhaps Eli was right about proving herself in Wyoming. She would have to convince Ben that she had no intention of leaving Wilder, especially if she asked him to take over the ranch. If only she'd had the courage to tell him from the beginning that she had nowhere else to run.

The sound of riders nearing the house startled them both, and Halley rushed to the window to see four men on horses nearing the house. She heard someone call her name but recognized none of the horses. Newfound instincts bid her to feel her pocket for her pistol.

"Halley!" A shout carried her name over the storm once again.

This time she recognized Ben's voice and rushed out onto the porch, her eyes scanning the group of men. Ben swung down from his horse and rushed up the front steps. She hurried into his embrace, not caring that he was drenched or that Eli stood in the open door watching.

"I want you to get into town." He raised her face to his. "Tonight if possible."

"Ben, what is it?" She reached up to smooth away the beads of moisture clinging to his face. "Are you all right?"

He covered her hand with his. "There's been a lynching."

She gasped, remembering Cooper Eldridge's vow to rid the territory of rustlers. "Oh, Ben, no."

"I'm afraid so." His face was grim. "They wanted a range war, and now they'll have one."

Halley placed the last of her baggage on the porch of the boardinghouse and returned to the wagon. Baby turned his knowing eyes toward her, accepting her touch on his face.

"I just can't make him stay in that livery stable." She wound her arms around the mule's strong neck and he pressed his forehead against the dark serge of her traveling suit. "He'd think I had sent him back."

She breathed the dusty scent of horsehair and leather as she whispered into his ear, assuring him of her devotion. The ear twitched, as if in response, and she swallowed hard against the lump in her throat.

"Now, missy, don't fret over this old mule." Eli climbed up in the wagon seat and gathered the reins. "He's got a nice warm stall, plenty to eat, and I bought the biggest bag of peppermint sticks Jim Tulley had in that store."

"I'll miss him." Halley blinked back tears, remembering how the mule had looked at her that day in the livery. It sounded so foolish, but he had been her first friend in Wyoming.

She stroked his velvety nose, the wiry hairs prickling her palm. A sadness stole into her heart, even though she knew she was doing the right thing. To keep him in town for her own comfort would be selfish, and she would be too busy with the school to take him riding every day.

"Will he forget me?"

Eli snorted in disgust. "It ain't like you're going off to join the army. You'll just be in town for a month. How 'bout I hang your picture in his stall?"

In spite of herself, she laughed. "I'll miss you, too."

Eli scowled and looked away. "You be careful . . . and keep your dang window locked this time."

The reminder of her last stay at the boardinghouse made Halley shudder. With her spending the next month in town and Tex Whitten walking around free, she doubted she would be lucky enough to avoid him entirely. After overhearing his coarse remarks about her in the general store, she knew such an encounter could prove dangerous.

"Now, remember what I told you." Halley fixed Eli with a menacing look. "I haven't had a chance to explain to Ben that I'm staying in town to teach school, so don't you mention it to him."

"You've had plenty of chances," he countered. "You're just too dang proud to admit you got in over your head with this here school. You belong on your ranch, not seeing after other folk's young'uns."

"I am just as qualified as anyone to teach the children," she replied. "Besides, Ben doesn't want me to be at the ranch now. He said it was too dangerous with all the rustlers and squatters shooting at each other. So I might as well be teaching school."

The old man snorted in disgust and slapped the reins across Baby's back. The wagon lurched forward, and he called out, "If it's so simple, why don't you just tell him?"

"I will!" she answered in kind.

As she turned toward the boardinghouse Halley knew nothing with Ben Parrish would ever be simple.

The simmering undercurrents of the land war put a damper on the first day of school. The children filed solemnly into the classroom, the hard soles of their shoes drumming against the pale plank floor. Halley waved to the mothers lingering in the school yard, their careworn faces shadowed with worry.

School was the safest place for the children, many had decided. Boys old enough to ride the range with their fathers were hastily enrolled in school by mothers unwilling to risk their sons even for grazing land. Attendance was more than Halley had hoped for, but the motive behind it lessened any sense of accomplishment.

The women returned her greeting with halfhearted smiles before slowly turning to go home.

Halley stepped inside the schoolhouse and closed the double doors behind her, drawing a deep breath. Neatly combed heads turned as she made her way to the front of the classroom and stood before the sea of anxious faces.

"Good morning, everyone," she began.

"Good morning," a few of the children murmured.

"I had hoped you would all be as excited about this day as

I am." A few weak smiles were managed, but mostly wary faces looked back at her. "Being a student is one of the most fulfilling experiences you can have."

"We ain't never been students before," a towheaded boy in the second row informed her.

Halley refrained from correcting his grammar. She wanted to instill a passion for learning in these children, a desire to learn, not a fear of reprimand. She glanced at the roll, hoping she could remember as many names as possible.

"That's not entirely true, Michael." She smiled at his doubtful expression, a strategy forming in her mind. "Do you know how to saddle a horse?"

" 'Course I do," the young fellow replied. "My pa showed me."

"Really, what else has he taught you?"

"Oh, lots of stuff." He paused thoughtfully, shifting slightly in his seat. "He showed me how to chop wood, feed the animals, and when I get a little bigger I'm gonna learn how to shoot a gun."

"So you see, you've been a student for quite some time." When his expression grew puzzled, she explained, "Life is a learning process. We will learn many things together, but you all are students already . . . good students."

An aura of confidence seemed to settle over the class, and the anxious expressions melted away. Halley crossed her fingers as she took her seat behind the teacher's desk, praying her ploy was working.

"Before we begin our studies this morning, I want us all to get to know one another." She peered down while cautiously sliding open the top drawer of her desk. Relieved to find it free of reptiles, she continued, "I want each person to stand, introduce themselves, and share something special that you have learned to do."

Beginning with the older students, one by one they stood hesitantly and stammered their names and declared a skill they were proud of. Halley discreetly jotted the names down and noted what they had shared.

There was James, who could play his father's fiddle; Martha, who could speak her parents' native German; Ross Carson's daughters, Emma and Iris, whose mother was teaching them to piece quilts, and on and on the list grew.

Finally, Megan, the youngest student, rose from her front-row seat and smiled, revealing a missing front tooth. "I learned how to whistle, but I can't do it no more."

Giggles filtered through the classroom, and Halley hid a smile at the child's genuine bewilderment over the loss of her ability. "Perhaps when your new tooth comes in, you can whistle again. In the meantime we will find something else you can do."

"What about you, teacher?" Michael piped up. "What have you learned to do? My pa said when you come out here you didn't know your head from a hole in the ground."

Stunned, Halley could only gape at the child as the older children smothered their giggles with open palms.

"Well, Michael . . ." She found her voice and began searching for an answer. "When I first came to Wyoming—"

"My ma says you were probably disgraced, and that's why you ain't got a man," the girl across from Michael announced. With a boastful smile, she added, "She wouldn't tell me what that meant, but I know it's something really bad."

Halley's eyes narrowed as she studied the sassy redhead, and she had a pretty good idea who would be clapping erasers after school.

"Disgraced can be a bad thing, Janie." Halley spoke slowly, bolstering her patience. "But that's not why I came to Wilder."

"Then why did you come here?" Michael asked again.

"My uncle wanted me to live on his ranch after he died," she explained in her most matter-of-fact voice. "That was reason enough."

The morning went as well as Halley could hope. Many of the children, she was pleased to learn, could read a little and possessed basic math skills. Megan and the other younger pupils, however, would require patient tutoring in all areas.

When she announced that time had come for lunch, the children scrambled for their coats and dinner pails and out the back they ran. Halley hurried after them, her own coat tossed over one arm and the lunch Mrs. Porter had packed for her in the opposite hand.

Benches had been arranged on a grassy spot near the pump,

and the smaller children scrambled to sit beside Halley. The older boys rummaged through their lunches, anxious to try out the baseball gear Mr. Tulley had donated. Selecting only what they could manage with one hand and play baseball with the other, they assembled on the lot behind the school.

Halley and others sat in the waning autumn sunshine and looked on as balls were tossed back and forth, smacking loudly into stiff leather gloves.

"What did you bring for lunch, Miss Halley?" Megan's timid voice drew her attention.

"Let's see." Halley removed the white linen napkin, revealing tiny bundles neatly wrapped in similar cloth. The first was a sandwich of sliced hard-boiled egg on buttered bread, along with a large piece of gingerbread.

Each of the girls began rooting through her pail and declaring the contents. Trades were proposed and agreed on, and soon everyone was content. Halley discreetly divided her gingerbread with Megan.

"Good afternoon, Miss Halley," Jim Tulley called as he rounded the schoolhouse. "I see you're having recess."

Halley went along with the storekeeper's pretense of just happening by the school when the boys were playing baseball. "It's such a pretty day, we came outside for lunch, but the boys are more interested in sports than food."

"You've got a good day for it." He glanced up toward the fat clouds herding toward the plains. "Won't be long before winter sets in."

His gaze drifted back to the game. "Jimmy Franks!" he called out. "That's no way to hold a baseball bat, and John Robinson, you've got that glove on the wrong hand!"

Within minutes, Mr. Tulley himself stood with a bat in hand, demonstrating the proper stance. He leaned over the horseshoe marking home plate, his apron fluttering in the breeze, and swung the bat.

"See there?" He straightened and looked at the boys. "Easy as pie. Who wants to take a turn?"

They all shrugged and looked at one another. Finally, Daniel stepped forward. "I can do it."

The girls looked on as the boys took turns swinging at Mr. Tulley's pitches. There was great debate over what was a strike and what was a ball. On occasion, the bat would make solid contact, and the boys scrambled to retrieve the ball.

After a several boys had taken their turn, Janie rose from the group in disgust and trudged toward the pump.

"This ain't no fun," she grumbled, filling a dipper with water. "Just sitting around watching the boys have all the fun."

Halley hated to agree, but she knew Janie was right. She waited until the child had taken her seat. "What kind of games do you like to play?"

Janie drew herself up proudly and declared, "I can jump rope better than anybody."

"Well, I will see that we have a rope tomorrow," Halley assured her. "And you can teach the rest of us."

With very little grace or concern, Halley flopped across the narrow bed in her plain room at the boardinghouse. The lumpy mattress accepted her body without complaint, and she released a shuddering sigh of contentment.

By the second week, teaching school had ceased to be an adventure and had turned into a job. She arrived an hour before the students each morning and barely had everything ready when they arrived. The older children devoured their lessons as quickly as she could prepare them, and the younger ones required painstaking effort. Even now, she had a satchel full of papers to grade.

She cast a guilty glance toward the valise, knowing she should get started on them before supper. Just a quick nap, she rationalized, would enable her to stay up later and finish the work. *Forty winks and I'll be good as new.*

When next she opened her eyes, the room was draped in shadow, eerie shades of gray and purple. From somewhere in the distance, she heard her name.

"Halley! Are you all right in there?"

Dimly, she recognized Hazel Porter's voice, followed by an insistent knock.

"Coming," she managed, and forced herself to rise from the bed. She stumbled across the room and opened the door just enough to see out into the hall.

"Were you asleep?" Mrs. Porter asked, peering through the

open wedge. "You're not sick, are you?"

Halley was unable to suppress a yawn as she answered, "No, just a little tired."

"Well, get yourself tidied up, girl, you have a gentleman caller."

Her heart leaped. Had Ben ridden all the way into town just to pay her a call? Surely not, unless something was wrong. Eli! she thought, couldn't he ever keep a secret?

Hurriedly, she smoothed her sleep-mussed hair back in place and straightened her collar. In the dim shadows, she could only guess whether or not her face was flushed as she stared into the mirror.

Steadying herself as she went downstairs, Halley decided the best approach was to feign innocence until the last. She peered into the tiny parlor of the boardinghouse and found Ben standing before the fireplace. His back was to her, and she could only judge his mood by the relaxed stance.

"Good evening." She managed a cheerful tone as she entered the room.

He turned toward her. "Evening."

She thought he looked tired, but he returned her smile as she closed the door behind her. "This is a surprise. How are things on the ranch?"

"We're keeping busy," he assured her. "That's what I need to talk to you about."

She tensed.

"A man came through town today wanting to buy beef for the army," he explained. "I wanted to let him have fifty from your herd . . . better to sell them now than lose them during the winter."

"That sounds like a wise decision." Her relief over not being confronted about the school was swept aside by disappointment. In two weeks, the only thing he thought important enough to discuss with her was selling cattle.

"I think so," he agreed as she crossed the room. "All you need to do is sign these papers, and I'll deliver the cattle."

Once seated on the sofa, Halley bid him join her as she scanned the brief agreement. She glanced up to ask him a question and found him studying her with a hooded expression, and she knew cows were not what was uppermost in his mind. She swallowed hard when he reached out to smooth back an errant lock of hair from her temple, his fingers softly tracing the shell of her ear.

He breathed her name, and the paper slipped from her fingers and floated to the floor. His fingers steadied her head as he lowered his lips to hers, and she smoothed her palms over the fabric of his shirt.

The door suddenly burst open, and Mrs. Porter bustled into the parlor, bearing a tray of cookies and steaming cups of coffee. "Here you are, the coffee is fresh made, and the cookies just came out of the oven."

"Thank you," Halley managed as she fumbled to retrieve the fallen document and Ben rose from the sofa.

"Miss Halley!" Hazel's son, Brian, burst into the parlor. "After supper, will you help me study for the spelling test?"

She glanced toward Ben, standing by the fireplace. "Of course I will."

Mrs. Porter glanced at her son and chuckled. "He thinks having the teacher stay with us gives him the right to private lessons."

"Aw, Ma, she said she didn't mind."

"Miss Halley's tired after you young'uns run her ragged all day long," Mrs. Porter maintained. "Run along now, and get your chores done."

"All right, but she said she didn't mind." Brian crammed his hands in his pockets and left the parlor.

His mother shook her head. "Ben, I reckon Halley wishes you hadn't offered to work her place. Then she would have *had* to hire a teacher."

Mrs. Porter followed after her son and closed the door behind her, her lecture on manners audible. "Don't go busting in the parlor when grown folks are talking."

"Well, you do it all the time."

Their voices faded as they made their way toward the kitchen. Halley quickly reached for the plate of cookies, offering them to Ben with her most sincere smile.

He pushed the plate away. "How long did you think it would take me to figure out that you're teaching school?"

Halley winced. "I tried to tell you . . . but the time was never right."

To her amazement, he laughed. He raked a hand through his dark hair and laughed again.

"What are you laughing at?"

"Myself," he answered; and shook his head. "For the past two weeks I've been killing myself trying to work two herds of cattle. Now I find out you tricked me into working your place while you play schoolmarm."

"I didn't trick you," she insisted. "I told you, the right time just never came for me to explain everything."

"Right time for what?" he demanded, his humor disappearing. "You could have told me that night in the kitchen, instead of making your little speech about wanting to stay in Wyoming."

She glared at him. "I do want to stay in Wyoming."

"Sure you do." He crossed the room, advancing toward her until she was forced to sink down on the sofa. He stood over her, deliberately emphasizing his advantage of size. "You think I'll fight your battles, protect your cattle and land, and then when spring is here, you'll go back to playing cowboy just in time to cash in?"

"Ben, I *had* to teach school."

"Spare me, Halley. I don't want any more of your lies."

She rose to her feet, her sudden movement surprising him enough to move him back a step. "I never lied to you."

"No, you just don't tell the exact truth." He gripped her shoulders, roughly bringing her up against him. "Well, I've got a little truth for you. I won't run and fetch like one of those lapdogs who courted you in New York.

"Olson said I could take that land whenever I saw fit. The way I see it, I'm entitled to at least half of everything right now . . . land and cattle."

Halley stared up at him, torn between anger and desperation. She hated him for his threats and accusations, but she refused to plead with him not to take her home. All he would see was another advantage he held over her.

"Well, at least you're finally willing to admit that's what you really want." She twisted from his grasp and rushed toward the door and escape. "How dare you expect any woman to trust you?"

She jerked the parlor door open and rushed toward the stairs, barely reaching her room before giving way to sobs.

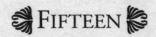

❧ FIFTEEN ❧

ROY TEAL SLAMMED the cell door and glared at his prisoners. "You fellas settle down. I don't tolerate no cussin' or fightin' in my jail."

He crossed the office and tossed the keys on his desk, grinning slightly at Ben. "Fine thing, taking a man away from his breakfast to accommodate cattle thieves."

"I did the hard work," Ben reminded him over a strong cup of coffee. "All you have to do is hold them until the marshal picks them up."

"Fair enough, but that could be three days." Settling behind his desk, the old lawman turned his attention to Clayton. "You all right, boy?"

A nod was the only response.

"He just got the wind knocked out him." Ben dismissed Roy's concern, not wanting to embarrass his brother. Clayton had ridden into a stand of trees after a stray and come face-to-face with three armed rustlers.

Fortunately, Ben had not been far behind and heard the startled exchange of voices. He drew his gun and rounded the corner just as the man in front raised his weapon and aimed at Clayton.

"They're lucky," Roy maintained. "Most that get caught don't live to see the inside of a jail."

"They almost didn't."

Ben thought of the man hanging facedown across the back of his own horse behind the sheriff's office. He had fired without thinking, knowing that Clayton would be dead if he didn't.

The sheriff nodded. "Anyone else would have strung those two right up alongside of him."

Ben shook his head. "I don't believe in lynching—it's a waste of good rope."

The sheriff laughed at that as he bent over and opened the bottom drawer of his desk. "Hell, I'll almost be glad to see bad weather set in. Maybe the rest of these thievin' bastards will find a nice fire to set by and forget about stealing beef."

Producing a bottle of whiskey, Roy poured a liberal amount into an empty cup and passed it to Clayton when Ben nodded in approval. "Here, boy, this'll put your legs back under you."

Clayton gulped the whiskey, still visibly shaken by the episode. By the age of twenty, most men had faced death a dozen times, but his years in Wyoming had been relatively uneventful.

The door burst open, admitting Warren Olson. "Good morning, Ben, I saw you ride in. We need to talk."

Ben set his coffee aside. "What's wrong?"

"Well, nothing, technically." The attorney glanced first at Roy then at Clayton, and then back to Ben. "I understand you're running your cattle on Miss St. John's land."

"No, that's not true." Ben hid a smile when he realized the attorney still had his nightshirt on under his expensive wool suit coat. "I've combined the herds; easier on the hands to keep them together, and easier to protect them."

"Legally, that could be construed as forfeiture on Miss St. John's part." Olson crossed the law office and poured himself a cup of coffee. "A judge could rule that she has violated the terms of the will and relinquished her rights to the land by living in town."

Ben folded his arms across his chest. "She's only staying at the boardinghouse while she teaches school."

"But that only makes things worse!" The attorney tasted the coffee and nearly choked. He gawked at Roy, demanding, "You call this coffee?"

The sheriff only shrugged, and Ben didn't wait for him to answer. "What do you mean, that only makes things worse?"

"Don't you see?" Olson set the coffee aside. "If she's living and *working* in town, that means she's not dependent on the land as her only source of income or a place to live."

Ben groaned inwardly. "She asked me to see after her place while she teaches school, that's all."

Olson shook his head. "It could still backfire. You have to convince her to move back to the ranch—immediately."

"If she does that, they'll have to shut the school down," Ben pointed out. "She'll never agree to that."

"She could lose the place if she doesn't." Olson fingered his chin thoughtfully. "The only other option is for you to seize the property."

Ben rose to his feet. "What?"

"I don't mean take it away from her, literally," Olson quickly amended. "You would only be transferring ownership to your name to protect her legally. Of course, no else must know that. For all practical purposes the ranch would still be hers."

A bitter taste settled in his throat, and Ben knew it had nothing to do with Roy's powerful coffee. He crossed the tiny room and stared out the window, watching a wagon jolt over the ruts in the muddy street. He still hadn't forgiven himself for making Halley cry, and he had practically promised to take the ranch away from her. She would only see this as a means of carrying out his threat.

No, she would never believe anything else, so she would have to make her choice. If she wanted to be a rancher, it was time she started acting like one, or, by God, go back to her comfortable life in the East.

He glanced back at the waiting attorney and shook his head. "She won't sign it over to me."

"Then you'll have to take it," Olson replied without hesitation. "If you don't, someone else will."

*　　*　　*

"Do you feel better now?" Halley smoothed Megan's bangs away from her face.

"Yes'm, I do." The little girl managed a smile, sniffling slightly.

Megan had stumbled trying to hurry down the steps during recess, scraping her knee. The injury was not serious, but Halley had rushed her to Mrs. Porter for a bandage and a cookie.

"We'd better get back." Halley replaced her lace handkerchief in the pocket of her skirt. "The others will think we've gotten lost."

As they neared the schoolhouse Halley could hear angry shouts and frightened cries. She dashed toward the back and found Jimmy Franks and Daniel Webber rolling on the ground, their faces streaked with dirt and blood.

"Stop it!" She rushed toward them, pushing past the other students who stood watching, some frightened, some cheering for a friend.

She rushed to pull Jimmy off of Daniel, but his strength surprised her. Daniel reached out and knotted his fingers in Jimmy's hair, gaining the advantage and rolling his opponent to the ground.

Halley's long skirts tangled in the exchange and she lost her balance and fell, still struggling to separate the two. Jimmy swung blindly, landing a doubled fist across Halley's cheek. She gasped, dimly aware of the smaller children crying hysterically.

Daniel fought back, his elbow colliding with Halley's bottom lip, and she tasted blood. She struggled to get between them, even if she separated them for only a moment, it might be enough to stop the fight. But the two boys were a tangle of swinging arms and legs, kicking up dirt. Halley tried to wedge herself between them, but the two boys just rolled over her in the heat of the battle.

Suddenly the weight was lifted from her and she looked up to see Ben holding Daniel at arm's length.

"What the hell is going on here?" he demanded, standing over Halley's prone form, staring at her in astonishment.

"He called my pa a thief!" Jimmy advanced, his face filled with blood and anger.

Clayton, who had arrived with his brother, moved quickly,

catching him by the collar, and holding him back.

"Your pa *is* a thief!" Daniel maintained, struggling to free himself from Ben's grasp. "A dirty, no-good horse thief, and my pa'll hang him if he comes snooping around our place again."

"That's enough!" Halley struggled to her feet, mortified to have Ben see her so out of control. "I'm ashamed of both of you. Fighting like commoners."

The younger children rushed to hide themselves in her skirts, their tiny fingers knotting in the black wool. She reassured each child with a touch and a hesitant smile.

Ben looked at her in disbelief. "Are you all right."

"Of course I am." She dismissed his concern and focused on regaining control of her class. "Clayton, will you take the children inside while I speak with Jimmy and Daniel?"

He nodded and released Jimmy with a warning look. He rounded the others toward the schoolhouse, assuring them that Halley would be along as soon as possible.

"Let's give them a chance to cool off and clean up first," Ben suggested. "I'll take Daniel over to Tulley's; there's a pump behind the store."

Once they were gone, Halley looked at Jimmy, but he wouldn't meet her eyes. She pumped water into the pail and bid him wash his face. When he had finished, she handed him the towel that was kept on a peg beside the pump.

"Jimmy, please, tell me what this is all about."

"Ever since we come here, folks have tried to run us off." He ran the towel over his face, leaving traces of blood on the white linen. "Men like Daniel's pa think they own whatever land they're standing on."

Halley remembered a discussion at the boardinghouse regarding the way smaller herds were scattered by the larger outfits in an attempt to maintain control over the free-range grazing land.

"Fighting won't solve such problems."

"Well, it's better than rolling over and taking it." He pinned her with dark, troubled eyes. "My pa just packs up and moves us off when trouble starts. He's never stood up to nobody."

*   *   *

Daniel Webber had definitely suffered the least physically, but his pride was hurting more. He splashed his face with water from Tulley's pump, and Ben didn't miss the sullen expression on his face.

"You ought not to have pulled me off him." He toweled water from the back of his neck. "I had him beat, if you'd stayed out of it."

Ben had always thought Daniel was a little big for his britches, but he'd never known the boy to be a bully. "What's your argument with Jimmy Franks?"

"My pa says those dirty nesters are taking over the territory." He scowled and tossed the towel over the pump handle. "Grazing their mangy cattle on our land."

"That's between your pa and Jimmy's."

Daniel glanced toward the school yard and then back at Ben. "You gonna tell my pa about this."

"I think that's something you need to do." When the boy made no reply, he added, "I think you owe Miss Halley an apology."

Daniel only nodded and turned toward the school. Ben followed him and found Halley waiting behind the school with Jimmy. He decided that Halley had gotten the worst of the fight. He should have ignored her staunch denial of any injury and checked for himself.

The two boys refused to look at one another, but Ben nudged Daniel forward to stand beside Jimmy. The look Halley leveled at them would have shamed a politician, and they both hung their heads.

Clearing her throat, she managed to speak in a steady voice. "You've upset the entire class, and someone could have been seriously hurt. I'll expect you both to stay after school this week and do cleanup work."

The two boys kept their eyes on the ground, nodding reluctantly.

"For now, I won't ask you to shake hands and be friends," Halley concluded. "But I expect you both to behave like gentlemen while you're in school. Now go inside and take your seats."

When she turned to follow after them, Ben reached out and caught her arm. She frowned at him over her shoulder and said, "I have to get back to class."

"You'd better get cleaned up first," he advised.

She felt her lip and grimaced at the blood on her fingertips. She nodded and allowed him to lead her to the pump. Despite her protests, he carefully felt her ribs and arms to be sure nothing was sprained or broken.

Satisfied that she was not seriously hurt, Ben unknotted the bandanna at his throat and dabbed at Halley's bloody lip. She tried to look away, but he turned her face back to his. He grazed his thumb over the already puffy bruise under her eye and she winced.

"You're going to have quite a shiner," he warned as he held the bandanna under a stream of cold water from the pump. He squeezed the excess water from the cloth and pressed it against her face.

She was so damned pretty, even with her face bruised and dirty. He gently drew the cloth off her delicate features, erasing the smudges of dirt and the blood smeared on her chin. With his other hand, he smoothed her disheveled hair from her face, tracing her swollen lip with the damp cloth.

Her eyes widened slightly, and he knew she wouldn't turn away if he kissed her. He leaned forward to brush his lips against hers, but even the slightest pressure against her mouth caused her to flinch.

She took the cloth from his hand and held it to her mouth. "I suppose, now, you'll tell me that I shouldn't be teaching school."

That was exactly what he had come to tell her, only it had nothing to do with the fight between the two boys. He hadn't planned on seeing her the moment he left the sheriff's office, nor had he decided the best way to convince her to move back to the ranch. How could he tell her it was to save the land, after he'd all but vowed to take it from her himself?

"Well, it won't do you any good." She raised her chin in defiance, not waiting for his answer. "The students do respect me, and if I quit now, they'll never trust or respect anyone who takes my place."

"*Is* there anyone who could take your place?"

Her eyes widened slightly in surprise. "Of course not. That's why I'm teaching; there wasn't anyone."

"When you spoke to the school board, you said that there were plenty of women applying for teaching positions in the West."

"Well, no one wanted to come to Wilder." Flustered, she glanced back toward the schoolhouse. "If I don't teach, the school will close. Don't think for a minute that I'll let that happen."

Winter was late in arriving, but when it did, it seemed determined to make up for lost time. Since before sunup, Ben had ridden with the hands to round the herd toward a sheltered spot where they might wait out the storm. The snow had finally stopped, but the wind felt colder than before.

They had done all they could to protect the cattle, but it never seemed enough. Even a mild winter could cost a man a fourth of a herd, and he wished now he'd sold more to the army.

He motioned for the hands to follow him as he turned for the nearest shelter—the bunkhouse at Halley's ranch. When they rode into the lot, Eli stepped out of the rickety building and waved in greeting.

"Get these horses in the barn," Eli ordered one of the men. "There's plenty of hay and grain, and I'll have a pot of coffee waitin' on you when you get done."

The old man followed after the younger ones, advising them on the best way to care for horses that have been out in the cold. Ben didn't hear what one man told Eli, but the chorus of laughter that followed and Eli's bluster of curses gave him a pretty good idea. The old man couldn't bear to have his counsel rejected.

Ben stood in the lot, glancing toward the little cabin, and thought of Halley. He still faced the task of convincing her to return to the ranch, but how?

He scaled the front steps and glanced around the snow-covered porch. A forgotten cup, filled with snow, sat waiting on the railing as if someone would be right out to claim it. He picked up the cup, knocked the snow onto the ground, and opened the door with the excuse of returning the mug to the kitchen.

Ben hesitated only a moment before closing the door behind

him. He stood in the center of the room, acutely aware of the
way Halley's presence lingered in the house. Subtle changes
were everywhere—lacy curtains, a starched white tablecloth,
and the delicate hint of lavender, which teased his senses as
if she were just in the next room.

He moved into the kitchen and leaned against the doorjamb,
taking note of the tiny feminine touches. When Pete was alive
the room had been neat and serviceable, meeting the basic
needs, but this was a woman's kitchen, a sweet mixture of
beeswax, scoured pots, and the mingled scents of clove and
starched linen.

He crossed the scrubbed floor, fingered the cheery gingham
curtains framing the kitchen window, and thought of Halley
hanging them. He noticed the sill contained other remnants of
her—a jar of hand cream, a forgotten thimble, and an opened
letter. Curiosity outweighed guilt and he lifted the envelope,
not surprised by the New York City postmark.

A newspaper clipping slipped from the torn envelope and
fell into the empty, dry sink. He retrieved the clipping and
read the words HEIRESS FLEES FOR THE FRONTIER. Ben rea-
soned that there was nothing dishonest about reading a newspaper clipping—it was not the same as reading someone's
mail.

Ben read in disbelief the almost gloating account of how
Halley had been relieved of her family's fortune by a swindler.
With her bank accounts depleted and stock in the family business worthless, creditors had seized her home and all property
deemed salable to pay the mountains of overdue debt and
taxes.

Very little was said against the man who had taken her
money, but Halley was soundly criticized for blindly trusting
someone of questionable character.

Now he understood her outrage over Pete's arrangement
regarding her inheritance. The very idea of anyone having control over her property was without a doubt her worst night-
mare, and his threats to take the land away had undoubtedly
confirmed her every fear.

Ben glanced out the frosted glass of the kitchen window
and studied the prairie, lightly dusted with the early snow, and
cursed the plans he had made for the land when Halley left

Wyoming. The fact that he would have paid her a fair price didn't ease his conscience. He had justified everything with the rationalization that she would be returning to a life of wealth and privilege.

The ranch was all she had in the world, her home, her only refuge, and no amount of money could compensate her for such a loss twice in one lifetime. If Halley left Wyoming, she would have nowhere to go, and she would never sell the ranch for enough money to sustain her for a lifetime.

His dilemma over the ranch instantly became a burden. She would never willingly give him title to the land, but he couldn't risk doing nothing and seeing her lose everything she owned. He would have to persuade her, somehow, to return to the ranch.

He folded the clipping and opened the envelope to replace it. The letter within would reveal more of Halley's carefully guarded secrets, but he couldn't bring himself to read it. She would be mortified if she knew he had learned what he had.

The thud of footsteps jolted him from his thoughts, and he hurriedly replaced the envelope where it had been. He braced his hands against the counter and pretended to stare out into the frozen morning.

"Coffee's on in the bunkhouse, and I got a batch of corn bread ready for the skillet." Eli made his way into the kitchen, his scraggly beard frosted with new snowflakes. He glanced pointedly toward the window before saying, "I ain't gonna cook in here. Lord knows I'd never get it back clean enough to suit her."

A halfhearted smile touched his lips as Ben imagined Halley scolding Eli over a dirty skillet. Reluctantly, he turned away from the window and asked, "Did you get the horses put away?"

The old man nodded. "The boys are rubbing them down now. They'll be good as new after a good feed. It's that mule I'm worried about."

"What's wrong with the mule?"

"The fool critter's pining away for Missy!" he exclaimed. "Won't even eat his oats."

Ben thought back to the first day he'd met Halley and re-called taking her to the livery. She had walked into the dusty stable in her fine clothes looking for a sturdy mount, and she had purchased an abandoned mule instead, because he ate candy out of her hand.

Did she somehow feel akin to the beast? Two lost souls needing a place to call home. What it must have cost her to know he could take her security away from her at anytime.

He looked up to find Eli watching him through narrowed eyes. "She sets a great store by that critter. I'd sure hate to see anything happen to him."

Halley looked up to find the children watching her with guarded expressions, their lessons forgotten on their desks. Her solemn mood had dampened the usual high spirits of the classroom, and she knew she should be ashamed for letting the children suffer for her unhappiness.

She was miserably homesick, and longed to return to the beauty of the ranch. The lamb would be fully grown before the semester ended, and she worried how the old hen and her brood of chicks were faring the cold weather. She had missed New York, but she grieved for the ranch.

Even when she did return home, she would still face the loss of her ties to Ben. She couldn't forget the anger on his face or the hard edge in voice when he had accused her of tricking him. Maybe she had.

She was accustomed to the social sparring of the Manhattan elite, where Ben's brutal kind of honesty was reserved only for deathbed confessions. All she wanted to do was save face and save the school, never dreaming she would hurt Ben in the process.

"Miss Halley, you ain't—*haven't* smiled one time in two days"—Michael finally spoke up—"and you haven't read none to us."

"I've had worries on my mind," she said by way of excuse. "I'm sorry if I've neglected you."

"Well, you could make it up by reading a story," the little boy suggested. " 'Specially one of them adventure stories."

The other students were quick to agree, and Halley surrendered, instructing them to put their lessons aside for now.

She rose from her seat and opened Mr. McClinton's journal.

Perching herself on the corner of the desk, she turned the pages and began to read aloud.

" 'One of my most harrowing experiences was the time I single-handedly foiled a bank robbery in progress. I had business at the Farmer's Trust Bank of Kansas City and entered the establishment, never dreaming such a simple act would put my very life in jeopardy.' "

A ripple of excited whispers reached her ears, and she cleared her throat and forced a dramatic note to her voice.

" 'The clerks stood like scarecrows, motionless, with arms raised toward the ceiling. One culprit, whose face was hidden behind a dirty bandanna, whirled to face me, sunlight glinting off the barrel of his pistol.' "

"I'll bet it was Jesse James!" Michael cried out, enthralled by the thought.

"Jesse James only robs trains," another boy contended. "I say it was the Daltons."

Before she could silence the debate over the identity of the bank robber, Halley turned at a sound from the frosted window—a muffled thud. She listened, but didn't hear it again.

She cleared her throat, and silence fell over the room. She returned to the story and read, " 'I could feel the hair on the back of my neck stand up, and I knew I would have to act quickly or—' "

She heard it again! This time the tapping was forceful enough to rattle the pane slightly. She rose from the desk and approached the window. Again, she heard a muffled thud against the glass.

She hesitated only a moment before raising the window. Immediately, the mule's head crowded the opening, his long tapered ears ducking under the sash.

"Baby!" she gasped, placing her hands on either side of his face. Tears sprang to her eyes as she pressed her forehead against his, and the children scrambled from their desks and crowded around the window. The mule bravely endured their groping hands, content at last under the loving touch of his mistress.

Halley forced the window fully open and looked out to see Ben leaning against the schoolhouse, watching her with a gratified expression. She gaped at him in disbelief. She barely managed words enough to ask, "Baby let you ride him to town?"

"I'm not fool enough to risk my neck on that ornery beast." He motioned toward his own horse nearby, harnessed to a large wagon. "I hitched him up with the General, and he knew who was boss."

The look that passed between them spoke volumes, filling her heart with love, and she was overwhelmed at the thought of anyone realizing how much she had missed the ranch. Seeing Baby was the next best thing to going home. Ben Parrish might be stubborn and arrogant, but he understood her heart, if nothing else.

She wanted to run to him and tell him that no one had ever done anything so thoughtful for her, and that she was sorry for not telling him about the school.

"Why?"

"He missed you."

Ben turned toward the wagon and retrieved a set of sleigh bells from the back of wagon, shaking them, as if to test their loudness. "Besides, children don't want to waste the first day of snow sitting indoors."

Chimes of agreement rose from the cluster of children, each child begging her, *please*, to let them go.

"Ma always lets us play out in the snow," Michael insisted. At Halley's dubious look, he added, "If we bundle up."

Halley glanced over the collection of anxious, pleading faces and then back at Ben. The man was stingy with smiles, but when he gave one, it was enough to melt her heart. She returned the grin and ordered, "Everyone get your coats and hats, and don't forget your mittens!"

The unexpected attack sent the boys diving for cover, and Ben swore as a second snowball disintegrated into a thousand tiny slivers of ice and slipped past the collar of his shirt. He whipped his head around to find that Halley had led her battalion behind them. An ambush!

In the boys-against-girls battle for the hill, the boys were losing badly. Halley was crouched behind a pine tree, ordering her troops to take the hill, and he hastily began making a snowball. The boys had let their ammunition run out, and he would have to hurry before she ducked back behind the tree.

Just as he prepared to fire he heard the distinct whir of a snowball coming toward him and made the mistake of looking up. The ball knocked his hat from his head, and Halley laughed with delight.

"I'll get you for that." He scooped enough snow from the ground to double the size of the snowball in his hand and advanced toward her.

She screamed and turned, running toward cover, but he was on her heels. He caught her around the waist and they tumbled to the ground, rolling a little ways down the hill. She laughed even harder, collapsing in the powdery snow.

"You're a cheat," he railed, staring down at her smiling face. She laughed again, her face flushed pink with delight.

"And you're a sore loser," she countered, reaching up to brush snowflakes clinging to his face.

He caught her fingers in his and kissed the inside of her palm. Her hand was cold from wielding snowballs, and he reached for her other hand, warming them in his gloved palms. "You shouldn't take your gloves off like that."

"You have to make snowballs with your bare hands," she insisted. She trembled when he kissed her fingertips. "The heat from your skin packs them solid. That's why my team won."

"I'll remember that." He kissed the tip of her nose, resisting the urge to taste her lips. He needed to talk to her about the ranch and somehow convince her to give up the school for now. "Halley, there's something you need to know—"

"There's something I need to tell you." She pressed her fingertips against his mouth, silencing his well-chosen words. "Ben, I was wrong for not telling you that I would be teaching. I should have trusted you, but I was so afraid something might go wrong and the school would fail. I just couldn't take that chance."

"No one would blame you."

"I would blame myself," she countered. "It's the first thing I've ever done that was worthwhile. All my life, so much has been taken for granted, but this was the first thing I ever had to fight for, and I won."

The solemn expression on her face mingled pride and gratitude. "I couldn't have done it without you, and I promise never to mistrust you again."

He drew a troubled breath and pressed his lips into her palm once again. "No matter what, I want you to know that I would never do anything to hurt you."

"Ben, I never really thought you would," she was quick to reassure him, smoothing her hand over his jaw. "It's just that . . . well, I know the consequences of trusting the wrong people."

He should have let it go at that, but he didn't. If only she would tell him about the trouble in New York, he could then warn her that she stood to lose her ranch without wounding her pride. He certainly couldn't admit to reading her mail.

Cautiously, he pressed the subject. "People in New York?"

Her expression became guarded, and she shifted to free herself from beneath his weight. "It was a long time ago."

He knew better than to ask anything else, and rose to help her to her feet.

She glanced around the clearing. "Do you think it's safe out here for the children?"

"We'll be all right this close to town," he assured her. "But I want to get everyone home before dark."

Before she could answer, a snowball smashed against Ben's shoulder, showering her face with icy flakes. They looked up to find that the opposing forces had united in a mutiny against the grown-ups. Suddenly the air was filled with flying snowballs, and Ben and Halley were forced to surrender.

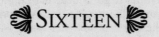

SIXTEEN

"Good night, Miss Halley!"

"Good night, girls," Halley replied as Ben hefted the Mitchell children down from the wagon. They ran toward the front porch, where their parents stood waiting in the open door.

"Ma! We had a snowball fight!" Ella exclaimed breathlessly.

"The *girls* won," Polly declared, making her way up the stairs after her younger sister.

"That's fine, girls." Delia prodded them into the house. "Supper's waiting for you on the table."

Halley waved to Delia, who closed the door once the girls were inside and followed her husband down the front steps.

"You folks come on in for supper." Mr. Mitchell extended his hand to Ben. "There's always plenty."

Delia made her way to Halley's side of the wagon. "Don't tell me you've been playing in the snow like a young'un."

"Yes, indeed." Halley smiled at her friend. "I believe Mr. Parrish was quite surprised by my ability to throw a snowball."

"She cheats," Ben clarified.

Tom laughed out loud. "Never knew a woman yet to fight fair."

"How about some supper?" Delia offered.

"Thank you, but I have to get Halley back to town," Ben explained. "It's getting late."

"You'd better not be on the road after dark." Tom Mitchell's face sobered, and Delia was quick to agree.

"In fact, I was just fixing to send Tom looking for you all." Delia exchanged a troubled glance with her husband.

Ben's shoulders tensed and he asked, "What's happened, Tom?"

"Coop came riding through here, 'bout two hours ago, with his pack of hired guns." The older man shook his head. "He claims those nesters up in the northern tip of the county are cutting his herd."

"He's just looking to stir up trouble," Delia cut in. "Wanted Tom to ride up there with him and chase them out."

"Everybody knows he's been running his cattle on that land without offering to buy it."

"We've all been guilty of that," Ben reminded him. "But that doesn't give the cattlemen any more claim on the land than the nesters."

"Cooper Eldridge doesn't think so," Delia informed him. "He's determined to run them off, and he wants to drag the rest of us into the fight."

"You folks had better get somewhere safe before dark," Mr. Mitchell advised. "And stay there."

Ben glanced at Halley before answering. "Don't worry, Tom, we will."

"Give me just a minute to pack up some supper for you," Delia insisted, turning toward the house. "I don't want it said that anyone went away from my house hungry."

The house and the bunkhouse had been deserted when they arrived, and Halley was alarmed for Eli's safety.

"I told him he ought to go to my place for the night," Ben assured her. "I hadn't planned on coming back here."

"Should we join them at your house?"

He considered it but decided that traveling any farther

would be dangerous, now that night had fallen. "We'd better stay put. You go on in the house; I'll put the horse away."

She was still lighting the kerosene lamps when he entered the house. It was cold and musty from being shut up for so many weeks, and he quickly went about building a fire. Soon the kindling blazed, and she sought out the coffeepot, filling it with water, and the tin of coffee.

Halley settled herself before the hearth and spread her palms over the warmth of the new fire. She shivered, unable to keep from complaining. "I'm freezing, Ben."

He gave her a slight grin and continued stabbing the logs with the poker. The coffeepot sat on the grate, hissing as the flames grazed its pewter bottom. "The coffee will take a while, but the fire should knock the chill off the room pretty soon."

Halley sat back on the blankets they had spread before fireplace, hugging her knees against her. It felt so good to be back in her little cabin, despite the cold.

Ben reached for the supper basket Delia had packed, sliding it between them. "I don't know about you, but I'm starved. Let's eat; the coffee should be ready soon."

Grateful for Delia's thoughtfulness, Halley pulled back the linen cloth and studied the basket's contents—fresh bread, sliced beef, yellow cheese, and a thick wedge of Delia's famous applesauce cake.

With her mother's silver, Halley sliced the bread and forked the beef onto plain tin plates and they ate in companionable silence. When the coffeepot quieted, Ben filled their cups.

"I'm sorry we couldn't get back to town before dark." He set his plate on the hearth and sat back, balancing his weight on one elbow as he tasted the coffee.

"That's all right," Halley answered as she popped the last bite of cake into her mouth. "In fact, I'd rather be here, even if it's just for the weekend."

"The boardinghouse doesn't suit you?" he asked, fingering the rim of his cup

"It's not home."

She gathered the dishes and remnants of their supper and carried them into the kitchen. She glanced around her little home, then studied the shelf containing her keepsakes from

New York. She plucked a forgotten snow globe from behind a picture frame—a scene of Central Park in winter with skaters on the pond.

Returning to the fireside, Halley held the delicate piece out to Ben, the amber glow of the fire shining like sunshine over the skaters. Ben took the globe from her hand and gently swirled the snowflakes into a flurry of white.

"When I was a child, I loved to skate in the park," she whispered, taking the globe from his hand. The snowflakes slowly settled to the bottom of the globe. "I would bribe the servants to take me."

She studied the scene. "I was there this time last year, never dreaming the next winter would find me on a cattle ranch in the middle of Wyoming."

"Are you sorry about that?"

The question was a whisper against her ear, and she looked up to find herself lost in the pale blue of his eyes. "No," she managed. "Are you sorry you came to Wyoming?"

A wry grin touched his lips. "I've never really thought about it. I suppose not."

"I thought perhaps you wished you had remained in Texas," she hinted shamelessly. "Were you happy there?"

"I thought I was." He stared into the fire. "I had everything that should make a man happy, but I couldn't pretend anymore."

Her heart leaped at the revelation, and she held her breath hoping he would tell her the rest.

"I married the daughter of a prominent judge. Her daddy saw to it that I received my commission as an officer in the Rangers." He shook his head at the absurdity. "I was foolish enough to believe it was because I had done a hell of a job."

Halley reached to cover his hand with hers. "I'm sure you were a fine lawman."

"I was," he assured her. "That's the hell of it. I really busted my ass, but all anyone saw was the son-in-law of a crooked politician."

Halley gasped. "He was dishonest?"

Ben chuckled and squeezed her hand. "I was surprised myself. The day soon came when it was time to pay him back for my rank. He wanted some evidence to disappear . . . without a trace.''

"Oh, Ben, you didn't—''

"No, I was still young enough to believe in ethics. I refused and found myself facing the threat of a court-martial.''

"Your wife allowed her father to mistreat you so?'' Halley felt her anger rise against the woman who'd betrayed him, and she laced her fingers with his.

"I didn't blame her at the time, and really not even now.'' He stared into the crackling fire, no trace of bitterness on his face. "Judith had known money all her life, and choosing me over her daddy would have left her without a cent.''

Judith. Halley tried to put a face with that name. She repeated the name silently, deciding that it suited someone cold and unfeeling. How could anyone turn her back on love for the sake of money?

"Money isn't everything.'' Halley thought of the friends she'd had in New York; during her ordeal, not one had offered her a word of comfort or a deed of kindness.

"It is when you find yourself without any.'' He pinned her with a knowing look. "If I had stayed in Texas, he would have ruined me and my family. I had to think of my mother and Clayton.''

"So you came to Wyoming,'' she concluded, struck by the similarities in their lives. They had both known betrayal and loss, and they had both come to Wyoming to start again.

Only Ben had succeeded whereas she had just begun, and even now her claim on the land and her home remained precarious. Guilt assailed her that she lacked the courage to confess her own misfortune after he had so honestly shared his painful past. But while Ben's past was safely behind him, hers still lingered in the shadows, waiting to pounce on her and destroy any remaining chance she had for happiness.

"In answer to your question, no.'' His voice drew her attention and she looked up to find him studying her. "I'm not sorry I came out here. What about you?''

"Me?''

"Are you sorry you left New York and came out here?'' He leaned forward and studied her face, as if not expecting a truthful answer.

"No, I'm not sorry." At that moment she was almost grate-
ful to Richard Farnsworth for leaving her broke. She touched
Ben's face and thought how empty her earlier life had been.
"I would have never met you in New York."

His mouth brushed against hers and Halley felt a shiver that
had nothing to do with the chill of a winter evening. His mouth
quickly became more demanding as he leaned over her. Her
arms went around his neck as he eased her to the floor, passion
washing over them like an unrelenting storm.

His lips were gentle, molding hers like hot wax. He deepened the kiss, and there was no shyness as his tongue joined
with hers.

She knotted her fingers in the dark hair spilling over his
collar, and his mouth became hot and urgent. He leaned over
her, their bodies a tangle of legs, boots, and skirts.

Halley stared up at Ben, her eyes widened, but not with
fear. He smoothed her tousled hair back from her face and
gently traced her kiss-swollen lips.

"Ben, I—"

"Shh." He pressed his fingers against her mouth, fearing
any protest she made would make sense. "I've wanted you
since the day you stepped off that stage. Don't tell me why
we shouldn't be together, just tell me whether or not you want
me. I'll understand."

Halley swallowed. She wanted Ben, loved him with all her
heart, and she hoped that love would be enough to make up
for the bitterness of his past. She lightly kissed his fingertips
and whispered, "I don't want anything to keep us apart, now
or ever."

She trembled as his fingers left her lips and trailed up the
delicate line of her face. He lowered his head and claimed the
sweetness of her mouth in a long, languid kiss, a kiss that left
no doubt as to his intentions.

Halley felt crushed beneath his weight, but her arms tightened around his neck, as if to draw him closer. She knew she
should protest, but her mind couldn't form the words.

He deepened the kiss, and she felt his breathing grow labored. The hand that had gently caressed her cheek now tangled in her hair, holding her still for the demands of his

passion. She felt his other hand moving over her shoulders to gently knead her breast.

His fingers tugged at the buttons of her blouse, and his hand eased the garment back from her shoulders.

The shirtwaist fell down her arms and her breasts were visible through the thin material of her chemise. Without warning, Ben claimed one rose-peaked mound with his mouth, and Halley gasped at the searing heat. Her whole body tingled, and she moaned aloud as his tongue teased the taut nipple.

Sensing her arousal, Ben reclaimed her mouth with a savage kiss, and she felt his fingers hook in the straps of her chemise. Once the fragile garment was removed, he rose to his feet and shed his jeans and boots. He returned to her side quickly, tossing his shirt to the floor.

Claiming her lips again, Ben settled her against the makeshift bedding. She shuddered at the feel of his masculine chest pressed against the softness of hers. His hand skimmed her waist and loosened the buttons securing her remaining undergarments.

The lacy drawers slid easily over her hips and down her legs, and she had to look away from the searing expression of pure lust on his face as he beheld her nakedness. She jumped at the feel of his palm sliding over her thigh, and he kissed her, long and deep, as his hand slid between her legs.

"Halley?" He gazed into her eyes as if searching her soul. "I don't want to hurt you, so I have to ask—"

"Never," she whispered the answer.

He kissed her and she tried not to stiffen as his fingers explored the nether regions of her body. Heat pooled between her thighs, and the muscles in her belly tightened. She gave a startled cry, tearing her mouth from his, as he eased one long finger into her.

"Shh, relax, sugar," he whispered, tracing the shell of her ear with his tongue. He began to move his finger in and out of her body, increasing the pleasure. His thumb brushed over her mound, finding the sensitive nub.

She gasped at the exquisite pleasure of his touch and clung to broad shoulders, her hips moving against his hand. He kissed her, easing his body over hers, and the feel of his skin against hers caused her to whimper.

Balancing his weight on his forearms, Ben parted her silken thighs, the feel of her creamy skin cool against the heat of his. He drew a ragged breath, knowing he had to maintain control over the lust that was pumping through him. He didn't want to hurt her more than what was inevitable.

He settled himself in the cradle of her thighs and kissed her as he nudged the tip of his throbbing length into the warmth of her body.

She stiffened at the first tentative intrusion of her body, and he kissed her, long and deep. He felt her relax beneath him and eased his body into hers in one swift thrust. He groaned as her warm tight flesh enveloped him, and her keening gasp of pain tore at his heart.

Halley had known what to expect, but the reality of penetration was something she could never have anticipated. The sharp pain was startling, but Ben kissed her until she was drugged with desire. The pain subsided and he began to move within her, sending waves of pleasure rippling over her body.

His lips left hers only to travel the line of her throat, seeking the tender swell of her breast. He anticipated her every reaction, and she felt awkward, wanting to please him but not sure how.

Heat washed over her, coiling between her thighs, and her nails dug into shoulders. He caught her hips in his large hands and guided her movements in rhythm with his own. The heat became unbearable, and she cried out as her body went rigid and then shattered into a million fragments of pleasure.

He began to move faster, his flesh slick with perspiration, and he groaned her name as he collapsed, sated, in her arms.

Ben stepped out into the eerie stillness of the dawn, relieved that the snow had stopped. The landscape was draped in the first blush of sunrise, and he scanned the ground for telltale tracks in the snow. Satisfied that no riders had been anywhere near the house or the barn, he made his way to tend the waiting livestock.

He opened the barn door and stepped into the warmth of the shadowed building. His own horse nickered in welcome, anticipating the morning oats. The mule, however, gave him an accusing stare before looking away with a swish of his tail.

Ben shook his head at the mule's arrogance. He peered into the stall to see that the lamb had moved in with the mule— only he wasn't a lamb anymore. His wool was thick and shaggy, and he had grown considerably, taking up more than his share of the stall.

As he scooped the oats his thoughts returned to the previous night. Everything had been so simple then. He wanted Halley, and she had wanted him. Afterward, when she had remained in his arms before the fire, he'd waited for her to reveal her true reason for coming to Wyoming. Instead she had drifted off to sleep, with her secrets still unshared.

The attorney's warning about Halley's precarious legal situation still preyed on his mind. He should have come right out and told her that she had to forget the school and get back to the ranch, and he should have told her the minute they returned to the house.

Now he faced the insurmountable challenge of convincing her that their lovemaking had nothing to do with wills or deeds, but that she stood to lose the land if she continued to teach. Either way she would be miserable . . . and either way she would blame him.

Halley squeezed her eyes against the sunlight streaming through her window. She stretched beneath the bedclothes, painfully aware of her bare skin against the sheets. The room held no morning chill, and she realized that Ben must have built up the fire. She strained to hear any sound coming from the room below, but only silence met her ears.

During the night, they had left the fireside for the comfort of her bed, savoring each other until the wee hours, when sleep had overcome her. The morning brought uncertainty, and she was grateful to awaken alone.

She combed her tousled hair back from her face and glanced around the room. Ben's clothes were nowhere in sight, and hers were neatly draped over the rocking chair. Had he left, or was he merely outside?

She tugged the tangled comforter from the bed and wrapped it around her bare body before crossing the tiny room. Staring out the window, she was awed by the snow-covered scene. A lone set of footprints in the snow led from the house to the barn, and she could only guess that Ben was inside the barn, caring for the animals.

The thought of Ben contending with Baby made her smile. She still marveled that the mule had allowed him to hitch and drive him into town, and that a man would go to such trouble for the sentimental love of an animal. In all her life, no one had ever done anything so thoughtful for her.

She still felt a twinge of guilt over all the accusations she had made toward him. Surely, *surely*, if Ben had any dishonorable intentions toward her or the land, he would have acted by now.

Besides, Uncle Peter would never have appointed Ben to be her adviser if he were a scoundrel. She bit her bottom lip and pondered the situation. She could, quite possibly, be putting herself in more jeopardy by not making him aware of how important the ranch was to her.

The barn door swung open and she caught sight of Ben emerging, his hat low on his head. He huddled deep inside his coat and made long, quick strides toward the house. Desperately, she glanced back toward her neatly folded clothes, knowing there wasn't time to dress.

She heard the door open downstairs and the sound of him stomping snow from his boots. He closed the door, and she could hear him moving about the living room. A log was dropped on the fire, and she heard the lid to the coffeepot clink shut.

You can't stay up here all day.

If she was going to tell him about her misfortune in New York, she had better do it now.

Steeling her nerves, Halley wrapped the comforter more securely about her and made her way down the ladder. When she reached the bottom rung, she felt his hands on her shoulders, his touch burning through the thick down.

"Good morning," she managed, shivering at the feel of his lips grazing the nape of her neck.

"Hmm," was his only response before turning her around. His clothes were cold from outdoors, and she shivered against him, gasping as his hands slid under the comforter.

He kissed her, and the carefully thought out words left her mind. She hung in his arms, and the comforter pooled around her feet. His hands slid over her nude body, cupping her buttocks and grinding her hips against his.

"Ben," she gasped, turning away from his hungry mouth. "I need to talk to you."

He pulled back and studied her for a moment, then dropped his head to nuzzle her neck and whispered, "I need to talk to you, too."

The peaceful moment was suddenly shattered by riders barreling into the lot, shouting for Ben. He glanced toward the window and breathed a curse. Snatching the comforter from the floor, he thrust it into her arms and ordered, "Get dressed, quick!"

Ben slammed the door behind him and stepped out onto the porch just as Frank Morgan swung down from his horse.

"Mount up, Ben," Frank told him. "Tom Mitchell's barn burned to the ground last night, and they shot two of his men."

"Dead?"

"No, Creek says they'll make it, but they won't be of any use to Tom if those bastards come back." Frank leveled his gaze with Ben's. "This thing is getting out of hand, and it won't be long before someone does end up dead."

Ben glanced up toward the tiny window of the loft bedroom, grateful now that his lust had gotten in the way of discussing the ranch with Halley. He had every intention of telling her that she had no choice but to give up the school and move back to the ranch. One look at the comforter sliding off her bare shoulders, and all he could think about was getting her back up to that bedroom.

He couldn't stay behind to protect her, and he damn well wasn't leaving her alone with packs of hired killers on the loose. He would deal with Olson later, but for now Halley's safety was all that mattered.

He turned back to Frank and nodded in agreement. "We'll just have to put a stop to it, once and for all. Where is Eli?"

"He's helping Creek tend those boys. Why?"

"Someone will have to take Halley back to town. I don't want her traveling alone."

Frank quirked an eyebrow and glanced up toward the window himself. He barely hid a smile when he met Ben's scowl.

"Tom is sending his womenfolk into town until the danger passes, I reckon they can pack her along."

Before Ben could decide whether to ignore Frank's obvious amusement with the situation or knock the hell out of him, the front door burst open and Halley stood looking out at him with wide, frightened eyes.

"Ma'am," Frank said, and touched the brim of his hat.

She nodded and asked, "Ben, what's happened?"

"They burned Tom Mitchell's barn last night." Her face went pale, and he reached out to steady her against him. "Delia and the girls are going into town, and I want you to go back with them."

"Yes, of course," she breathed. "Poor Delia, she'll need me to help her get the girls packed."

"Get your things," he instructed. "I'll saddle the horses."

When he emerged from the barn, leading the horse and mule, she was waiting for him on the porch. She descended the steps, her buttontop shoes sinking in the snow. He hurried to meet her, taking her in his arms.

"Frank will take you to the Mitchells," he whispered against her hair. "I'm going to check on my place. I left Clayton there alone."

She nodded, tightening her arms around his waist.

"Please be careful," she whispered against his lips. New snowflakes whirled between them, clinging to the thick fringe of lashes. Her eyelids fluttered and he kissed the flakes away.

"I'm always careful," he reminded her.

❧ SEVENTEEN ❧

"I AIN'T HAVIN' no sheep in my livery stable!"

Halley patiently listened to Gus Mahoney's tirade against sheep and sheepherders and how he had no intention of boarding her lamb, now a full grown sheep, in his place of business.

"Every cattleman in the territory will be looking to stretch my neck!" He glowered down at the woolly sheep at her side. "No, ma'am, I can't help you."

"Mr. Mahoney, I understand your reservations," she responded in her most self-possessed voice. "But, please, consider my predicament—Baby and Niles have become attached to one another. I cannot separate them, and I cannot leave them alone on the ranch with no one to tend to them while I teach school."

The mule nudged Halley's shoulder, and she stroked his forehead, hoping to reassure him. She could sense his reluctance to enter the livery, and she hoped having the lamb with him would ease his fears.

"I wouldn't feel right leaving them with anyone else," she explained, favoring Mahoney with her most cajoling smile. "Ben says you're the best blacksmith in the territory, and I know I can depend on you to see after them.''

Mahoney's frown lessened somewhat and he studied the animals flanking Halley. "Baby and Niles?"

"I named the lamb after my butler in New York, because he is so impatient," she explained, even as he struggled against his lead, "and Baby . . . well, the name just suited him."

The blacksmith blinked, his anger dissolving in the struggle to trudge up a logical argument against that. "Miss Halley, you'll have to admit, you never shirk from asking the most from folks."

Again, Halley smiled up at the burly man. "The worst anyone can ever do is say no."

He propped the pitchfork against the wall and motioned for her to follow him toward the back of the stable with both animals.

"Now, they won't be a bit of trouble," she assured him, tugging Niles away from a bin of cracked corn. "I'll come by before school and immediately after. They will share a stall, of course, and all I ask is that you see that they are fed and cared for."

He stopped in his tracks, turned, and asked, "Why will you be coming by every day?"

"To keep them from getting homesick, of course."

Without reply, Mr. Mahoney resumed his steps, leading the mule toward a stall in the back, and Niles followed docilely. The stall was clean and spacious, and Halley nodded her approval. Mahoney forked hay into the trough while she slipped a peppermint to Baby.

Once they were settled, Halley paid Mr. Mahoney a week's board. She thanked him again and turned toward the entrance, coming face-to-face with Tex Whitten, the intruder from her first night in Wilder.

Surprise got the better of her and she gasped aloud, taking a few quick steps backward.

"Well, if it ain't the fancy miss." He sneered, gallantly bowing at the waist.

Her eyes narrowed. "Let me by."

"You just ain't very friendly, are you?"

He stepped toward her, and she glanced desperately at the

pitchfork Mr. Mahoney had left propped against the wall. He anticipated her move, and his fingers closed around her wrist the moment she reached for the weapon.

"You're just a regular hellcat, ain't you?" He fingers dug painfully into her wrist. "What's the matter, leave your gun at home?"

"Unhand me this instant." She refused to scream or cower, rather facing him with a countenance of disdain.

"Or what?" he taunted. "Thought you only talked big around that man of yours."

"Leave the lady alone, Tex, you've got work to do." Cooper Eldridge appeared from nowhere. "I want those horses unsaddled and back in the livery. If I have to pay Mahoney another day's use of them, it's coming out of your wages."

Whitten released her wrist immediately, glaring at Halley before making his way toward the back of the stable. She rubbed her wrist, not looking at Eldridge.

"Howdy, Miss Halley." Eldridge spoke politely, touching the brim of his hat. "I'm sorry about that. Whitten can be crude as they come."

"I know all about Mr. Whitten's lack of character," she reminded him. "Frankly, Mr. Eldridge, I'm disappointed in you for hiring someone like that."

He only shrugged. "When a man rides with me, all I care about is how good he is with a gun. I can't worry about his morals."

She frowned. "You may regret that outlook someday."

He only shook his head. "By the time a man gets out here, there ain't nothing left to regret."

"An empty conscience is no substitute for a clear one." She moved toward the doorway of the livery. "Good day, Mr. Eldridge."

"Give me just a minute, Miss Halley," he implored, twining his fingers around her arm. She glanced pointedly at his offending hand, and he withdrew his hold immediately. Coughing slightly, he said, "I understand you're teaching school."

"That's right," she responded hesitantly.

"So, you're tired of ranching already. I knew you wouldn't like it," he assured her. "But don't worry, you won't have any trouble selling the place; in fact, I—''

"My ranch is not for sale, Mr. Eldridge."

"Just how do you figure to hang on to that place and live in town?"

"I do not live in town," she corrected him. "I'm merely staying at the boardinghouse while I teach school."

"You can't keep that up forever." His smug smile grated on her nerves. "A ranch can't see after itself."

The snow swirled down in flakes the size of silver dollars, and Ben cursed the howling wind, his words lingering before his face in a puff of steam. Leaning forward, he urged his horse down the ridge, his eyes scanning the ground below for any sign of wayward cattle.

For two days he and the few ranch hands had ridden the range in the wake of an early blizzard, bringing the combined herds to sheltered areas in an effort to prevent them from wandering off and dying of exposure. The men used axes to chop drinking holes in the frozen ponds, and wagonloads of hay were put out, but it was never enough.

He rode on toward a particularly high snowdrift and caught sight of several carcasses, partially covered with snow. He counted eight, but there could have been more beneath the higher drifts.

"Hey, Ben!"

His head snapped around at the sound of the voice. A rider approached, and Ben strained his eyes to see who it was. It was Clayton, he recognized the horse the way the rider was steering the animal down the ridge.

"What are you doing out here?" Ben had to shout to be heard over the gale.

"I rode out with Creek, on the chuck wagon."

"Chuck wagon?" Ben repeated in disbelief.

Clayton grinned. "He said you fellas were bound to be tired of stale biscuits and jerky."

"Lead the way."

Ben followed his brother to the clearing where Creek had set up his wagon. Tom Mitchell was already seated by blazing fire, the bright flames a beacon in the cold gray afternoon.

Several pots hung on hooks over the fire, and the battalion

of aromas was overwhelming—coffee, hot and strong, stew bubbling in the pot, thick and spicy, and rabbit roasting over a spit, juicy and tender.

Clayton led Ben's horse away with a promise to feed him well with grain brought on the wagon. Assured that the horse would be cared for, Ben accepted a tin cup of black coffee and seated himself near the fire, nodding to Tom.

As he drained the cup Creek appeared with plate of stew and hot biscuits and refilled the cup from the enormous coffeepot.

Ben hesitated over his food only long enough to ask, "Where are the others?"

"Been straggling in and out for the last hour," Creek assured him. "One whiff of that coffee, and they hightailed it in to eat."

With a fire at his feet and hot food inside him, Ben felt almost content for the first time since leaving Halley. He carried in his heart the picture of her standing in the misting snow, draped in black wool, with tears in her eyes for his safety.

The only thing that made being away from her bearable was the knowledge that she was safe in town, where a sheriff and the grateful parents of her students would protect her. He stared into the fire and realized that Pete's will had held nothing over him. It was Halley. She had stepped off the stage into his arms and into his life, bringing laughter and love. He had spent so much time trying to uncover her secrets—only to realize at last that they meant nothing. Whether Halley had riches to return to or not, he couldn't imagine letting her leave Wilder.

"I don't believe this weather is going to let up." Tom Mitchell's voice intruded on his thoughts. "How are you holding up, Ben?"

He shrugged. "I've seen worse than this. What about you? You're the one who took the worst blow."

"They burned an empty barn." He sopped the last trace of stew from his plate with a biscuit. "I was able to save the cow and the horses got out. My family is safe, and I can buy new lumber and nails."

Ben admired Tom's tenacity; losing a barn full of hay and

grain would be enough to discourage most men, but he was taking it in stride.

"The horses can stay at my place as long as necessary." Ben knew a man hated nothing more than being dependent on friends, but even Tom Mitchell wasn't going to allow livestock to suffer for the sake of pride. "We'll just keep running the herds together so there will be fewer stops to make for dropping hay."

Tom rose to his feet, a hint of his usual humor returning to his face. "Delia was right about you."

"Right about me?"

"She said, 'Ben Parrish has turned plumb soft since Halley came to town.'" He chuckled slightly and turned from the fire to claim his horse and return to the work awaiting them.

Ben stared after his retreating back and decided he'd never agreed with anyone more. Damn, if that woman hadn't wormed her way into every part of his life. She made him laugh, and she'd made him love her without even trying.

Clayton returned to the fire, taking a seat beside Ben. He balanced his elbows on his knees and waited for his brother to finish eating.

"Ben, there's something I have to say to you." He leaned forward, staring into the dancing flames, and drew a deep breath. "Miss Halley is a fine lady, and you're a fool if you keep trying to send her away."

Glancing sideways, Ben was struck by the firm set of his brother's jaw, darkened with a heavy growth of whiskers. There was nothing boyish about Clayton anymore—he had made the choice to return to the ranch and face the dangers because it was the right thing to do. Now he stood up to his older brother, not for his own benefit but for the sake of someone he cared for and wanted to protect.

"She *is* a fine lady," Ben agreed. "But there's more to consider than my intentions. Halley has to decide what she wants as well."

Clayton didn't waiver. "You need to declare your intentions first. Eli says Halley is too stubborn to tell you how she feels and you need to quit sniffing around and make your move."

Ben laughed and his brother's eyes widened. "What's so funny?"

"You and Eli sitting around gossiping like old women." He took a deep gulp of coffee. "You let me worry about Halley."

"You won't think it's so funny when she gets tired of waiting on you and goes back home."

Before he could respond, riders made their way into the clearing. As they neared the fire Ben recognized Cooper Eldridge

"Howdy, Ben," he called, leaning forward on his horse. "Coffee smells good."

Ben nodded toward the cook, who in turn waved for the men to ride into the camp.

The men hurried to dismount and picket their horses, lured by the promise of hot coffee. Creek doled out cups and each man filled his own from the pot. A pan of biscuits was passed and devoured without benefit of butter or jelly.

Only Eldridge took a seat by the fire. "Heard you carted three fellas into the sheriff a few days back," he began.

"They were cattle thieves," was the only explanation Ben offered.

"Just whose cattle were they thievin'?" Eldridge asked, leaning forward. "Yours or your lady friend's."

Ben's eyes narrowed. "What difference does it make? They were breaking the law and I took them in."

"I say it makes a lot of difference." He flashed a self-assured smile over his coffee. "In fact, I got plumb curious as to why you would work so hard to keep her herd together, so I sent a wire down to Cheyenne. Did you know that land is still in Pete's name?"

"Pete wanted her to have that land," Ben reminded him, struggling to keep his anger in check. Eldridge was trying to goad him into revealing the truth about Pete's land. "It's not your place or mine to judge the wishes of a dead man."

"If he wanted her to have it, why doesn't she?" Eldridge pressed. "A woman can own land same as a man out here, if it's really hers to own."

"I have enough trouble of my own to tend to," Ben cautioned. "Don't become part of it."

* * *

"Breakfast is ready, girls!" Delia called up the stairs. "Hurry, or you'll be late for school."

Halley looked up from the table she was setting and gave her friend an encouraging smile. Mrs. Porter rushed into the dining room, bearing large platters of fried potatoes and scrambled eggs.

"I can't find my stockings, Ma!"

"Ma, my hairbrush is gone!"

Delia closed her eyes and sagged against the stair rail, the strain of being uprooted from her home visible on her face. Before she could reprimand the children, Susan's voice called, "Don't worry, Ma, I'll find their things. We'll be right down."

"I swear to goodness, I feel like I've been away from home a month." Shaking her head, Delia turned back to the dining room and began folding napkins. Her fingers shook and she twisted a linen napkin in frustration before tossing it to the table. "Damn those rustlers."

Halley rushed to put a comforting arm around the woman's shoulders. "Don't be discouraged."

Delia managed a brave smile. "Tom and I haven't been apart since he left Missouri and come off out here to buy land. He wanted me to wait until he had a house built, but I wrote him right back and threatened to have Sitting Bull himself bring me out here if he didn't come for me."

Halley smiled, but she could sense Delia's despair. The men had not sent word in two days, and they each tried to allay the other's fears while clinging to her own.

"I must sound silly as a schoolgirl, but I miss that old man of mine."

Halley felt the sting of her own tears as Delia dabbed her eyes. She had to turn away, not wanting to have her friend worrying over her. She concentrated on the task of laying silver at the place settings, but the gleaming china blurred before her eyes.

She felt Delia's hand on her shoulder and shuddered, retrieving the crumple napkin. She folded the square of cloth and tried to smooth out the wrinkles.

Delia took the napkin from her hand and positioned it beside an empty coffee cup. "Halley, you know you can talk to me . . . about anything."

Halley managed a tearful smile. "Is it that obvious?"

"I've been married a long time, girl. I know that look."

Halley pressed her palms to her face and blinked back the tears. "I suppose you think I'm awful."

"Do you love him?"

Halley nodded. "Yes, I do, but—"

"But you didn't tell him," Delia concluded. "And you didn't make him say how he feels."

"The situation is more complicated than that."

Shaking her head, the older woman finished doling out napkins. "What's so complicated about two people in love?"

Halley gripped the back rail of one of Mrs. Porter's dining-room chairs. "I know he cares for me, but I can't assume that he would ever be willing to risk falling in love again."

Delia raised an eyebrow. "You sound like you're giving him a choice."

Before she could respond, the girls bounded down the stairs, stockings matched and hair combed. They paused long enough to hug their mother before taking their seats. Halley helped Delia with the chore of filling their plates, cutting their meat, and buttering their biscuits.

Soon everyone was situated, and Delia poured coffee for Halley and herself. Mrs. Porter entered the dining room carrying a large pitcher of milk.

"Anyone need a refill?" she asked. When everyone shook their head, she placed the pitcher on the table and took her own seat. She spooned eggs onto her plate and asked Halley to pass the biscuits.

"Delia, I declare, I wish my biscuits would turn out this light." Mrs. Porter took a second biscuit before returning the platter to the table. "You'll have to share your secret with me one of these days."

The two women smiled at each other in truce, and Delia replied, "Only if show me how to make that wonderful chicken gravy."

"Miss Halley." Sara, the youngest child, spoke up, "Can we have a Christmas tree at the school?"

"A Christmas tree?" Halley hadn't given much thought to the approaching holiday. "Well, I suppose we could. What made you think of that?"

The little girl slid from her seat and rushed into the parlor, returning with one of Mrs. Porter's periodicals. "I saw this last night."

She thrust the gazette into Halley's outstretched hands and pointed to the illustration on the cover. "See?"

The drawing portrayed a group of schoolchildren decorating a tree in their classroom. Halley flipped the pages and scanned the articles detailing various Christmas projects for children.

Sara turned the page and directed Halley's attention to a rendering of youngsters acting out the Nativity scene. "Why can't we have a play?

"A Christmas play!" Polly exclaimed.

"Ooh, I want to be an angel." Ella sighed in a wistful voice. "With big white wings."

Halley sat back and contemplated the task of producing a play. There would be a set to build and costumes to sew, but she knew the children would love it.

"It will be a lot of work," she warned the girls. "We'll have to practice every day after school, and you would have to memorize your parts."

"We can do that," Ella assured her.

Polly nodded in agreement. "Besides, it's too cold to play outside, and we can even build the set ourselves, if the boys help."

"Jim Tulley's always got scrap lumber and bent nails he could give you," Mrs. Porter suggested.

"Please, Miss Halley?" Sara implored.

"Please, let us try."

Halley nodded her consent, and the girls began chattering like squirrels about all that would have to be done.

"Everyone in town will be there," Delia said, and smiled for the first time in three days. "We can have a party afterward!"

"That sounds wonderful." Mrs. Porter heaved herself from the chair and began clearing away the dishes. "I'll make the applesauce cake."

"Mary and Joseph, take your places!" Halley clapped her hands loudly. "This is just a rehearsal, there's nothing to be nervous about. Where are the shepherds?"

Three boys rushed to their appointed places, snickering at their friend who was cast in the role of Joseph. What worse fate could befall a young man than being stuck with the role of a husband?

Halley glanced over her notes. "Alvin, you should be on that side of the stage."

"I don't want to be the innkeeper," the boy whined. "I only get to say one line and everyone boos at me."

Halley straightened his collar. "No one will *boo* at you."

"The innkeeper couldn't help it if there were so many people in town." Mrs. Porter rushed to the defense of her biblical colleague.

"It is a very important part," Halley reassured him. "After all, he did the best he could, allowing them to stay in the stable. Just think what might have happened if he had turned them out in the cold."

Alvin considered her words for a quiet moment, finally nodding in acceptance. With a shrug, he said, "I suppose so."

"Good." Halley smiled and patted his shoulder. "You'll do fine."

She glanced around, catching sight of the wise men lining up for Mrs. Porter to measure them for their costumes. The older boys were to portray the visitors from the East, and she kept a close eye on Daniel and Jimmy. There had not been any more trouble at school, but the pair had never completely buried the hatchet.

Hannah Carson and Delia were sifting through the assortment of donated items to be used as costumes. The banker's wife held up a faded blue blanket. "This will be perfect for the shepherds, and I can get two costumes out of it, I just know."

"We have to have something white for the angels," Delia insisted, digging through the box of material. "Some old bedsheets would do."

"I have a linen tablecloth that I don't use much," Mrs. Porter offered. "There's a gravy stain right in the center and I always have to set something over it."

"We could just cut around the stain." Mrs. Carson set the blue fabric aside. "It would be perfect, if you don't mind parting with it."

"Not at all, I'll go fetch it right now."

Soon scissors were snipping through the discarded fabric, and fidgeting children were forced to stand still to be measured.

Halley glanced toward the window and noticed that it was snowing again. She crossed the schoolhouse and stared out into the bleak weather. She pressed her palm against the cold glass and breathed a prayer for Ben's protection. The past few days had been unbearable, not knowing if he was safe or if he had been hurt.

She couldn't face the thought of losing Ben, and she knew Delia was right. If she wanted to keep him, she would have to declare her feelings, and not give him a choice about his.

The weather was finally easing up, but Ben felt no sense of relief. Winter had just begun, and there would be more blizzards to fight. Leading his horse inside the barn, he was enveloped by the welcoming warmth emanating from the animals. General Sherman was impatient to be unsaddled, and Ben didn't make him wait.

A thorough rubdown was the best reward for a hardworking horse. Ben spread a thick blanket across the General's back and scooped a generous portion of oats into the trough.

That done, he checked the other horses and made sure someone had milked the cow. Finally, he could turn toward the house and see about satisfying his own needs. A light was on in the kitchen, and he was suddenly filled with longing to enter the warmth of the house and find Halley waiting for him. He ached to feel her in his arms and taste the sweetness of her lips.

So much time had passed since Ben had felt love for anyone, but the feeling rushed through him like a spark set to tinder. He knew she had nowhere else to go, but he wanted her to stay in Wilder because she loved him.

The wind nearly cut him in two as he made his way to the house, but he was grateful to be headed toward a hot meal and clean clothes.

He entered the house by way of the side door and stepped inside, stamping snow from his boots. The aroma of brewing coffee was intoxicating and the room was almost unbearably warm, a shock after so many hours in the cold.

He shrugged out of his coat and hung his hat by the door. He entered the kitchen and found Eli hunched over a cup of coffee, deep in conversation with Warren Olson.

"Good evening, Ben." The attorney rose to his feet and held his hand out in greeting.

"Evening." Ben shook the proffered hand. "What brings you all the way out here?"

"Business, I'm afraid."

He didn't miss the anxiety in Olson's voice, and he hesitated before lifting the coffeepot from the stove and filling a cup for himself.

"It's about Missy." Eli cut to the heart of the matter. "That goldurn Eldridge has been nosing into her business."

Ben folded his arms across his chest and leaned against the counter. "You didn't tell him anything, did you?"

"Not a word!" Olson was indignant. "Nothing is more sacred to me than a client's confidence, but I'm afraid Mr. Eldridge will not be put off. He is threatening to wire a judge in Cheyenne regarding Mr. St. John's will."

"Can he do that?"

"A will is a matter of public record," Olson said with a sigh. "It won't be easy, but if he hires a smart enough lawyer, well . . ."

"I say we just send a few boys over there to beat the tar out him." Eli slammed his hand against the tabletop. "And tell him to stay the hell out of Missy's business."

"That won't solve the problem," Olson said ruefully. "Once word gets out that there might be a problem with the will, everyone in the territory will be curious."

"Damn Pete St. John," Ben growled under his breath, placing his cup on the counter. "If he wanted her to have the damned place, why didn't he just give it to her?"

"He wanted her to be protected," the attorney reminded him. "Ben, there's only one thing that can be done to save that land."

He knew the answer without having to hear if from Olson. If he took ownership, the land would be safe from those who wanted to take it from Halley—but by taking it, he would make himself no better than they.

"When does this have to be done?"

"I brought the papers with me." Olson bent to retrieve a thick stack of legal documents from his valise. "If you sign everything tonight, I can be on the first stage to Cheyenne in the morning."

"Shouldn't we explain what we're doing to her first?" Ben frowned at the numerous papers being spread across his kitchen table.

"You can explain everything to her tomorrow, but we need to get this done tonight." The attorney scanned the documents, nodding with approval, and offered a fountain pen to Ben. "If you don't do this, she may very well find herself in court, and there's not a judge in Wyoming that will rule in favor of an Eastern woman over a resident cattleman."

Olson wasn't telling him anything he hadn't told himself a hundred times the past few days, but the reassurances did little to ease his conscience, and the hand holding the pen hesitated over the document.

He hated doing this behind her back, but Halley would never agree to hand ownership of the land over to him, and there wasn't time to persuade her. If Eldridge got hold of a judge in Cheyenne, she could easily lose any claim to the ranch. This way it would always be there for her ... as he himself intended to be.

"She may question your intentions," the attorney advised. "The sooner you tell her the better."

❧ EIGHTEEN ❧

DINNERTIME AT THE boardinghouse was always a hectic affair, and sometimes guests were even fed in shifts to avoid crowding. Tonight was especially frenzied as everyone prepared to attend the Christmas pageant at the school.

Halley coiled her braided hair into a chignon and craned her neck to judge the results in the tiny mirror. She wanted to appear as mature and dignified as possible tonight; after all, she would surely be scrutinized by the citizens of Wilder.

"Dinner everyone!" Mrs. Porter called from the bottom of the stairs. "If you don't want to go hungry, get down here!"

Her warning was quickly answered by the pounding of footsteps on the stairs.

Halley smoothed her hair one last time and hurried to don the ivory shirtwaist she had ironed herself. A cranberry wool skirt lent a festive note to the outfit, and she carefully pinned her mother's cameo at the base of the ruffled collar.

She turned before the mirror, an eager smile marring her sensible image. She was looking forward to the play as much as the children, doubly so in hopes that Ben would be there. Clayton had ridden into town the day before yesterday to check on the women and assure them that no one had been hurt.

Delia would have packed and headed for home then and there, but Clayton had strict orders that the women were to remain in town. Disappointed, Delia made Clayton swear to tell Tom about the play and ask him to be there if he could.

If Tom Mitchell came to the play, Halley hoped Ben might ride along. There would a party after the performance, but she planned to talk to Ben alone.

Tonight would mark the end of the semester and she would return to the ranch, danger or no. The ranch was her home, and she meant to fight for it. She would tell Ben all—about Farnsworth, about losing everything, and that she wanted to spend the rest of her life in Wyoming, with him.

The thunder of footsteps storming down the stairs subsided, and Halley took one last look in the mirror before leaving her room. She could hear silverware clinking against china and conversation, which consisted mostly of Delia hurrying her children with their dinner.

Halley slipped inside the crowded dining room, and Mrs. Porter directed her to a chair in the center.

"Land sakes, girl, you'd best hurry if you're going to get there before everyone else." The landlady refilled coffee cups and water glasses. "Pass that pot roast, Mr. Hawkins, folks are waiting."

Halley spooned mashed potatoes onto her plate and Mrs. Porter ladled gravy over them. The serving platter of roast beef was passed to her, and when she took the plate she looked up to see a stranger smiling at her from across the table.

"Good evening," he said.

"Good evening," she replied, serving herself quickly before Mrs. Porter snatched the plate and sent it on to another guest.

The stranger didn't look away; in fact he was almost studying her. She guessed him to fortyish, graying at the temples, and very well dressed.

He broke a biscuit in half, buttered it, and passed the butter dish to her. "So you're the schoolmarm I've been hearing so much about."

The Mitchell girls giggled, but Halley pretended to ignore them. "I'm afraid you have me at a disadvantage, sir."

"I beg your pardon, miss," he said, with a telltale drawl, betraying him as a Southerner. He paused to pour a generous amount of cream into his coffee. "My name is Robert Brandon, I'm an attorney from Cheyenne."

"An attorney?" she asked, passing the butter to a clerk from the bank. "I take it you are here on business."

"What makes you so sure?" He raised a forkful of potatoes to his mouth, pausing long enough to say, "This could very well be a pleasure trip."

"I've never known an attorney to find anything more pleasurable than business."

He chuckled, dabbing his mouth with his napkin. She noted the way he neatly folded the linen and replaced it across his lap. "Obviously, I am the one at a disadvantage."

"What does bring you to Wilder?" the bank clerk asked.

"Business, just as the lady suspected," Brandon confessed. "A local rancher is interested in contesting a will."

Halley's fork clattered to the floor, and she nearly choked on a mouthful of pot roast. She quickly raised her napkin to her mouth, coughing hard. Delia passed her a glass of water.

A traveling salesman was intrigued at the mention of a will, and began recounting his own misfortune with a widow in Omaha who had vowed to leave him a sizable inheritance.

"Of course, her children denied that she'd ever written a new will," he concluded, spooning gravy over his second helping of potatoes. "So I was left with nothing but fond memories."

Halley looked up to find Robert Brandon watching her closely, his chin resting on his steepled fingers. Mrs. Porter handed her a clean fork from the sideboard, but eating had become impossible.

Robert Brandon smiled and returned to his dinner. Without looking up, he said, "You'd better toss a pinch of salt over your shoulder. My mama always said dropping silverware was a sure sign of bad luck."

"Megan, you must be still," Halley muttered around the pins clamped between her lips. "Please, honey, I might stick you."

The little girl craned her neck, determined to get a look at her angelic costume. Finally, the pins were secured and Halley stepped back and held up the mirror for her to see.

She turned this way and that, clapping with approval. "Oh, Miss Halley, I look just precious!"

"You certainly do," she assured the child. "Now take your seat and don't muss your costume."

Armed with pins, Halley checked each costume, securing shepherds' robes and a wise man's turban. Delia was waiting to usher each child into place to await their cues. Halley marveled at the woman's ability to be cheerful under the circumstances, but Delia maintained that hardships made folks strong.

"Miss Halley?"

She whirled at the voice, taking a pin from her teeth. Automatically she ordered, "Turn around and hold still."

To her chagrin, she came face-to-face with Warren Olson. His eyes widened, and he stumbled backward, well out of her reach.

"Pardon me, Mr. Olson." She laughed at the astonishment on his face and gestured at the chaos surrounding them. "I'm afraid I'm a bit overwhelmed by all these last-minute details."

"You certainly have your hands full," he observed, keeping his distance. "I just arrived home and found your note. I rushed right over. What on earth has happened?"

She took his arm and led him away from the others. "There's an attorney in town, all the way from Cheyenne. He says he's here to contest a will. He didn't say, but it has to be Uncle Peter's. No one else has died!"

Olson only chuckled and patted her arm. "Just as I suspected, but not to worry. We outsmarted them."

"We?"

"Ben Parrish, you, and me," he clarified. "I've just returned from Cheyenne myself, filed the papers personally."

He smiled at her and waited, as if expecting her to thank him. "Mr. Olson, I'm afraid I have no idea what you are talking about."

"Haven't you spoken with Mr. Parrish?"

Halley closed the distance between them and demanded in a hushed whisper, "Spoken to him about what?"

"Oh, dear." The attorney cleared his throat and nervously fingered his collar. "It appears I have spoken out of turn.

Perhaps it would be best if Ben explains this to you.''

He turned to leave, but Halley held tight to his sleeve. ''I want to know what is going on around here.''

''Miss Halley, Ben was forced to exercise his obligation as adviser to the estate and seize the property.'' He gave her a sympathetic smile. ''I filed the papers today, transferring everything into Ben's name.''

''Everything?''

He nodded. ''The house, the land, the cattle, everything.''

''Everything,'' she repeated, releasing her hold on his arm. ''Just like that?''

Halley felt her legs dissolve and she groped for the edge of her desk. Mr. Olson continued to speak, but she could comprehend nothing he was saying for the great roaring in her ears. Ben had seized the property, her property.

The reasons rushed by; why would he have done this without telling her, without asking her?

You trusted him, my dear, because it was the easiest thing to do.

Memories of that awful day in the New York City Jail made her dizzy. She had been so close to poverty and homelessness, only to be saved by a windfall inheritance.

Now it was all gone—again. Everything. And this time there would be no miracle, no unforeseen fortune plopping into her lap.

She had trusted Richard Farnsworth because he came highly recommended by longtime family friends. His betrayal had infuriated her, but at least she had the small comfort of knowing that she was one of many fooled by his smooth talk and fictitious references.

What Ben had done was a thousand times worse. She had trusted him because she loved him.

Halley stood in the shadows, watching the play she had worked so hard to produce with little joy. The tiny schoolhouse was packed; even the aisles were crowded with those who could not find a seat.

Entertainment of any form was hard to come by in frontier towns, and it was obvious everyone had come to see the play. It wasn't hard to pick out the parents. They sat clustered toward the front, exchanging anxious whispers as they strained their necks to get a glimpse of what was behind the curtain.

Jimmy Franks made his way onto center stage and faced the audience of proud parents and townsfolk. "Good evening, ladies and gentlemen," he announced. "On behalf of the students and our teacher, Miss Halley St. John, we want to welcome you to the first annual Christmas play of the Wilder Township School."

The polite applause increased in volume as the curtain was pulled aside, revealing the set. Halley held her breath and nodded for Jimmy to begin.

"And it came to pass in those days, that there went out a decree from Caesar Augustus, that all the world should be taxed. And Joseph also went up from Galilee, to be taxed with Mary, his espoused wife, being great with child."

Mary and Joseph took their places and Halley glanced up to see Delia smiling, her eyes shining with parental pride as she watched Polly kneel before the manger.

Once they were seated, Jimmy continued: "While they were there, the days were accomplished that she should be delivered. And she brought forth her firstborn son, and wrapped Him in swaddling clothes, and laid Him in a manger; because there was no room for them in the inn."

The Star of Bethlehem hung crookedly over the rickety stable, and Halley almost forgot to cue Polly to place the swaddling-clothed doll in the manger. As they had rehearsed, the children sang the first verse of "O Little Town of Bethlehem," their voices filling the tiny schoolhouse.

When the verse ended, Jimmy continued, "And there were in the same country shepherds abiding in the field, keeping watch over their flock by night."

Niles, who had been cast in the role of "the flock," was overcome with a bout of stage fright. He balked at being tugged onto stage and was literally shoved into place. Titters of laughter rose from the audience, but the shepherds finally took their places, as if huddled against the cold night air.

"And lo, the angel of the Lord came upon them and the glory of the Lord shone round about them, and they were sore afraid."

Halley nudged Megan forward onto the stage. The little girl

stood in her robes of bedsheets and her wings of cheesecloth, but no angel in heaven could have been more beautiful.

Halley leaned forward and whispered, "Fear not . . ."

Megan grinned. "Fear not. Behold, I bring you . . ."

"Good tidings." The loud whisper could be heard throughout the building, and Halley cringed, hoping no one would laugh.

"Good tidings of great joy for all people." Megan glanced at Halley for a nod and continued: "For you is born this day a Savior, which is Christ the Lord." She paused to point dramatically toward the Nativity. "Find him wrapped in swaddling clothes, lying in a manger."

The children broke into song—"Hark the Herald Angels Sing"—and this time the audience joined them. Megan obediently waited for Halley's signal before waving to her mother and leaving the stage.

A shepherd rose to his feet, adjusting his costume before clearing his throat and saying, "Let us go now, even unto Bethlehem, to see this thing that the Lord hath made known unto us."

Niles bleated loudly in protest as the shepherds led him even unto Bethlehem to stand before the manger. Parents hid smiles behind their hands, and Halley felt tempted to laugh herself when Joseph discreetly reached out to pet the squirming lamb.

The wise men then filed onto stage, leading the chorus of "O Come All Ye Faithful," and again the audience joined in the song.

The door opened, admitting a blast of cold air, and Halley looked up to see Ben slip into the back and stand against the wall. Despite the shadows, she could feel his eyes upon her.

All she wanted was to get through the evening for the sake of the children and then find somewhere to indulge in a good cry. She was in no mood to confront Ben tonight, but she knew him well enough to know he would not be put off.

The entire class joined the cast on stage, leading the audience in all four verses of "Silent Night." For all the second-hand costumes and forgotten lines, Halley decided then that the children had surpassed themselves. Their voices were clear and strong, and the audience was greatly impressed. The final verse ended, and the audience members rose in a standing ovation.

After several minutes the applause subsided and Halley motioned for the children to step down from the stage. They stood in place, and she again signaled toward the stage exit. Jimmy smiled and spoke. "Miss Halley doesn't know about this part."

She glanced toward Delia, who only smiled innocently, keeping her attention on the stage.

Reaching into his pocket, the lanky teenager withdrew a folded piece of paper and read the words for all to hear. "We decided to take this opp-opportunity to tell our folks what this school has meant to all of us. We've learned to read and write, and to figure our sums, but the most important lessons weren't in the books."

Halley felt the tears threaten, and Delia discreetly placed a handkerchief in her hand.

"We've learned to believe in ourselves," Jimmy continued. "And to believe that we can do anything we put our minds to.

"We owe it all to our teacher, Halley St. John. She knew a school was needed here in Wilder, and she did something about it. She went out and made it happen."

Polly reached beneath the manger and withdrew a box wrapped in tissue paper. She crossed the stage and held the package out to Halley. "We wanted you to know how much we appreciate all that you've done."

Delia shoved Halley forward when her legs wouldn't work. Polly placed the box in her hands and bid her open it. With shaking fingers, Halley tore the delicate wrappings and opened the package.

"Oh, children," she gasped. She reached inside and withdrew a beautifully carved jewelry box. "Oh, it's lovely."

"Open it!" Megan cried, clapping her hands.

Halley found the catch and opened the lid; the box chimed the melody of "Beautiful Dreamer." She swallowed hard, but tears slipped down her cheeks. The audience applauded, and Halley hugged each student.

Mayor Riales made his way on stage and shook her hand. Everyone grew quiet and he grasped his lapels, saying, "First off, I want to congratulate the children on the hard work they put into this play. You all did a fine job.''

Applause rose once again, and the mayor shook Jimmy's hand. He waited until the audience quieted before continuing.

''You all know that it was Miss Halley who went before the school board and convinced them that we deserved a school as much as any town, but there's something I'll bet none of you knew.''

Niles gave a sudden bleat, startling the mayor and sending a ripple of laughter through the audience. The mayor smiled and continued: ''When money got tight, Miss Halley took on the job of teaching the students herself, refusing any salary, and made sure our youngsters got the best learning there was.''

He turned to Halley, withdrawing an envelope from his pocket. ''The town council decided that no amount of money could have hired a better teacher, but we wanted to present you with the equivalent you would have earned from the board of education.''

''But there are so many things we still need for the school,'' Halley protested.

''The main thing this school needs is a good teacher,'' he countered. ''And we want you to know the job is yours as long as you want it.''

Halley was completely overwhelmed. There was too much to consider. If she left Wilder, she had nowhere to go, but could she remain in the same town with Ben?

She looked up and saw him standing in the same spot, his expression solemn. She then glanced at the expectant faces in the audience and back at the mayor. She couldn't decide now, but she didn't want to put a damper on the wonderful evening.

She managed a sincere smile and nodded.

The audience cheered, and Jim Tulley rose to his feet. ''Everyone over to the store for a party!''

The children scrambled to keep up with the adults, and Halley let the crowd rush ahead of her. Ben stood waiting for her, his eyes solemn.

''I need to talk with you.''

''Do you?'' She sneered. ''Well, let me tell you a thing or two—''

''It's Eli. He's been shot.''

❧ NINETEEN ❧

HALLEY PEERED INSIDE the guest room at Ben's house, where Eli lay in a narrow bed. Mrs. Gunter hovered over him, sponging his forehead with a cloth. Even from across the room, she could see the pain etched on his face, and she sagged against the doorjamb. Ben took her elbow and led her inside.

The room was filled with the strong odor of antiseptic and fresh blood. She caught sight of a basin filled with blood-stained bandages, and her knees buckled. Ben held her steady and steered her across the room.

She stood over the bed, refusing to believe her eyes. Eli's face was so pale and he looked so old, she hardly recognized him. Ben moved a chair near the bedside and helped her find her seat.

She covered the old man's fingers with her own, horrified by the coldness of his hand. "Oh, Eli," she whispered. "You old coot."

"He is weak," Mrs. Gunter declared. "Much blood was lost, and he needs to rest."

"Will he be . . . all right?" Halley had tried to prepare herself for the worst as she rode Baby back to the ranch, but it was more than she was ready to face. Ben would not have brought her all the way from town unless Eli's chances of survival were slim.

The housekeeper only shook her head. "If he survives tonight . . . we can only hope for the best."

The somber words filled Halley with dread, and she wanted to run from the room and hide. She had never been good at pretending to be brave, but she would hate herself if she left Eli when he needed her the most. His eyelids fluttered and she gazed into his sunken eyes, trying her best to smile.

She tried to think of something cheerful to say, but all she could muster was a shaky, "How are you?"

"Missy," he managed, his voice trembling. "You ain't missin' your play, are you?"

"No, it's over," she assured him, tightening her hold on his hand. "The children did a wonderful job."

" 'Course they did." With great effort, he managed to squeeze his fingers around hers with a faint grip. "They got a fine teacher."

She nodded. "I wish you had been there."

He smiled weakly. "Somebody had to keep them bastards off'n your land."

"No more talk," Mrs. Gunter ordered. "He must rest or the bleeding with start all over."

Alarmed, Halley glanced up at the housekeeper. She hated to think how much blood he had lost already. If only Wilder had a doctor, she could be certain he would get the care he needed.

She started at the feel of Ben's hand on her shoulder. "Let Mrs. Gunter get him settled," he murmured in a gentle voice. "You can come back later."

Reluctantly, she rose from the chair, never taking her eyes from Eli. His eyes fluttered shut and her heart lurched. She thought of the night her father had died. The doctor wouldn't let her in the room until it was too late. Poor Father had died alone, and there had been so many things she wanted to tell him.

Ben applied light pressure to her back, easing her from the room, but she struggled against his touch. She didn't want to loose Eli without telling him how much she cared. For all his grit and bluster, he had befriended her when she might otherwise have been alone. No one had ever called her missy, or worried over her having a heavy coat.

"I can't leave him," she implored, peering up at Ben. "He's so weak, and he might need—"

"Mrs. Gunter has tended a few bullets in her time," he assured her. "She knows what to do, but he has to rest in order to get his strength back."

She followed him out of the room, and he led her toward the kitchen, where she collapsed into a chair at the table. Tears burned her eyes, but she refused to cry. If she succumbed to tears, he would hold her, and if he held her she would be lost.

"Here."

His voice drew her attention and she looked up to see him pouring a generous amount of brandy into a glass. She accepted the liquor, with grudging gratitude, and drank deeply.

"Go easy on that," he warned. "You don't want to get drunk."

"I hope I get completely pixilated," she retorted, and turned the glass up. The liquor burned pleasantly, feeding her wounded pride. She swallowed hard, but the lump in her throat only grew. "Why would anyone want to hurt a helpless old man?"

"That helpless old man was wielding a double-barrel shotgun, and he knows how to use it." Ben filled a glass for himself. "I'm sure he got more than one of them before he took that bullet."

"And that makes it all right?" She drained her glass and slammed it down on the table. "Ben, he could die, and all you can think of is how many rustlers he was able to pick off first?"

"That's not what I meant, and you know it." He seated himself across the table from her and tossed the liquor back in his throat.

"How do I know what you mean by anything you say?" She lifted the bottle and poured herself a refill. She was already feeling the first drink rushing through her veins as she downed the second. "All that matters to you is land and cattle."

Her frayed nerves began to loosen and she giggled slightly.

"Aren't you going to congratulate me on my new job?"

His eyes narrowed, but she didn't wait for his reply. "I am going to be the old-maid schoolteacher. Of course, you won't tell them that I'm not technically a maiden, will you?"

He reached to take her drink, but she quickly drained the contents and handed him the empty glass with a smug expression. He rose to his feet and removed the bottle from the table. "You don't need any more of this."

His patronizing tone was more than she could take, and she jumped from her seat, scraping the chair across the floor. He placed the bottle on a high shelf just as she reached his side, as if she were a child he didn't want to reach the cookie jar.

"You arrogant son of a bitch." She could hold her temper no longer, and the hurt and anger poured out of her. She drew her arm back to slap him, wanting somehow to hurt him as he had hurt her.

He caught her wrist in a tight grip, pulling her up against him. Her eyes widened slightly, and she twisted to free herself from his hold. He caught her other wrist and held it at her side. "Don't make threats you can't carry out."

Her struggles didn't cease, and he could see the anger burning in her hazel eyes. "How dare you?" she bit out. "Take your hands off me this instant."

"Not until you settle down." He pinned her body with his, crushing her against him from breast to knee. His body readily responded to the feel of her, and he deliberately let the evidence of his arousal grind against her belly.

She went still, her breath coming in short gasps, but he knew better than to release her yet. He expected her to be upset about Eli, but not furious with him. Did she blame him for the old man getting shot?

They stared at one another, a silent battle of wills raging between them. He bent his head to kiss her, wanting her to know that needing him was something she should never fear. Abruptly, she turned her lips from his and his temper snapped.

His mouth covered hers with a bruising kiss, and he clenched his fingers in her hair when she tried to tear her mouth from his. A protest rose in her throat and he thrust his tongue past her parted lips. She tasted sweet, a heady blend of brandy and her own warmth, and his tongue mated with hers until he felt the tension drain from her body.

Her palms remained against his chest, but she wasn't fighting him anymore. He heard her whimper slightly and felt her palms slide over his shoulders.

The kiss became gentle but no less passionate, and his desire was only heightened by her yielding. He caught her bottom in his hands and lifted her onto the kitchen table, easing her onto her back.

He slid one hand under her skirt, feeling the warmth of her skin through the thin material of her underclothes. His jean-clad thighs eased her legs apart, and his mouth left hers, seeking the hollow her throat. A sob caught in her throat just as he hooked his fingers in her lacy stockings.

He raised his head and saw tears welling up in her eyes. She blinked against them, but soon her face was streaked with tears. She looked away from him and asked, "Is this all I ever meant to you?"

As if cold water had been splashed in his face, Ben pulled back and raised her to a sitting position. She began a hasty attempt to straighten her clothes, not looking at him. He caught her by the shoulders, forcing her to meet his gaze.

"You listen to me." Even to his own ears, his voice sounded eerily calm. "I don't know what you thought you'd find when you came out here, but don't be mistaken. If you stay in Wilder one more day, it will be on my terms."

Her face paled, but a quick spark of anger flashed in her eyes. "What terms are those? The same ones you made for your wife, or will there be a new set for me?"

He released her immediately, so angry that he didn't dare touch her in any way. He crossed the room toward the back door. He needed to get the hell away from her before he did something they would both regret.

Placing his hand on the doorknob, he paused only long enough to turn and say, "Just remember, Halley, my wife had a choice; you don't."

When Ben returned to the house, the only light burning was in the room off the kitchen, where Eli slept. He moved to the doorway and looked inside. Halley sat in the chair, her head slumped forward and her hand still holding Eli's.

He crossed the room and stood over the bed. Eli's breathing was stronger and his lips had regained color. He felt the old man's forehead and found it warm but not fevered.

Eli's eyes fluttered and he scowled up at Ben. "You, too? If'n this bullet don't kill me, I'll die from lack of sleep." He glanced over at Halley. "She wouldn't do as I told her and go lie down."

"She's worried about you." Ben was glad to hear the agitation in Eli's voice: soon the old goat would be back to his ornery self. "Looks like she's gotten attached to you."

"I reckon she's gotten quite attached to you, too." Eli shifted in the bed, wincing with the effort. "Danged if I know why. Why don't you make her lie down for a while? I might even get some sleep with you two not hovering over me." Ben scooped Halley from the chair, and she managed a muttered protest. Pillowing her head against his shoulder, she didn't make another sound as he made his way down the hall. He considered taking her upstairs and placing her in his bed. She would be more comfortable there, but mostly he wanted to see her curled beneath his sheets with her dark hair spread across his pillow.

He thought better of it, not wanting to upset her more than he already had. He'd been a complete bastard tonight, and she wasn't going to be in any hurry to forgive him for spreading her out on the kitchen table like a saloon girl.

The fire in the parlor fireplace was no more than a glowing pile of embers, barely enough light to allow him to study her face as he placed her on the sofa. Her mouth was still swollen from his kisses, and her eyes were puffy as well. He cursed himself for making her cry, realizing the years in Wyoming had made him completely unsuited for the tender emotions of a lady.

She huddled against the velvet upholstery, and he rose to his feet, searching for a cover for her. Several blankets were stored in an old trunk by the window, and he returned to spread a soft coverlet over her shivering form. He tucked the blanket around her shoulders, his touch gentle so as not to wake her.

Ever since she had arrived in Wilder, he had been trying to protect her, whether she was willing or not. He traced the line of her face, remembering the way she had charged the stage driver when he threatened to destroy her trunk. Ben had never dreamed at the time that the trunk probably held everything she owned in the world.

How frightened she must have been, alone in a rough cowtown, armed with nothing but a gun she didn't know how to fire and the journal of a man who'd never been farther west than Dodge City.

He was tempted to take her in his arms right then, but she was exhausted from the play at school and the emotional upheaval of seeing Eli so near death. He would let her sleep tonight, but in the morning they would talk. And for once in her life, Halley St. John was going to face the truth.

Halley woke with a start, unsure of her surroundings. Her eyes darted around the unfamiliar room, and she realized that she was in the parlor of Ben's house, lying on the sofa. Still wearing her dress from the evening before, she surmised that someone must have placed her there.

Her mind was fuzzy, and she groaned as a dull throbbing began in her temples. She remembered drinking more brandy than she meant to and quarreling with Ben. All she could recall after he stormed out was going to sit with Eli.

"Oh, my God," she breathed. If someone had moved her from the bedroom, and no one was needed to sit with Eli . . . he might be—

She bolted upright and threw back the soft blanket, refusing to contemplate the possibility. Her legs were shaky, and she reached out to steady herself along the back of the sofa. The sudden movement set her head to pounding, and she was forced to wait until her stomach calmed before hurrying toward Eli's room. Halfway down the hall, she met Ben.

"Easy," he said, catching her against him. "He's better this morning. Mrs. Gunter fed him some broth, and she's changing the bandages right now."

"You shouldn't have moved me," she insisted. "He might have needed something during the night."

"You were exhausted, and he wanted you to rest." Ben took her elbow and led her back to the kitchen. "Besides, I sat with him the rest of the night."

Chagrined, Halley nodded. She should have known Ben would not have left Eli alone. She crossed the large room and stared out into the frozen morning.

"Halley, we need to talk."

She turned to find him filling two cups with coffee and motioning for her to be seated at the table. She accepted the coffee, but returned to the window. "This sounds like something I need to hear standing up."

"I told you Eli is going to be fine," he reminded her. "This has nothing to do with him."

"I realize that." Her fingers tightened around the cup, but she dared not drink it for fear her stomach would revolt against the potent brew. "Why don't you just get to the point?"

His eyes narrowed. "You know that there has been a lot of trouble lately. Tom Mitchell was lucky they didn't burn his house or hurt his women."

She folded her arms across her chest and waited. She wondered exactly how he intended to convince her how lucky she was that he had taken everything she owned.

"At least, he was waylaid by strangers." She smiled sweetly. "One always looks so foolish when ransacked by a friend."

"What the hell are you getting at?" he demanded.

"I'm getting to the truth, finally!" Her anger spilled over and she could hold her tongue no longer. "You took everything I own, Ben Parrish, and I suppose you want me to thank you for it."

He stared at her in disbelief. "Who told you about that?"

"Mr. Olson assumed *you* had told me," she said, the irony almost striking her as amusing. "He seems to think you did this with my complete knowledge and consent."

"There wasn't time to discuss the situation with you, and I didn't want you to lose the place."

"So you took it for yourself?" she countered. "Tell me, sir, how much rent do you intend to charge me?"

Anger darkened his face, and she knew she had pushed him too far. His voice was dangerously calm when he said, "I did it because I didn't want you to get hurt over that land."

She just couldn't keep quiet. "Well, that is a strange way of showing you care for someone."

He crossed the room and stood within inches of her. "At least, I didn't stand by and watch bill collectors cart everything you own off to auction."

The color drained from her face, but he didn't retreat. "Is that what society people call loyalty?"

"How did you . . . there's no way." Her mind raced; she had told no one about Farnsworth, not even Delia, whom she considered her dearest friend.

"I didn't wait around for you to tell me, that's for damned sure." The disdain on his face was almost palpable. He tasted his coffee before casually asking, "What's wrong, Halley? Were you afraid I'd find out you're no better than I am?"

Silence fell between them, and Halley felt a numbing cold settle into the very marrow of her bones. She set the coffee on the counter, her movement stiff and jointed. "How long have you known this?"

"Long enough to know you couldn't afford to lose the fight that was coming."

That wasn't what she wanted to know, and she didn't believe for a minute that he misunderstood the question. She drew a deep breath, but her voice was a mere whisper when she said, "You know what I'm asking."

"Yes, Halley," he replied without flinching. "I knew everything before we made love. I knew you were penniless, and I knew you had no choice but to go along with whatever I decided to do about the ranch."

❦ TWENTY ❦

Eli was feeling well enough to sit up in bed the next morning, and Halley insisted on preparing his breakfast and bringing it in to him on a tray.

Ben's hurtful words the previous day had caused her to flee to Eli's side and she had spent all of the day and night tending to the old man, determined to avoid Ben as much as possible. She was amazed that her body had any tears left, but she cried every time she recalled the coldness in his voice when he'd told her she had no choice but to accept his terms.

As she approached the door to Eli's room she knew that she would have to make a decision today. She had to leave Ben's ranch, that was certain. The strain of pretending to ignore him was tearing her apart; the decision she faced was where to go when she left.

School would resume in the spring, and Mayor Riales had assured her the teaching position was hers. She had enough money to rent a room from Mrs. Porter until then, but could she really live in Wilder? Could she face each day, knowing that she might encounter Ben every time she walked down the street?

Balancing the tray, she steeled her frayed nerves and forced a bright smile before opening the bedroom door.

"Breakfast in bed, sir," she announced upon entering the room. "Very cosmopolitan."

"Pete used that word from time to time," he commented as she placed the tray on the bedside table and plumped his pillows. "Didn't know it had anything to do with taking a bullet."

"Normally, it does not." Despite his protest, she felt his forehead and was relieved to find no hint of fever. "But this may be as close as you'll come to it in Wilder, Wyoming."

She tucked a napkin into the neck of his nightshirt and helped him arrange the tray. He looked doubtfully at the food. "What is this?"

"Soft-boiled eggs," she answered, stirring a steaming bowl of porridge. "And this is cornmeal mush, with a little molasses. Mrs. Gunter says that you must eat light for the next several days."

The old man scowled. "What does she know? I've had lead cut out of me and ate buffalo steaks the same day."

"She said you lost a lot of blood." Halley sank into the chair near the bedside. "You had a very close call, Eli."

"Don't let that old crone scare you, missy," he advised, raising a spoonful of mush to his mouth. "She thinks 'cause she tied a few bandages around me that she can boss me."

Halley looked on as he tasted the porridge and made a loathsome face. She was still amazed by Eli's speedy recovery, given his age and the severity of the wound. "She did save your life," she reminded him.

"I'd say Ben is the one who saved my life." Eli tasted the egg and nodded in approval. "Seems like he's always pulling folk out of bad scrapes."

She looked up at that. "You're talking about the ranch?"

"I'd say you were in a pretty bad scrape." He pinned her with a knowing look. "Wouldn't you?"

"Eli, he took everything I had." She stared down at her hands folded in her lap. "The least he could have done was tell me."

"And what would you have done?" He didn't wait for her answer. "You'd have put up a scrap, that's what. And while

Ben was trying to sweet-talk you into signing the land over to him, Eldridge would have bought himself a judge and put you off the place."

Exasperated, Halley struggled to maintain an argument. "But he just *took* everything."

"Missy, what Ben took was your fight and made it his own." He finished the egg but left the mush untouched. "Take this stuff back to the kitchen when the old pruneface goes to the henhouse and bring me back something to eat."

"He spied on me, read my mail." Halley wasn't going to let Eli win the argument by changing the subject. "I had that letter put away, and he searched the house until he found proof that I had no means to protect the land. Then he took it."

"That letter was in plain sight," he informed her as she moved the tray, placing in on the table. "Ben didn't pilfer through your things."

"I put that letter—"

"In your dresser drawer, I know," he finished the thought. "Took me an hour to find it."

"You?" She gaped at him, tempted to laugh at the irony. "Why, you nosy old goat. Why on earth did you do that?"

"Missy, Pete didn't think you'd come out here, but he wanted to make the offer because you was his kin. He told me how grand your life was back there, and that you wouldn't want to give all that up. I just figured that there had to more than you was tellin'."

"I didn't want to be know as a poor relation," she confessed. "I still had my pride."

"And not much else." Eli smiled sympathetically. "It wouldn't have made no difference to me . . . or Ben neither."

She crossed the room and peered out the window. The grasslands lay buried beneath the white mantle of snow. Spring would come and they would grow green and fragrant once again. Knowing she wouldn't be there to see the rebirth of the land tore at her heart.

She had lost her fortune in New York and blamed an unscrupulous con man. She had lost her home in Wyoming, and there was no one to blame but herself.

As long as she lived on the ranch, squatters would see an opportunity to run her off and take it for themselves. Ben would continue fighting, for the land if not for her. With her gone from Wilder, he could publicly claim the property and hold it easily, without the danger of being gunned down.

Eli had been lucky this time, and she didn't want to be the cause of another shooting. She pressed her palm against the windowpane and thought of the danger she had already caused for Ben. She loved him, and all that mattered was his safety and happiness.

She glanced back at Eli, who had dozed off. He would never forgive her for leaving, but if she told him, he would talk her out of going, and she would listen.

Ben led General Sherman into the welcome warmth of the barn and unsaddled the weary horse. The General wasted no time in trotting to his stall, anxious for the food and care that his master would never deny him.

Spreading a heavy blanket over the horse's broad back, Ben felt a twinge of guilt for having the animal out in the cold longer than necessary. He should have returned hours ago, but he hated being in the house with Halley, knowing she hated him. She hadn't left Eli's side since yesterday, claiming she didn't want to leave him alone.

Ben scooped a generous portion of oats into the horses' trough and decided he probably deserved her contempt. He had treated her like a child, assuming she wouldn't have sense enough to see the danger in leaving the land in her name. Perhaps what he had feared most of all was that she would lose the land and leave Wyoming.

He had acted to give her a means to stay and, in doing so, had done the one thing that would drive her away. If he let her go.

And that wasn't going to happen. He had humored her wounded pride for two days, but no more. He would apologize, get down on his knees—whatever it took—but if Halley left, it wouldn't be because she didn't know how much he loved her.

He noticed the empty stall first. The mule . . . Baby was not in the barn. He doubled-checked the stalls toward the rear of the building but found no sign of the animal. In the tack room he found Halley's saddle missing, and he swore a long steam of obscenities.

Damn that foolish woman! He was tempted to slam his fist into the wall; instead he settled for kicking a wooden bucket halfway across the room. Surely to God she hadn't taken off for town with a snowstorm on its way.

He stalked out of he barn toward the house, hoping to find her and any other reason for the mule being gone. Not twenty yards from the barn, he found an unmarred set of tracks. The hooves were too narrow for a horse, and the prints weren't deep as they would be from a man's heavy weight.

There was only one explanation. Halley had ridden away on her mule in the direction of the ranch he had taken from her.

Halley closed the door behind her and stood in the center of the little house she had come to regard as home. She placed the box she had found in the barn onto the floor and began gathering her belongings. There would not be much to take. The furniture would have to be left behind, and the supplies that remained would be useless in the city.

She would ask Delia to take whatever she could use, especially the things she had given her. She dreaded Delia's reaction to her leaving, knowing she would try to stop her.

She carefully folded tablecloths and gathered books from the shelves. She reached for the snow globe, but her hand stilled over the object. She wished moments from life could be preserved in glass, stilled forever against the damage of hurt and disappointment.

Everything she had brought from New York now held memories of Ben. She decided to pack her clothes first, leaving the downstairs for last. The moment she stood in her tiny bedroom she realized her mistake.

The last night she'd spent in this room had been in Ben's arms. The memory of that night weakened her, and she was struck with the realization that she would never be with him in that way again.

She sank to the bed and gave way to tears. Leaving New York had been easy compared with this. There had been nothing left for her in the city, but her heart and soul would always remain in Wyoming. Wherever she went, the memories would torment her.

Curling on her side, Halley clutched the pillow in her arms, as if she could relive the feelings Ben's touch had awakened in her. She wished now she had told him she loved him, not that it would have made any difference.

She closed her eyes and indulged in a daydream of growing old in Wyoming with Ben. The peaceful image was suddenly shattered by rifle fire, and her eyes flew open in panic. Someone was firing at the house!

She rolled onto the floor, desperate to find cover. She considered crawling under the bed, but she would have no weapon to use to protect herself. She couldn't just cower and wait for them to come after her.

As he topped the ridge Ben heard the ring of rifle fire and urged the horse on faster. Drawing his own weapon, he surveyed the house from the cover of the trees. A second shot rang out, shattering the front window.

He had no doubt Halley was inside, trapped, and nothing he could do would draw their fire away. He had to reach the house and get inside.

Looping his reins over a nearby limb, Ben cocked his own rifle and skulked down the hillside. Another shot splintered off the front porch, and this time he heard Halley's frightened cries.

He swore under his breath. He had to get inside that house. Raising the Winchester, he fired toward the trees, bringing immediate return fire. He cursed and fired again, scrambling toward the barn.

"Make tracks, mister!" a voice echoed from the line of timber. "This ain't your fight."

"I'm making it my fight!" he answered, firing in the direction of the voice. An agonized cry assured him that he had hit the spokesman for the bastards.

He wasted no time in closing the remaining distance toward the barn. If he could get inside, he could hold them off better, but he still needed to get to Halley. His mind refused to believe that she might already have been shot.

Just as he reached the barn door he heard a rifle in the

distance and immediately felt an explosion in his shoulder. The impact of the shot hurled him through the door, and he landed hard against the dirt floor. He groaned and kicked the door closed, grateful his own weapon had not discharged in the fall.

The right front of his shirt was quickly stained with blood, and he knew his collarbone was broken. The rifle was useless to him now, and he groped for his pistol with his left hand. He struggled to remain lucid, wondering how he would hold off the raiders and protect Halley at the same time.

Halley huddled against the stone fireplace, hoping bullets would not penetrate the rocks as easily as they would the frame walls. Another shot rang out and this time voices did as well.

"This ain't your fight."

"I'm making it my fight!"

Ben! Her heart soared. He had come for her, rushing to her defense, now, when he stood to gain nothing. She strained her ears and listened for his voice.

Another shot rang out, followed by silence.

Then: "I got him! He's in the barn!"

Halley felt her blood run cold. They would easily overtake and kill him if he was wounded. Desperation dissolved her fear, and she rose on wobbly legs, searching the room for anything that could be used as a weapon.

Her pistol was safely packed away at Mrs. Porter's. In her haste to reach Eli, she had forgotten to retrieve the weapon.

She thought of Mr. McClinton's encounters with bank robbers and highwaymen, always with his Colt .45. He would never have survived the mining towns without the weapon.

Mining! Her mind raced, recounting the descriptions of the rugged miners and their strenuous labor. Mr. McClinton had advised that dynamite should always be stored in a dry area to prevent moisture from ruining the charge.

She scurried into the kitchen and snatched the wooden box down from the top of the pie safe. She reached inside and withdrew three perfectly dry charges of dynamite and snatched the matches from near the stove, hoping she could remember Mr. McClinton's instructions on using dynamite.

Be certain the fuse is securely attached to the charge.

Cautiously she moved to the broken window and flattened herself against the wall. She peered out long enough to see three men advancing toward the barn, their menacing voices reaching her ears.

"Here we come, boy!"

"Don't worry about the little lady. We'll keep her plenty of company."

"After you're dead."

Allow ample distance between yourself and the intended blasting area.

She waited for Ben to reply, but the only the crack of a pistol answered.

"Still got a little fight in you, eh?"

She sneaked a second glance out the window. They were less than thirty feet from the barn. She hoped it would not be too close. Breathing a prayer, she struck the match, lit the fuse, and hurled the explosive out of the window.

Take cover immediately.

The explosion rattled every pane of glass in the house, and Halley was pelted with flying snow and dirt.

"What in the hell was that?"

"Dynamite, you idiot!"

"Hurry, get to the barn!"

Halley wasted no time in repeating the process, this time shattering windowpanes.

"I ain't getting paid enough to get blown to kingdom come!"

"Me, neither! Let's get the hell out of here."

Halley peered out the window once again, just in time to see their retreating backs. Fleetingly, she wondered if they would return, but she knew it would not be soon. She hurried out of the house, anxious to reach Ben.

The barn door opened as she approached, and Ben stood in the doorway. She gasped at the sight of his bloody shirtfront. Taking his arm, she eased him to the ground and began tearing at the blood-soaked chambray.

"Oh, Ben," she gasped. She removed the bandanna from around his neck and held the cloth against the wound. There was so much blood that she couldn't tell just how bad the wound was. "What should I do?"

"I'll be all right," he assured her, covering her hand with his. "I'm pretty sure the bullet went all the way through, and I just need a splint for this arm."

She searched his face, needing confirmation of his words. He smiled slightly as she smoothed her hand along his face.

"Halley, why did you come out here by yourself?" he asked in a reproachful tone. "You knew it was dangerous."

She looked away, the courage she'd mustered fading fast. "There were some things in the house I wanted to take with me. I didn't meant to . . . Oh, Ben, you could have been killed because of me."

Tears slipped down her face, pooling in the palm of his hand, and he pulled her against his good shoulder. "Don't fret so," he soothed. "I've been shot before, and this won't be the last time."

She looked up at him, swallowing back the sobs. "I want you to claim the land, Ben, make it part of your ranch. It's rightfully yours, and no one would dare challenge you for it."

"I have every intention of doing just that." He smoothed the tears from her face with his thumb. "At our wedding."

She raised up and studied his face, noticing the spark of humor in his eyes. "Wedding? Ben Parrish, are you proposing?"

"I guess I am." He laughed. "A man would have to be crazy not to marry a woman so savvy in a shoot-out."

"Mr. McClinton always said, 'A cool head in the face of danger is the best defense.' "

Ben winced as she resumed inspection of the wound in his shoulder. "But dynamite? You could have blown yourself to bits."

Halley sat back. "No risk is too great when faced with losing the one you love."

"Is that what Mr. McClinton says?"

"No, it isn't," she answered, leaning forward to kiss him. "That's what I say."

Our Town

...where love is always right around the corner!

__Take Heart *by Lisa Higdon*
                  0-515-11898-2/$5.99
In Wilder, Wyoming...a penniless socialite learns a lesson in frontier life — and love.

__Harbor Lights *by Linda Kreisel*
                  0-515-11899-0/$5.99
On Maryland's Silchester Island...the perfect summer holiday sparks a perfect summer fling.

__Humble Pie *by Deborah Lawrence*
                  0-515-11900-8/$5.99
In Moose Gulch, Montana...a waitress with a secret meets a stranger with a heart.